THE BRADING
COLLECTION

Titles by Patricia Wentworth

THE BRADING COLLECTION

PATRICIA WENTWORTH

HARPER & ROW, PUBLISHERS, New York
Grand Rapids, Philadelphia, St. Louis, San Francisco
London, Singapore, Sydney, Tokyo, Toronto

This book was originally published in hardcover in 1950 by J. B. Lippincott Company.

First PERENNIAL LIBRARY edition published 1990.

ISBN 0-06-081226-5

90 91 92 93 94 WB/OPM 10 9 8 7 6 5 4 3 2 1

THE BRADING COLLECTION

CHAPTER 1

Miss Maud Silver picked up her knitting. She was using the odds and ends of wool left over at various times from jumpers knitted for her niece Ethel Burkett, stockings for the Burkett boys, woolly frocks and cardigans for little Josephine, and combining them in a striped scarf which she considered really "very tasteful, very artistic." As she knitted a narrow lemon-coloured stripe, her hands low, her needles held in the continental fashion, she allowed her glance to dwell with reserve upon the visitor who had just been ushered in. She judged him to be about fifty-five years of age, of no more than medium height, but very upright, spare, and grey. There was no look of ill health, but the greyness was noticeable in the well cut suit, in the close-cropped hair, in the cool eyes, and even in the tinge of the skin. Miss Silver was reminded of one of those slim fishlike insects which sometimes emerge disconcertingly from between the leaves of an unused book. The card which he had sent in lay on the small table at her elbow.

Mr. Lewis Brading
Warne House
Ledstow

1

Ledstow lay between Ledlington and the sea. She knew all that part of the country well. Randal March, an old pupil of hers, was now the Chief Constable of the county. She had been a governess before transferring her interest to detection. Her friendship with the March family was most affectionately maintained.

A number of her cases had taken her into Ledshire. She thought that she had heard Mr. Brading's name, but the connection eluded her. She made no attempt to pursue it, her attention being required for Mr. Brading himself. Like so many of her visitors, he was at the moment regretting that he had come. She had no means of judging whether the stiffness of his manner proceeded entirely from this cause, or whether some part of it was natural to him, but that he was embarrassed, uncertain, and engaged in wondering why he had come was plain enough to an experienced observer. Some of her clients were voluble, but whether they had too much or too little to say, most of them in that first five minutes would have been glad to be on the farther side of the front door with the bell unrung and the errand which had brought them there not yet committed to words.

The "Private Enquiries" which were her professional occupation had brought Miss Maud Silver some strange confidences and taken her into some dangerous places. They had also provided her with the modest comforts of her flat in Montague Mansions. They had bought the peacock-blue curtains, now drawn back from the two windows, and the carpet in a matching shade which had weathered the war years but was now beginning to show signs of wear. They had also indirectly provided the photographs which thronged the mantelpiece, the top of the book-case, and any other place upon which a frame could be induced to stand. While the frames were old-fashioned—plush, or silver filigree upon velvet—the photographs were for the most part quite modern pictures of babies. Sometimes a young mother was included, and there was a fair sprinkling of girls and young men, but very few older people. Every photograph was an offering of gratitude from someone who stood in safety or lived in happiness and contentment because Miss Maud Silver had fought a successful battle for justice. If the battle had been lost, most of these babies would never have been born.

Lewis Brading had been diagnosed correctly. He was wishing that he had not come. The room reminded him of schoolboy visits to his Forrest aunts. Yellow walnut chairs whose contorted legs and bad carving were scarcely atoned for by their wide, capacious laps. The same type of wall-paper, the same outmoded pictures—"The Soul's Awakening," Millais' "The Huguenot," "The Monarch of the Glen." The same litter and clutter of photographs. An old maid's room, and Miss Silver herself the period old maid in a state of perfect preservation.

It was at this point that his interest as a collector was awakened. Not his line of course, but he could recognize a museum piece when he saw one. The dowdy, old-fashioned clothes—where in heaven's name did anyone get such garments nowadays? The net front with slides of whalebone in the collar, the thick stockings, the shoes exactly like old Cousin Mary's, beaded toes and all, the rigidly netted hair with its Alexander fringe, the cameo brooch with its head of a spurious Greek warrior, the neat features, the mild deprecating air, the eternal knitting, made up a picture as disarming as it was out of date. His momentary feeling of embarrassment displaced by a convincing sense of male superiority, he said,

"I have been told a good deal about you, Miss Silver."

The change of mood did not go unnoticed. Miss Silver was aware of it, and of a flavour of condescension in Mr. Brading's not very pleasing voice. She did not care about being condescended to, she did not care about his rather grating tone. She coughed slightly and said,

"Yes, Mr. Brading?"

"From the Marches. I think you know them."

"Oh, yes."

The rather indeterminate-coloured eyes remained fixed upon his face. He began to feel annoyed with Randal March, and with the situation. Not that March had sent him here—he hastened to make that clear.

"He doesn't know that I have come to see you, and I shall be obliged if you will not mention it. He is, as you know, our Chief Constable. It so happens that I met him at dinner the other night, and the subject of detection having come up, he gave it as his opinion that the best detective he knew was a woman. He did not mention your name, but one of the other guests did. There was some talk about a case in which you had been concerned—the Melling murder—and I was suffi-

4

ciently interested to remember your name and to look you up in the telephone directory."

As he spoke he was recalling not so much what Randal March had said as his manner. It had impressed him. In retrospect he found it impressing him again.

Miss Silver regarded him thoughtfully.

"You were interested enough to make an appointment. You have kept it. What can I do for you, Mr. Brading?"

He made an abrupt movement.

"Does my name convey anything to you?"

She coughed.

"I feel that it should do so, but for the moment— no, of course I should have remembered at once— the Brading Collection."

The interest in her voice was mollifying. It made amends for a momentary lapse of memory.

He said, "Yes," with justifiable pride.

Miss Silver had finished the lemon-coloured stripe which she had been knitting, and was now attaching a thread of dark blue wool. This accomplished, she said,

"But of course—that was very stupid of me. Your Collection is quite famous. I have often felt that it would interest me to see it. Jewels with a history—that opens up a very wide field."

"A little too wide. I have some reproductions of famous jewels, but the collection is limited for the most part to articles of jewelry which have some connection with crime. The exceptions are a few pieces of family interest."

She continued to knit, and to look at him.

"The collection must be a valuable one."

5

His laugh had that grating sound.

"I have sunk a good deal of money in it. I sometimes ask myself why. When I am gone no one will value it."

Miss Silver coughed.

"I fear that is often the case. Each generation has its own tastes and interests. But I suppose that you have formed yours in order to please yourself, and not for the sake of your children."

He said still more harshly,

"I have no children—I am not married. My present heir would be a cousin, Charles Forrest, who would, I imagine, immediately convert the more valuable items of the Collection into cash."

Miss Silver's needles clicked. The striped scarf revolved. She said,

"You are in some anxiety, are you not? Perhaps you will tell me how I can help you."

Up to that moment he had not really made up his mind. He was not conscious of making it up now, but he said,

"Anything I tell you will be in confidence?"

"Of course, Mr. Brading."

March had said she was discretion personified. He frowned.

"I haven't anything very definite to say. I am uneasy, and I think I have grounds for this uneasiness. It really does not amount to more than that. I had better begin by telling you how I am placed."

Miss Silver inclined her head.

"I will be glad if you will do so."

He went on speaking, sitting rather stiffly upright, his right hand moving a little on the arm of his chair, the fingertips sometimes following the

6

pattern of the acanthus leaves which bordered the upholstery, sometimes tapping with a nervous movement.

"Until recently I owned Warne House, near the village of Warne in Ledshire. It is a very small village about three miles out of Ledstow. When I became seriously interested in jewels I realized that to house a valuable collection would require some thought. Eventually I decided to build an annexe to the house, which should be virtually a strong-room. I had experts down, and in the late nineteen-twenties such a strong-room was constructed. It is not built on to the house, but is connected with it by a thirty-foot passage which is kept brightly lighted at night. A hill rises up sharply on that side, and the annexe is partly built into it. I won't trouble you with technical details, but as far as concrete and steel can make a place burglar-proof, the annexe is burglar-proof. There are no windows, their place being taken by a first-class air-conditioning plant, and there is only one entrance—from the glazed passage, which terminates in a steel door. When that is opened there is still a small lobby and another steel door before the main building can be entered. Have I made myself clear?"

"Perfectly, Mr. Brading."

She was reflecting that he had the lecturer's manner, though fortunately it was not every lecturer who addressed his audience with so much dryness and precision.

He brought his fingertips together and resumed the address.

"Once you are inside the main building the plan is a very simple one. There is the large room which

7

houses my Collection, with my secretary's bed-room and a bathroom opening from it on the left. Facing you as you come in, there is another door which leads to a passage, and opening upon this passage is my own bedroom, a second bathroom, and a laboratory. I am engaged upon some inter-esting experiments with stones—but that is by the way. The whole structure has been designed to be, and I believe is, quite impregnable."

Miss Silver had continued to knit. She now gave her prim little cough, and said,

"Why are you telling me all this, Mr. Brading?"

His hand went back to feeling the pattern of the acanthus leaves. The platform manner wavered.

"Because I wish you to understand that every precaution has been taken."

"But you are not satisfied?"

He said with a drag in his voice,

"My reason should be."

"Pray continue."

"I have taken every precaution. During the war I had the Collection removed to a place of greater safety inland. I was myself occupied in the Cen-sorship—I am a considerable linguist. When the war was over I found myself no longer interested in keeping up Warne House. It was much too big for me. There were the consequent staff difficulties, and—in short, I was not interested. It was sug-gested to me that it was admirably suited for con-version into a country club. A syndicate was formed to purchase it, and I moved into the an-nexe. I hold a proportion of the shares, and I have retained my old study, which is situated on the same side of the house as the annexe and lies just to the right of the door which opens upon the glazed passage. To sum up, my secretary and I have all our meals in the club, and I keep my study, but the Collection is housed in the annexe and we both sleep there. A woman comes over from the club to clean, but she is never alone in the building. It is one of my secretary's duties to superintend her."

Miss Silver was accustomed to clients who expended themselves in detail upon non-essentials because they wished to defer the moment when something unpleasant must be said. The dark blue stripe finished, she returned to the lemon-yellow.

"You have been very lucid, Mr. Brading. You have taken all these precautions which you describe, but there remains the human element. This building in which you live with your Collection is not remote, but it is isolated by the very nature of the precautions which you have taken. In this isolation you live with another person. My attention is naturally focussed upon this person, your secretary. Who is he, what are his antecedents, and how long has he been with you?"

Lewis Brading leaned back in his chair and crossed one leg over the other. A very slight smile just changed the set of his lips. He said,

"Exactly. Well, here you are. His name is James Moberly, his age is thirty-nine. He started life in humble circumstances, took a scholarship, went in for experimental chemistry, and became involved in some rather ingenious proceedings of a fraudulent character."

Miss Silver said, "Dear me!" She continued to knit.

9

Lewis Brading's fingers began to tap out a little tune upon the acanthus leaves. He was not exactly smiling now, but he looked pleased.

"He was employed by a man who was engaged in the perpetration of a series of frauds. Articles of jewelry were stolen and some of the stones replaced by very clever copies. The reward offered by the insurance company was then claimed and a double profit made. The whole thing came to light during the war. The principal was a Frenchman who operated from Paris. He disappeared at the time of the collapse of France. The affair came my way through my work in the Censorship. I made it my business to follow it up. James Moberly served in the army—I don't think he ever got beyond being a clerk at the base. I kept track of him, and when he was demobilized I offered him a job as my secretary. That surprises you?"

Miss Silver said gravely,

"I believe that you expected it to do so."

He gave his dry laugh.

"Undoubtedly. And now I will give you my reasons. James Moberly has the technical qualifications which I require for my experiments. They are not so common as you may suppose. He served a useful fraudulent apprenticeship with M. Poisson—known, I believe, amongst his criminal associates as *poisson d'avril*, I imagine on the principle of *lucus a non lucendo*, since he was by no means a fool."

Miss Silver showed that she had taken the allusion in the manner of the governess who commends a pupil. She murmured,

"*Poisson d'avril* being, of course, the French

10

equivalent for an April fool."

A slight bleak pinching of the lips replaced the slight bleak smile. He had a feeling that he had been set down, but could not believe that that had been her intention. Miss Silver's gaze remained mild and enquiring. He said,

"In addition to Moberly's technical qualifications, I considered that his antecedents would give me a useful hold over him. He had never been brought to book, and if he behaved himself in my employment he never would be, but if he put a foot wrong, if he abused his position in the slightest degree, he would expose himself to prosecution."

Miss Silver said, "Dear me!" again. The busy needles checked for a moment in the middle of the lemon-coloured stripe. She observed,

"It seems to me that you have embarked upon a very dangerous course."

The grey eyebrows rose. He laughed.

"He won't murder me," he said. "You must give me credit for a little intelligence, you know. If anything were to happen to me, James Moberly's dossier would come into the hands of my cousin Charles Forrest, who is also my executor. If he is not satisfied that everything is above-board, the dossier will go to the police. There is a letter with my will instructing him to that effect, and James Moberly knows it."

Miss Silver's needles moved again. She did not comment. To anyone who knew her it would have been evident that she disapproved.

If Mr. Brading was not aware of this, it was because it did not occur to him that there was matter for disapproval. He was, in fact, quite pleased with himself and his expedient for ensuring his secretary's fidelity. He even invited applause.

"Quite a good idea, don't you think? I've got the whip hand, and he knows it. As long as he stays honest and does his job, I pay him well and he is all right. Self-interest, you see. That's as powerful a motive as you can have. It pays him to be honest and to do his job to my liking. You can't have a stronger motive than that."

Miss Silver reached the end of her row. She said in a tone of great gravity,

"You are engaged upon a dangerous course, Mr. Brading. I think you must be aware of this yourself, or you would not be here. Why have you come to see me?"

He had a sudden frown.

"I don't know. I have been—how shall I put it—obsessed. Yes, I think that is the right word—" he repeated it with a good deal of emphasis—"*obsessed* with the idea that something is going on behind my back. I am neither nervous nor imaginative, but I have that feeling. If there is any foundation for it, I should like to know what it is. If there is none—well, I should like to be assured about that."

Miss Silver coughed.

"Have you nothing more to go upon than a feeling?"

She saw him hesitate.

"I don't know—perhaps—perhaps not. I have thought—" He broke off.

"Pray be frank with me, Mr. Brading. What have you thought?"

He looked at her, at first curiously, and then with some intensity.

"I have thought once or twice that I have slept rather too heavily—and I have waked with the feeling that something has been going on."

"How often has this happened?"

"Two or three times. I have no certainty about it—it just presents itself as a possibility. I have had the feeling that someone else has been in the annexe—" He broke off with a shake of the head. "No, that's putting it too strongly. I can't get farther than what I said before—it presents itself as a possibility."

Miss Silver made an almost imperceptible movement. It did not get as far as being a shake of the head, but to anyone who knew her—let us say, to Inspector Abbott of Scotland Yard—it would have conveyed dissatisfaction if not dissent. She said after a slight preliminary cough,

"You will forgive me, Mr. Brading, if I do not see why you are consulting me."

"No?"

She repeated the word in a quiet thoughtful manner.

"No. You seem to have some vague suspicions, and I assume that these are directed against your secretary."

"I did not say so."

She laid down her knitting for a moment and said briskly,

"No, you did not say so. But you and Mr. Moberly are alone in this annexe which you have described. I suppose, like yourself, he has a key?"

"Yes, he has a key."

"Then what you have said amounts to this. You suspect that he admits, or has admitted, someone to the annexe after taking the precaution of drugging you."

"I have not said any of those things."

"You have implied them. May I ask what you had in your mind when you asked me to see you? In what way did you think I could be of any service?"

The smile was still there. If it afforded any evidence of pleasure, it was not the kind of pleasure of which Miss Silver could approve. He lifted his hand and let it fall again.

"I thought it might not be a bad thing to have Moberly watched."

Miss Silver had resumed her knitting. She was upon a grey stripe rather wider than either the lemon or the blue. Over the needles she contemplated Mr. Brading and his smile.

"I am afraid I cannot be of any help to you there. The case would not be at all in my line. I could give you some advice, but before I do so—" she broke off—"there is a question I should like to ask."

The grey eyebrows lifted a little.

"What is it?"

"Your secretary, Mr. Moberly—has he ever asked you to release him?"

"He has."

"Recently?"

"Oh, yes."

"Urgently?"

"You might put it that way. And now what is your advice?"

"That you should let him go."

The hand lifted again.

"I'm afraid that wouldn't suit me."

She said with some urgency,

"Let him go, Mr. Brading. I do not know what your motive may be, but you are keeping a man against his will, and you are keeping him by means of a threat. That is not only wrong, it is dangerous. I have said this before. If I repeat it now, it is because I feel it my duty to warn you. Resentment may pass into hatred, and hatred produces an atmosphere in which anything may happen. You would, I think, be well advised to house your Collection in a museum and adopt a more normal way of life."

"Really? Is that all?"

She looked at him steadily.

"Opposition stiffens you, does it not, Mr. Brading? Is that why you came to me? Did you, perhaps, feel the need of something to stiffen you? If that is the case, I think it is a pity that you came."

She laid her knitting down upon the table at her side and rose to her feet. The audience was over.

Lewis Brading had no choice but to follow her example. He took a formal leave and went out. A good deal against his will and his intention, he had been impressed.

CHAPTER 2

Stacy Mainwaring stood at the window looking out. She stood because she was feeling too restless to sit, and she looked out because she was expecting a client and she wanted to see her arrive. Sometimes you can get quite a good idea of what a person is like from walk, carriage, manner of approach. When two people meet, each is to some extent affected by the other, neither is quite the same as when alone. Stacy had a fancy to see Lady Minstrell before they met.

She looked down from her third-floor window and saw the London street, very hot in the afternoon sun. It was a quiet street, the tall old-fashioned houses mostly let out in hastily improvised flats to meet the pressing need for accommodation. Stacy had two rooms and the use of a bath. A great many people only had one, and thought themselves lucky.

She looked down the street and wondered if the woman in the bulging coat was going to be Lady Minstrell. Even if the temperature was nearing ninety, London could always produce a fat woman swathed to the chin in fur. If this particular woman stopped at No. 10, Stacy was going to say no. Perhaps she would say no anyhow—she hadn't made up her mind. Ever since Lady Minstrell had rung her up and made the appointment she had been trying to make up her mind, but it just wouldn't play. Every time she got within sight of saying yes or saying no it balked and she had to start arguing with it all over again. Ledshire was a big county. You could probably live for years in Ledshire and never run up against Charles Forrest. You might even live there for years and never run up against anyone who knew him. On the other hand you might meet him pointblank in Ledlington High Street any day of the week, or find yourself at a cocktail party, or having tea with people who were discussing the divorce. "I see Charles has got rid of that girl. What was her name? Something rather odd, but I don't remember what."... . "Walked out and left him, didn't she? Something rather new for old Charles—what? It's generally been the other way on." That was the sort of thing people said, and if she went down into Ledshire to do a miniature of old Mrs. Constantine she might have to hear them saying it.

Her right hand closed hard upon itself. So what? If you did things, people talked, and if they talked, you had just got to get used to what they said. What did it matter? She had left Charles, and he had divorced her for desertion. What of it? It was three years since she had seen him. She had kept her head above water, she was making a name with her miniatures. There was no reason on earth why she shouldn't go down into Ledshire and paint Mrs. Constantine. There was, in fact, every reason why she should. The old thing was a celebrity. It would be a feather in her cap, she could do with the money. And London was baking hot. Quite suddenly she felt as if she couldn't bear it any longer.

17

Two rooms, and a row of grey houses to look at. Her feet ached at the mere thought of the August pavements. The hand which she had clenched relaxed. If she took this on, there would be a garden—grass, trees, shade. What did it matter if she met Charles or didn't meet him? They could say "Hullo!" and get on with whatever they were doing. They didn't matter to each other any longer. They weren't married any more.

A taxi came up the street and stopped at No. 10. A tall woman got out. Stacy saw the crown of a small black hat, the flutter of a thin flowery dress, and that was all. She stepped back from the window and waited. After all, the first view had told her nothing.

Lady Minstrell came into the room like a ship in full sail. If she hadn't had the money and the sense to put herself into the hands of a first-class dressmaker she would have been just a big raw-boned woman. As it was, she was imposing—a good six foot of her, with a lot of vigorous dark hair just threaded with grey and a set of handsome features. She made Stacy feel inconsiderable and wispy. When she spoke she had the carefully trained voice of the class into which she had married. No one could have found any fault with it, except that it might have been any other woman's voice.

"Miss Mainwaring—I am so glad you were able to arrange to see me. Letters are so unsatisfactory, don't you think, and a conversation on the telephone always seems so one-sided." She settled herself without haste, fixed her dark eyes on Stacy, and went on as if there had been no interruption. "You see, as I was trying to explain, this is not just an or-

18

dinary case of commissioning a portrait. My mother has always refused to have her portrait painted. Of course when she was on the stage she used to be photographed, but only in character. She has never had a private photograph taken in her life, and my sister and I are naturally most anxious to—to—" she broke off and made a little gesture with her hands—"I am sure you understand."

Stacy said, "Yes, of course." Her voice sounded cool and detached. Three years ago it would have been different. She could hear the difference herself. She hated it, and it pleased her. If you don't wear armour you get hurt, but sometimes the armour feels stiff and not to be borne.

Lady Minstrell went on talking.

"My mother saw some of your work in an exhibition. There was a miniature of an old man—Professor Langton. She liked it very much, and when she came home she said, 'You are always pestering me to be painted. Well, if you can get hold of that young woman, I don't mind if I do.'" She made the same little gesture as before. "I hope you don't think I'm too blunt, but the fact is my mother is a character and that's the way she talks. It wouldn't be any good your going down to paint her if you thought she was going to be like other people, for she never has been and she never will be."

Stacy found herself laughing.

"I shouldn't want to paint her if she were!"

"Do you want to paint her? I do hope you do."

"You are making me want to."

"Oh, I'm so glad! That is just what I hoped, because it's such an opportunity. My mother is

19

really interested. She still has the most wonderful energy, you know. If you had said no, she would have been perfectly capable of coming up to town and planting herself in this chair until she had persuaded you to say yes, so it will be much less tiring all round if we can come to an arrangement. Now, what about it? When could you come?"

Something in Stacy said, "I can't—"

The voice was a fainting one. When she told it not to be a fool it died away. She felt quite a little glow of triumph as she settled with Lady Minstrell about the fee and arranged to go down to Burdon in two days' time.

"It's seven miles from Ledlington, and we will meet the three-forty-five."

CHAPTER 3

When Lady Minstrell had gone Stacy went down and borrowed a map of Ledshire. Colonel Albury on the ground floor had all the maps in the world. In the days when he had a car he had driven it at a high rate of speed over most of the roads which were marked upon them. Now that he couldn't drive any more he spent a good many hours a day going over his maps, calculating things like mileage, and just where you could save petrol by coasting down a slope. Stacy did not want to become entangled in these calculations, so she was glad to catch Mrs. Albury, who gave her the map without asking any questions and was only too anxious to hurry back to the washing, or the cooking, or the cleaning, which she did so badly, and which took up all her time.

Back in her own room, Stacy unfolded the map and laid it out on the piece of furniture which was a sofa by day and a bed by night. She certainly had two rooms, but the one at the back was too small and hot to sleep in.

She spread out the map and kneeled down to look at it. There was Ledlington, with Ledstow seven miles away and a wavy line of coast beyond. Burdon wouldn't be marked, but the village was Hele, and that was seven miles from Ledlington too. She found it almost at once, on the opposite side from Ledstow, and drew in her breath. That would make it a good fourteen miles from the coast. Warne lay right on the coast. Even if Charles was there, she could go down to Burdon with a light heart. Fourteen miles was quite a long way. Besides, why should Charles be at Warne? He couldn't possibly afford to live at Saltings.

She stopped for a moment to think about the big grey house standing amongst the old trees which screened it from the Channel winds. She wondered if it was sold, or let, or parcelled out into flats. She wondered whether Charles would mind if it were. If he did he would never show it. He never showed anything. Perhaps that was because there was nothing to show. He kept a smiling face to the world and charmed it at his will, but whether he cared for anything more than that it should be charmed, she had not known and she would never know.

Stacy got up quickly. She bundled the map together and pitched it on to a chair in a manner which would have made Colonel Albury see red. Granted she was a born fool, she wasn't quite such a fool as to go all maudlin over a map and start thinking back about Charles. It didn't matter to her what had happened to him or to Saltings. She was going to Burdon to paint old Myra Constantine, and Burdon was fourteen miles from Warne.

She made herself very busy for the rest of the day. There was plenty to do if she was to get off in two days' time. She did it in a rush of energy which sent her to bed so tired that she fell asleep almost as soon as her head was on the pillow. And then she must needs dream about Saltings.

It was a most extraordinarily vivid dream. She was walking on the cliff path. There really was a cliff path, and she had hated it because the drop went down so steeply to the sea and the way was narrow, but in her dream it was narrower still. The drop was sheer, and on the landward side, instead of a bank easy and sometimes no more than head high, there towered a long unbroken wall. There was quite a lot of light, but she couldn't see the sea or the top of the wall. She could hear the waves come crawling up across the sand and go dragging back into the sea, and she could hear a landward wind that buffeted the wall, but she couldn't see the tide or feel the wind. She had to walk straight on. She didn't know why she had to—she was compelled, without knowledge or choice. The wall was Colonel Albury's map standing up on end with all the towns and roads and rivers marked on it. The cliff path was marked on it. Every step her feet

22

were taking was marked. She had passed Saltings, and presently the path would bring her to Warne. The path would stop there, because the cliff dipped to the village. Any minute now it would begin to run downhill, and she would see the trees which protected Warne House, and the roofs of the village houses below. Only there was something wrong—the path kept going on and not getting anywhere. A voice called from high overhead, "Where, Stacy—where?" and she said, "To Warne." The voice said, "Don't go. I'm warning you—don't go to Warne." Then it died away, and she saw Charles coming towards her along the narrow path. They would meet if neither of them turned. They couldn't turn, because the path had shrunk to less than a foothold, to one of those narrow lines traced upon Colonel Albury's map. Charles smiled at her as he used to do, and she fell down the face of the rustling map and woke.

For a moment she had no sense of where she was. There should have been rocks, and the sea. They were gone, and Charles was gone. All her armour was gone too. She put her face into her pillow and wept.

CHAPTER 4

Stacy sat in the train and felt elated. She had downed all the things which had tried to put her off, and here she was, on her way. She had a right to feel pleased. Even that morning Edith Fonteyne had said on the telephone, "*My dear*," with about six exclamation marks when Stacy murmured that she was going to Burdon to paint a miniature of Myra Constantine. The exclamation marks had been followed by a gasp.

"You're *not!*"

"Why shouldn't I?"

"My *dear!*" Edith was still gasping. "Well, if you don't *mind*—"

"What is there to mind?"

"Well, I should have thought—"

Stacy lost her temper.

"Oh, don't think!" she said, and banged the receiver down.

Edith might be a cousin, but she was one of the most irritating women in the world. What she really wanted was to hold Stacy's hand and say, "Confide in me." It was not the first time by a good many that the receiver had been jolted back in a hurry. As a rule Stacy was sorry afterwards, because Edith had known her in her cradle and she meant to be kind. But today she merely experienced a glow of triumph. She had downed Edith

24

just as she had downed her own misgivings and that really damnable dream. You could down things if you tried hard enough.

Someone had once told Stacy that doing things in a hurry was her besetting weakness. She couldn't remember who it was, but it was probably Edith's mother, old Cousin Agatha Fonteyne. Yes, it was. Stacy could hear her saying it—"You are always in too much of a hurry, my dear. If you see something you like you must have it at once. That dress you came home with last week—not in the least suitable or practical, but you had to rush in and get it without giving yourself time to think. And now this marriage—"

Of course, that had been the text, a whirlwind courtship and a lightning marriage—"Marry in haste and repent at leisure," and all the rest of it. Charles, like the offending dress, was neither suitable nor practical. An old place hanging round his neck, army pay and very little else, expensive tastes, and a good deal more charm than was good for him. Too much for Stacy, who had married him in haste and repented before the honeymoon was over.

A little hot spurt of rage made her face glow. Charles again! Bobbing up in such unlikely company as Agatha Fonteyne! She thought of them, and had to laugh. And there she was, back to being pleased with herself.

When she got to Ledlington there were a good many people on the platform, some getting out, and some getting in because the train went on to Ledstow. In the crowd, head and shoulders above the ruck, Lady Minstrell looked even more imposing than she had done in the flat. As soon as she saw Stacy at the window she came forward, met her at the open door, and with no more than a murmured greeting stepped up into the train and ensconced herself in a corner seat.

"I hope you don't mind—we're going on to Ledstow. I hadn't time to let you know."

Before Stacy could answer or do anything except feel completely out of her depth a porter thrust two suitcases into the carriage and followed with a hamper of fruit. By the time Stacy had said, "Ledstow?" he was helping three children up the steps and hoisting a very stout woman in after them. The children all wanted to wave to someone on the platform, and when the stout woman had finished mopping her face she stood looking over their heads and waved too.

Stacy got as close to Lady Minstrell as she could. Her mouth was dry. She said, "Ledstow?" again, and then something like "I can't—"

The children were shouting farewells to a group of assorted relatives. Lady Minstrell raised her voice and said,

"My mother has gone to Warne."

It was like a bad dream. She couldn't possibly go to Warne, but in about half a minute the train would begin to take her there. No, that was nonsense. It couldn't take her any farther than Ledstow, and what she had to do was to get out there and go back to town. She could even get out now. She half rose from her seat, and as she did so, a porter shouted, "By your leave!", flung the door open with one hand, and pushing the children back with the other, made room for a wiry middle-

26

aged woman to dart through the opening. As he banged the door on her and shouted, "All right, George!" the train gave a preliminary jerk, the children squeaked and giggled, the newcomer cleared two of them out of the corner opposite Lady Minstrell and, sitting down, said briskly,

"Hullo, Milly! Nice to see you. Where are you off to?"

Lady Minstrell said,

"Warne. Mama had a sudden urge. You know how she is." She turned to include Stacy. "This is Miss Mainwaring whom we have persuaded to come down on a visit. She is going to do a miniature. Miss Mainwaring, this is our friend Miss Dale. I expect you know Miss Mainwaring's work, Dossie. Mama admired it so much that she has given way and is going to sit to her."

Theodosia Dale took a good sharp look at Stacy. She not only knew her work, but she knew all about her. She knew that she had married Charles Forrest and left him, and that they were now divorced. If there was anything to know about anyone she always knew it. She had, unfortunately, been away from home at the time of Stacy's brief visit to Saltings as Mrs. Forrest. If she had been on the spot she would naturally have made it her business to know why the honeymoon had come to such a disastrous end. Of course the girl had found Charles Forrest out—that went without saying. But just what she had found out was what nobody seemed to know. There were plenty of stories, but she did not feel sure that any of them were true. Lilias Grey? Nonsense! She was his adopted sister, and though she was obviously a fool about him,

Theodosia was prepared to eat her sensible felt hat if Charles was, or ever had been, in love with Lilias. Of course quite idiotic to bring the girl he had married down to Saltings with Lilias still in the house and a general clutter of relations knocking about. He probably thought they were all going to be bosom friends. Men were like that. Stupid beyond belief.

As these thoughts went through her mind, she glanced sharply at Stacy sitting over the way from her by Milly Minstrell. The children—very badly behaved—had come to blows over a piece of chocolate, and two of them were screaming. Conversation was for the moment quite impossible. She sat stiffly upright in the iron-grey tweeds which matched her quite abundant hair, the thick country shoes, the sensible hat, and looked at Stacy Forrest who had gone back to calling herself Miss Mainwaring. Not very tall, not very anything. Brown hair made the most of—girls spent all their money at the hairdresser's nowadays. Grey eyes rather widely set. Good lashes, with none of that filthy mascara on them. A clear, pale skin, and a reasonable shade of lipstick. A neat blue linen dress. The girl looked like a lady. Good hands and feet, good ankles. But just why Charles Forrest should have fallen for her was past guessing. No particular figure—just slim. Probably never had a decent meal. Girls were just as stupid as men, only in less revolting ways. This—what was her name—Stacy? Ridiculous! She probably ate in snack bars perched up on a high stool with her feet off the ground. Lunacy!

The wails of the combatants had died away. The

stout woman was fanning herself with a pair of black kid gloves, and all three children were smearing their faces with fresh pieces of chocolate. Lady Minstrell went on speaking as if there had been no interruption.

"Mama is like that—if she wants anything she wants it at once." She turned to Stacy. "I would have let you know about the change in our plan if there had been time, but there really wasn't. My mother just suddenly took it into her head that she had been long enough at Burdon and that what she wanted was sea air, so she packed up and went off to Warne this morning. She didn't even let me know. I just came down and found she'd gone, and by that time it was too late to ring you up, so I thought the best thing I could do was to get into your train."

Stacy felt amused, angry, relieved, all at the same time. She began to say, "Oh, but then of course—" but Lady Minstrell caught her up.

"No, no, there is no change about the sittings. My mother has gone, as she always goes, to Warne House."

Stacy's hand contracted in her lap. Lewis Brading's house! And she was to go and stay there, presumably as his guest, and paint Mrs. Constantine! She had a quick picture of him in her mind, thin and grey, with dislike in his eyes, and one of his famous jewels held out for her to see—the sapphire ring which had belonged to Marie Antoinette.

Theodosia Dale leaned a little forward from her upright position and said drily,

29

"Warne House has been turned into a country club."

Stacy thought, "She knows me. She wouldn't have said that if she didn't know me."

And then Lady Minstrell was going on.

"It belonged to a Mr. Brading, a friend of ours. But of course much too big for him, so he very wisely decided to sell. He keeps the annexe which he had built to house his Collection, and he lives there and has all his meals in the club. It saves him a lot of trouble. The annexe is quite shut off of course, with steel doors, steel shutters—all that kind of thing. Because his Collection is immensely valuable—jewels of historic interest. That is one of the things that takes my mother to Warne. She loves fine jewels, and some of Mr. Brading's are very fine. The annexe is really like a strong-room, but I shouldn't like to have so much valuable stuff about."

Miss Dale gave a short laugh.

"Like it! Sticking your neck out, that's what I call it. Lewis will be getting himself murdered one of these days, and then what good will all that junk be to him?"

Lady Minstrell sounded shocked. She said, "Dossie!" and Miss Dale tossed her head.

"Much better collect postage stamps. Something abnormal about a man going soft in the head over jewels."

Stacy found her voice.

"I'm afraid I couldn't undertake to do a miniature of Mrs. Constantine in an hotel—it really wouldn't be possible."

She caught a sardonic gleam in Miss Dale's eye.

30

And then Lady Minstrell's hand was on her arm.

"Oh, please don't say that—it's all been so difficult! But do let me explain. It isn't an hotel, it's a club, and my mother has her own suite of rooms. You wouldn't know you weren't in a private house."

Theodosia watched them. The girl would like to get out of it, but Milly wouldn't let her. Nice hot water she'd be in with old Myra if she turned up at Warne without the tame artist. After refusing to so much as have her photograph taken for about forty years Myra had swung round and was all set to be painted. Snatch her miniaturist away at the last moment and there would be the devil to pay.

She watched Milly being soothing, and the girl hanging back. And then they were at Ledstow, with Myra Constantine's chauffeur on the platform touching his cap and saying,

"The car is outside, my lady."

CHAPTER 5

In the car Stacy told herself that she had behaved like a mesmerized rabbit. But what on earth could she have done? Impossible to go on saying no without giving a reason. Impossible to explain in the interested hearing of Theodosia Dale, a fat woman, and three children eating chocolate. She hastened to make amends to herself. Much better to do as she had done. She could go up to Warne House, put the case quietly before Mrs. Constantine, and catch a morning train. It wouldn't hurt her to spend the night in Lewis Brading's house. She need not even come down to dinner. Much better and more dignified than having a scene at the station.

Lady Minstrell's voice came through her thoughts.

"Dossie and I were at school together. Her father was the Rector. She has a little old house in the village, and she knows all about everyone. I have asked her to come up this evening. My mother likes to know about everything too."

Stacy couldn't think of a thing to say.

Lady Minstrell flowed on—schooldays, Dossie's good heart, Dossie's sharp tongue.

"She really is the best friend in the world, but of course she wants knowing. She never wears anything but those thick coats and skirts winter and summer. I don't know how she does it in this heat. There—we're coming to Warne now—down in the dip. Such a pretty village. Really it was a pity Dossie was having tea in Ledstow, or we could have given her a lift, but there is quite a convenient bus service. Look—that is Warne House, half way up the slope on the other side among the trees. It is very tiring travelling in this heat, don't you think? We shall both be glad of some tea."

Stacy felt as if it was going to take more than a cup of tea to get her through arriving at Warne House. Lewis Brading was the sort of cousin who had always been there. She and Charles had dined with him, driving over from Saltings on a summer evening, turning in between the trees as they were turning now, and just as they came in sight of the house Charles had taken his hand off the wheel and touched her lightly on the cheek.

"Cheer up, darling, it'll be all the same by to-morrow. Anyhow, what's the matter?"

"He doesn't like me."

His smile flashed out, fleeting, impish, charming.

"He doesn't like anyone—much. What used to be his heart is completely bunged up with the Collection—there really isn't room for anything else."

"How grim."

She could hear him laugh.

"Cheer up! It takes all sorts to make a world."

The whole scene came back in a flash, the two of them all warm and happy, and sorry for Lewis Brading who was out in the cold. That cut deep, because two days later Stacy was out in the cold too—the bitter freezing cold that kills your heart.

"Here we are," said Lady Minstrell in a tone of relief. "We'll go straight up to my mother. She is longing to see you."

Mrs. Constantine's sitting-room looked over the tree-tops to the sea, unbelievably blue and still under a cloudless sky. Mrs. Constantine herself sat well up to the window in the largest armchair with her feet resting upon an embroidered footstool. They were pretty feet, and she was inordinately proud of the "only bit of prettiness I ever had, so no wonder." Stacy saw them before she saw anything else, pretty, elegant feet in pretty, elegant shoes. And then a shapeless incongruity of figure, and the clever, ugly face with its flattened features, big chin, wide mouth, and astonishingly brilliant eyes.

33

In that first glance she was reminded of a toad—something about the big hunched body, the forward thrust of the head, the wide mouth and the eyes, not bulging like a toad's but with something about them, something that reminded her—

All at once she knew what it was. Words flowed into her mind: "Which like the toad, ugly and venomous, wears yet a precious jewel in his head." Myra Constantine's eyes were like the fabulous jewel, full of black fire. A voice that was almost as deep as a man's said,

"Well, Milly?" And then, "How do you do, Miss Mainwaring?" She put out a hand that felt square and strong. "I don't get up, because it is rather a performance. Come and sit down and have a good look at me. I'm an ugly old devil, but I daresay you get tired of painting pretty-pretties. Girls are all too much alike, especially nowadays—clothes, figures and complexions planned, controlled, and mass-produced. Het, ring for tea!" She waved a hand. "My daughter Hester." Then, with a grimace, "Miss Constantine."

Stacy shook hands with a tall, limp woman. There was a look of Lady Minstrell, but no more—older, meek, bullied, without colour or individuality. Stacy gave her a glance, and realized that that was all Hester Constantine would ever get from anyone whilst her mother was in the room. If she had worn scarlet to old Myra's black, she wouldn't have been noticed. But it was Myra who flaunted the loose coat of cherry silk over a gay flowered dress. She fixed her brilliant eyes on Stacy.

"Well, what about it? Are you going to paint me?"

34

This was the moment to explain that she simply couldn't stay, and it was quite impossible to do it. Myra Constantine had asked her in so many words if she was too ugly to paint, and if she came out with "I've got to get back to town," it was as much as to say, "Well, yes, you are." And it wouldn't be true. She'd be the most marvellous subject, just as she was, in that red coat, with the fuzz of white hair standing up in a golliwog frill. The artist in Stacy took charge. Her eyes shone as she leaned forward and said in most convincing tones,

"Oh, *may* I? I'd love to! You'd be marvellous to paint!"

Myra Constantine chuckled.

"That's the stuff! And now you and me'll have a talk." She turned her head for a moment. "Milly, you and Het can go and have your tea in the lounge. Me and Miss Mainwaring's going to have a talk."

The tall, imposing Lady Minstrell came to lay her hand on her mother's shoulder, and said, "Yes, Mama," in the voice of an obedient little girl. And then the tea came in and she and her sister went out.

Mrs. Constantine took charge. It was a substantial tea. When she wasn't pouring out she was eating with gusto, and whether she was pouring or eating she hardly ever drew breath.

"Now you just make a good tea. I've always liked my tea, and always shall. 'You may keep your cocktails,' that's what I said when they come in. 'Keep 'em and welcome,' I said, 'I'll stick to a nice cuppa.'" She shot a malicious glance at Stacy. "Vulgar old woman, ain't I? Well, I can talk common, and I can talk fine if I want to." Voice and manner altered in a flash. "I'm sure you must have had a dreadfully hot journey, Miss Mainwaring. Let us each take one of these small sandwiches and talk about the weather." She dropped back with a grin. "There—I can talk exactly like the Minstrells if I want to. Milly's in-laws, you know—perfectly well bred and damnably dull. She's made herself over to suit. 'Yes, Mama. No, Mama. Dear Mama, it's time for your rest.'" The mimicry was perfect.

"Tchah!" said Myra Constantine with violence. And then, "Oh, well, she's a good daughter, and so is Het. The bother with me is I can't stand being bored."

As she tossed off a cup of almost boiling tea, those black eyes of hers were searching Stacy's face. "Are you going to be any good?" they said. "Are you going to amuse me? I don't know, but I'm going to find out. Can I shock you? I don't know that either, but I'm going to see."

She set down her cup and filled it again.

"Not ready yet?"

Stacy said, "Mine's too hot." Her eyes met the questing look, wide and clear with a little laugh in them. What she would have liked to say was, "Do go on talking."

Said or unsaid, Myra Constantine obliged, this time with a sharp question.

"Well, what do you know about me?"

"You are Myra Constantine—"

"So what?"

"The greatest variety artist we've ever had."

Myra nodded.

"I knocked 'em," she said. "And do you know

36

where I started? In a slum. Drunken father—bullied, worn-out mother—seven kids one after another as quick as they could come. Quads hadn't been invented then, or I daresay she'd have had 'em, poor Mum. Nine of us in a basement kitchen—kids getting dragged up somehow." She gave a short laugh. "If it had been Milly or Het, they'd have stayed there. But I got out—pushed my way into panto. Can you see me as a fairy? That's how I started. 'Keep that kid well out of the way at the back! She's ugly enough to scare the crows,' that's what the stage manager said. So they put me in the back row, and I made faces at the kids that made fun of me. Like this." The wide mouth widened and curled up to show remarkable teeth, strong, white, and sharp. The eyes looked inwards in a horrifying squint, the ears under the golliwog thatch wiggled horribly.

"I can still do it," said Myra Constantine in a complacent voice. "After three kids had had high-strikes they hauled me out and asked me what I'd done, so I did it again. Old Sim Purcell saw it—he just happened to be passing. He took his cigar out of his mouth and said, 'Put her in as an imp, damn her! She won't want any make-up.' So they did, and I had a sort of hop-skip-and-jump dance and made faces. After a bit it got worked up into a kind of take-off of the fairy dance. Brought the house down every time. That's where I got my start, and that's where I learned that it paid to be ugly so long as you were ugly enough." She paused, and added in a deep meditative tone, "I was damned ugly. Have another cup of tea, my dear."

The laughter was clear in Stacy's eyes. She said,

"Do go on," and passed her cup.

Myra Constantine gave a sort of grunt.

"You'll have plenty more," she said. "I couldn't stop talking if I tried, and I don't try. Only turn and turn about's fair doos. Why did you walk out on Charles Forrest?"

Stacy felt exactly as if she had been slapped in the face. She said, "Oh—" and, "You *know!*" The sort of thing you say, and the minute you've said it you can hear for yourself how idiotic it sounds. She had the full cup in her hand. She had to put it down because it shook.

"Know?" said Myra Constantine. "Of course I know! That's why I went to see your stuff. I said to Het, 'A girl that can walk out on Charles Forrest, she's got guts—that's what. And I'll go and see her stuff,' I said. And when I saw it I liked it. There was an old man you'd done—like an old cross tyke snarling over a bone. 'Clever,' I said to Het right away, 'I wouldn't mind letting that girl do *me.*' And she said, 'Oh, Mama—' same as she always does. And I rang up Milly and told her to fix it. I'll say one thing for my girls, they do what they're told. And now are you going to tell me why you walked out?"

Stacy had got her balance again. She picked up her cup of tea.

"Did you really think I would?" she said.

Myra chuckled.

"You never can tell."

Stacy's colour rose. This time it was because she was angry.

"I should never have come if I had known that

you were going to be at Warne. I ought to have gone straight back to town from Ledstow."

"Why didn't you?"

"Miss Dale was there, and the chauffeur. I thought—"

The black eyes were mocking her.

"Yes?"

"I meant to come up here and explain—to you."

"But just now you were all for painting me."

"I got carried away."

The square ugly hands were clapped, a big diamond flashed. The wide mouth grinned.

"That's how I got where I am—I carried 'em away. That's better than letting them shunt you, you may take my word for it. Somebody started to hiss me once—a put-up job. Shall I tell you what I did? Stamped my foot and said, 'Don't be damfools! I'm a lot better than you think I am! I'll show you!' *And* I showed 'em. I had 'em shouting before I'd finished." She dropped to an affable conversational tone. "Well, are you going to let 'em drive you away?"

"I don't see how I can stay."

Myra shrugged.

"Have it your own way. The job'd be a big advert—you know that as well as I do. Funk if you like—you've got as much right to be here as anyone else, haven't you?"

Stacy was being carried away again. She didn't want to be, but she was. She tried to hold on to being angry, but it wasn't any good. She wanted to paint Myra Constantine in her cherry-coloured coat—she wanted it more than she had wanted anything for the last three years. She threw out her hands and said,

"It's not fair—and I ought to go. But I won't. I've got to paint you."

CHAPTER 6

They went down to dinner in a party, and sat at a table in the window. It was the best table, and it had the best view. You could see out over the lawn to the gap in the trees which framed a breadth of hyacinth sea, and you could look all down the long room and watch everyone who came and went, or sat talking at the other tables. Nobody was in evening dress, just light summer things.

Theodosia Dale came in and joined them. She had taken off the black felt hat, but was still wearing the iron-grey tweeds which matched her hair. Nobody could say it was becoming, but somehow it was so much part of her that it was difficult to imagine her in anything else. That she had once danced in this room in a frock of rose-coloured tulle was one of those incredible things that the mind rejects, but it was in the memory of a good many of the people present that they had expected her to be the mistress of Warne House and Lewis Brading's wife. He had given a ball for her here, and had had a famous ruby set for her engagement ring. It was all a very long time ago.

She came up the room, giving a nod here and there, slid into a chair, waved away the soup and, scanning the menu, said she didn't care what she had as long as it was something cold.

"Lobster mayonnaise," said Myra to the waiter. "Yes, everyone—except Miss Constantine. I can't think where she gets her weak stomach from. Thank God, I've always enjoyed my food. Didn't get enough of it when I was a kid. There's nothing like not enough crusts to go round in a cellar to give you a relish for lobster."

Lady Minstrell said, "Mama, *darling!*" and Lewis Brading came into the room and walked to a small table against the wall. Myra waved. He looked over at them, bowed formally, and sat down.

Theodosia Dale had taken no notice at all. She was disentangling her lobster from its shell. If he had come up to the table, she would have said, "Hullo, Lewis!" and gone on with what she was doing. When you live in a village, you have to get over feeling awkward about meeting someone whom you once thought you were going to marry.

Stacy didn't know whether she had been recognized or not. He was cool and bored, but then he always was cool and bored except when he was talking about the Collection. He looked as he had probably looked for the last twenty-five years or so, thin, upright, and rather distinguished. There wasn't any likeness to Charles, but there was something that made Stacy deny it every time she looked at him. All the Forrests were dark like that, and his mother had been a Forrest. But the Forrest charm had certainly passed him by. He looked as if he had swallowed a cold poker, and pokers do

not charm. His glance had passed over her as if
she were not there. Well, what did she expect—
that he would rush up to her and say, "Why,
Stacy—how marvellous!"? She couldn't help a
quick unwilling laugh.

Myra Constantine looked up from the salad
which she had deluged with mayonnaise and gave
her deep throaty chuckle.

"Makes you laugh, don't he? Think of the
women all over the world that'd give their eyes to
have the diamonds and things he's got locked up
next door—and he can't wear one of 'em!"

"Mama *darling!*" said Lady Minstrell.

Hester Constantine only spoke twice. She ate in
a picking sort of way. She left a good deal on her
plate, and once she asked for salt, and once for
vinegar.

Theodosia Dale talked a great deal. She had a
complete catalogue of births, engagements, mar-
riages, and deaths, with such additional items as
who wasn't getting on with whom, why, what they
had said and done, and what their friends thought
about it.

Right in the middle a party of four came in by
the door in the left-hand wall and made for the
empty table on their right. There were two women
and two men. One of the women and one of the
men were strangers to Stacy. She saw red hair, a
black dress, a string of pearls—broad shoulders,
an expanse of ruddy sunburn, bright blue eyes,
and a good-natured air. And then Lilias Grey, with
her flaxen hair piled high, her fragile, delicate look,
and behind her the tall dark ugliness of Charles.
Lilias was in white. She was much better looking

than she had been three years ago—better made up, better dressed, better groomed. Nobody would have guessed that she was three years older than Charles. Her whiteness, her fairness, and the scarlet thread of her lips were a swimming blur on the air in front of Stacy's eyes. When it cleared she saw Charles. He looked just the same. It was unbearable that he should look just the same.

He said, "Hullo, Lewis!" as he passed the table where Lewis Brading sat alone. And then Myra Constantine was waving, and he came right on into the window.

Myra's voice could be heard all over the room.

"Now if this isn't nice! But what are you doing here? Don't they make you work in the army any more?"

He said, "We get a spot of leave sometimes when there isn't a war on." Then he looked past her and said in a pleasant, ordinary tone, "Hullo, Stacy!"

Just for a moment it was like being in a trap with the steel teeth cracking down. And then she was too angry to feel anything else, because Myra Constantine had set the trap, and she had walked into it, like the rabbit she had called herself this afternoon. Well, if they thought she was going to let them see she minded they could think again. She looked at Charles, and she said in quite a good kind of casual voice,

"Hullo, Charles, how are you?" and that was all.

He said, "Going strong," and then he had turned away and was sitting down by Lilias Grey.

"Well, if that wasn't a surprise!" said Myra Constantine. She looked across at Theodosia Dale. "Did you know he was here, Dossie?"

Miss Dale nodded briskly.

"Came two days ago. He's on leave."

Myra called across to the other table.

"Where are you staying, Charles?"

"Up at Saltings. I keep a flat there."

Myra said, "Of course. Must have somewhere to put one's things." She came back to the conversational range of her own party. "They've made a very nice job of those Saltings flats—two rooms—three—four—and a kitchenette. You pay your money and you take your choice. Miss Grey's got a three-roomer." She raised her voice again. "What's your flat, Charles—two rooms or three?"

The smile which made his ugliness more attractive than other men's good looks jerked at Stacy's heartstrings. It always had, and she supposed it always would. It had nothing to do with love, or respect, or even liking—just a physical reflex. Just Charles.

He called back,

"Two. But quite palatial. Kitchen and bath thrown in."

Lady Minstrell said,

"Darling Mama!"

CHAPTER 7

There was dancing later on in the room which used to be the library. The books were still there, big handsomely bound sets like Gibbon's *Decline and Fall of the Roman Empire*, and the *Encyclopaedia Britannica*, with the Victorian novelists in their serried rows—Scott, Trollope, Charles Reade, Dickens, Thackeray, and the rest. There was no dust on them—Warne House was much too well run for that—but it was probably close on fifty years since anyone had taken one of the volumes down to read.

Stacy, with every intention of slipping away upstairs, found herself supporting Myra Constantine on one side whilst Lady Minstrell held her up on the other. It was Hester Constantine who had managed to slip away. Myra weighed fifteen stone if she weighed an ounce. She was not exactly lame, but as she put it herself, a bit apt to go over at the knees. She had to be walked slowly up and down the terrace for a constitutional, after which she signified her intention of going in to watch the dancing.

On two sides of the room there were windows, set back among the shelves, deeply embayed and furnished with comfortable seats. They had hardly reached the particular bay selected by Mrs. Con-

45

stantine, when she hailed a man who was coming towards them.

"Moberly—you're the person I wanted to see! Where are you off to?"

He was a thin man who stooped a little, dark and rather hollow about the cheeks. The features were good, but the lines about the eyes and mouth were too deeply drawn for his age, which might have been thirty or thirty-five, or perhaps five years more. A man should not be so lined at forty. When he spoke there was something in his voice which suggested that he might have had to learn his pleasant way of speech.

"What can I do for you, Mrs. Constantine?"

"I'm breaking Miss Mainwaring's arm. You can come and let me down with a thud. Some day I'm going to break one of these settees. There—that's better. Milly's used to it, but Miss Mainwaring isn't, and that's a fact."

Mr. Moberly performed his part with skill. It was, perhaps, not a first appearance. As he straightened up, Myra caught him by the sleeve.

"Are you dancing?"

"Forrest asked me to join his party, but there was something I had to finish for Mr. Brading, and I see they have a fourth."

"Arrived at the last moment—friend of Charles's, name of Constable. They had the table next to ours—that's how I know. No need for you to huff—he wasn't expected till tomorrow."

"I assure you, Mrs. Constantine—"

She laughed good-humouredly.

"No need for that either. And if you want a partner, here's Miss Mainwaring."

Stacy said sweetly, "I'm afraid I'm not dancing."

She might just as well have held her tongue. Myra said,

"Of course you are! You don't want to sit and talk to a fat old woman all the evening. Milly and me'll do fine as a pair of wall-flowers."

"Mama darling—"

Myra went on without taking any notice.

"You shan't say you've not been properly introduced. This is Mr. James Moberly who is Lewis Brading's secretary. He knows all about diamonds, and emeralds, and rubies, and sapphires, and pearls. Makes your mouth water, don't it? There—go along and dance!"

"If I may have the pleasure—" said James Moberly.

He could hardly have done less, and short of making a scene Stacy had very little choice. She was divided between sheer rage and a desire to laugh as they took the floor. In the hope of finding that her sentiments were reciprocated she looked up and met a polite and anxious eye.

"You are staying with Mrs. Constantine, Miss Mainwaring?"

"I've come down to paint her. I do miniatures."

"That must be very interesting."

Mr. Moberly was a fair dancer, you couldn't put it higher than that. Effortless floating on air would not be achieved in his company. Charles and Lilias, who were dancing together, were definitely floating. "And I dance better than Lilias—a whole lot better," said Stacy to Stacy in a horrid cattish way. Aloud she enquired after the Collection, and learned that some interesting items had been added to it.

They passed Charles and Lilias for the second time. They were laughing at something Charles had just said. They floated away together, warm and gay.

Stacy felt frozen with boredom. What did she care whether Lewis Brading had discovered the missing links which had been wrenched from the Albany necklace when it was stolen in '68? James Moberly told her all about it in an earnest voice, and when he was being earnest his dancing wasn't even fair.

"There they were amongst the odds and ends in a country jeweller's shop, with a label, 'Everything on this tray one and six.' There was just a small bow and a couple of links. The necklace, you know, has a pattern of true lover's knots. It was the shape of the bow that caught my attention. I went in and asked if I could have a look at the tray. There was an elderly woman behind the counter, and of course I saw at once that she didn't know anything at all. The shop was her father's, and he had just died. The stuff in the tray was rubbish he had picked up at the last sale he went to—just a lot of junk thrown in with a clock he wanted. She said there was always a good sale for clocks. Well, of course I bought the bow, and when I got back and showed it to Mr. Brading, I don't know when I've seen him so excited. 'The Albany necklace!' he said at once. And when I got it out, there it was—the missing bit without a shadow of doubt." He lost step, trod upon Stacy's foot, and said, "I'm sure I beg your pardon!'' After which he went on talking about the Collection.

The longest dance comes to an end. Unfortunately, the ice now being broken, Mr. Moberly had no wish to part with his audience. It was just as Stacy was beginning to feel that she could bear no more that Charles Forrest came over to them.

"Hullo, Moberly!" he said. "So you've got here. I see Stacy's been taking pity on you. Now we can shuffle round a bit. You go and take Lilias for the next dance. Jack Constable seems to have got off with Maida." He turned to Stacy. "That's the red-headed girl. Name of Maida Robinson. She's a newcomer up at Saltings. She's got the flat next to Lilias. Some sort of a widow, but whether grass or real, I haven't gathered. You'd better have a shot at cutting Jack Constable out, James."

James Moberly crossed the floor in a patient manner. Charles looked after him for a moment, murmured, "'On with the dance, let joy be unconfined,'" and then turned back.

"Going to dance with me, Stacy?"

That the party had been shuffled to this end was obvious. She felt an agreeable glow as she said,

"I don't think so."

His eyebrows went up.

"Too lame? I saw him hack you. Come along! Think how amusing it will be for everyone! Spread a little happiness as you go by! I don't suppose our steps go any worse together than they always did."

As the record started, his hand was at her waist. They slid into the rhythm. Now it was she and Charles who were floating together as they used to do. She heard him take a long, soft breath.

"Two minds with but a single thought. You've still got all the others beat."

She looked up gravely.

"You say that to everyone you dance with, don't you?"

The corner of his mouth twitched. He said,

"With variations. Only in your case it happens to be true."

"That being one of the variations, I suppose."

He shook his head.

"Oh, no, darling—that's the original air. All the rest are just me making myself agreeable. One's first social duty. I'm considered to do it quite well."

She said, "Oh, yes," still with that grave look.

They floated the length of the room before he said,

"What are you doing here?"

Her colour rose. Infuriating, because there was nothing in the world to make it rise. She explained in a voice which she hoped was merely bored,

"I'm doing a miniature of Mrs. Constantine. And of course I thought she was at Burdon. I was actually getting out of the train at Ledlington, when Lady Minstrell got in and said her mother had suddenly taken the idea of coming down to Warne."

Charles nodded.

"She comes here a good deal. Actually, I believe, she holds most of the shares in the club. It's quite a good show—much better than Burdon, which can't be run on a present-day staff. You're well out of it."

"I wouldn't have come if I'd known, and I didn't mean to stay, but I couldn't explain in the train because there were other people there. And then

50

when I saw Mrs. Constantine I felt I'd give practically anything to paint her."

"She being a first-class advertisement—or am I being earthy?"

She couldn't help an answering glint of laughter. It didn't get beyond her eyes, but of course he knew it would be there. She said in a reproving tone,

"You are rather. It's a bit of incredible luck getting a subject like that." Then, after the least possible pause, "I didn't know you were going to be here."

"You can look upon me as a bonus. Fortunate, aren't you? Well, now that you are here, and I am here, I think we'd better have a business talk."

"We haven't any business to talk about."

"You mayn't have any, but I have. Let us make an assignation. What about tea in Ledlington tomorrow? There's a café there where the sixteenth-century interior is plunged in almost total gloom and the buns are still quite good. If you take the bus from here at a quarter past two and get off at the next halt beyond Ledstow station, I will pick you up—unless, which of course would be much simpler but not so much like an assignation, you just let me call for you here in a perfectly ordinary way."

She was startled into another change of colour.

"No—I won't do that."

His odd crooked eyebrow went up.

"Not a breath of scandal? All right, darling—your lightest wish and all the rest of it. The first halt beyond Ledstow."

Stacy's colour ebbed.

"I don't think so. We have nothing to say to each other."

"My sweet, we haven't drawn breath. Personally I could go on without repeating myself for a month of Sundays. There will be no need for you to compete. Didn't Solomon say that a silent woman was like an apple of gold in a frame of silver?"

"No, he didn't!" said Stacy indignantly. "You made that one up!"

"Perhaps. But how profoundly true. And so beautifully easy. I will discourse, and you shall sit and eat buns."

"No!"

"Well, I think you'd better. I really have got something to say. I'll be at the first halt."

The music stopped. Stacy felt robbed. They ought to have danced, not talked. There was no divorce between their steps. The smooth, gliding rhythm could have carried them away for those few minutes at least. But she wouldn't dance with him again. She said abruptly,

"I'm going up now. I don't want to dance any more."

Charles kept his hand on her arm.

"Oh, but you must give Jack Constable a turn. He can't just monopolize Maida. I want to have a look in myself. I always fall for red-heads, especially the green-eyed kind. Attractive, isn't she? What I can't make out is the immediate status of Robinson—whether disembodied, looming, or relegated to being a mere provider of alimony. Take Jack off her hands and give me a chance to find out. By the way, what are you calling yourself? Did I hear Myra say 'Miss Mainwaring'?"

"I expect so."

Charles said, "Damn silly!" He looked down at her left hand and found it bare. "So you've taken off your ring?"

"Three years ago."

He had his hand on her arm, steering her across the emptying floor. As she said, "Three years ago," they fetched up beside the red-headed Maida and Jack Constable. Still holding Stacy, Charles took him also by the arm.

"Here, Jack, I want you to meet Stacy Mainwaring. She dances like a dream. Have this one with me, Maida?"

CHAPTER 8

Major Constable was a hearty soul and a good if daring dancer.

"Look here, I'll show you a new step you can do to this tune. Rather amusing—picked it up in Chile. I danced it with the belle of the local party, and her boy friend got so worked up he ran a knife into me."

Stacy said,

"You must find Warne dull—no new steps, no boy friends with knives."

"But a much better floor."

He had missed his chance to say, "A much better partner." It seemed to come over him suddenly.

53

He dodged between two couples in a very agile manner, and said,

"I missed my cue there, didn't I? Take it as said. You really are a better partner than the girl friend."

Stacy couldn't help being amused, but she thought she would probably have to watch her step. One of those fast workers. She said, "Thank you," and put a touch of frost into her voice. More to change the subject than for any other reason, she added,

"Have you known Charles long?"

Because if he had, it was odd that she hadn't heard of him before.

It appeared that they had knocked about together in the desert—Tobruk, Hell Fire Corner, Alamein, and so forth. He sounded all over Charles, and began to tell her stories about him, the sort that had made it so easy to fall in love with him three years ago, concluding with,

"Very dashing fellow. And always something to say to make you see the funny side. Pity about that girl he got tied up with."

Stacy said,

"Perhaps girls are always rather a pity."

He laughed.

"Oh, well, Charles likes them. She wasn't the first, and she won't be the last."

Conversation with Jack Constable seemed to involve a constant change of topic. Her colour becomingly heightened, Stacy enquired whether he was staying at Saltings. It appeared that he was.

"I ran into old Charles the other day in town, and asked myself down. I say, he's done pretty well out of converting the house into flats. Lucky to have had the capital to do it with."

Stacy's heart did a horrid sort of sidestop. But he hadn't any capital, he hadn't any capital at all. That was just the trouble. She said,

"I thought he sold Saltings."

Jack Constable shook his head.

"Oh no, he did much better for himself than that. Sold the family diamonds, or something and put the proceeds into converting the place. He's made an awfully good job of it. Haven't you been up there to see?"

Stacy said, "I only came this afternoon." She leapt for yet another subject. "Talking of diamonds, have you seen Mr. Brading's Collection?"

He laughed.

"Sounds like the sort of thing nobody's got enough money for nowadays. Who is he—and what about it?"

She made the Collection last until the dance was over.

She did get away after that. Pausing to say goodnight, she had a brief interchange with Mrs. Constantine, who wanted her to stay but finished up with saying,

"All right, all right—you go and get a good night's rest. There's always another day tomorrow, isn't there? There was a little German Jew fellow played the piano in a road-show I was in, he used to say that—in German, you know, 'Morgen ist auch ein Tag.'" She produced an accent fearfully and wonderfully British. "Sounds funny, don't it? All right, my dear, off you go! And you can start doing my picture tomorrow. Half past ten, if that suits you."

As Stacy looked back at the room before she left it she saw Jack Constable dancing with Lilias, and Charles with the red-haired girl in his arms. Lewis Brading was standing against the wall watching them.

Her room was the small one at the end of Mrs. Constantine's suite. It was really the dressing-room of a bigger room next door. Hester Constantine slept there, and Myra had the bedroom and dressing-room opposite, with the sitting-room beyond. Like her bedroom it looked out towards the sea. Stacy's room looked sideways to the annexe, built against the hill to house Lewis Brading's Collection. Thirty feet of bare glazed passage connected it with the house, and in that passage a light burned all night long.

When Stacy was ready for bed she pulled back the curtains and looked out. It would not be dark for half an hour yet, and she was in no hurry for sleep. She looked out to the annexe and the dark trees surrounding it. There were no windows. Electric light and an excellent air-conditioning plant did away with the need for natural light and air. Even the light-hearted Stacy of three years ago had found something rather horrid about that. And Lewis Brading didn't live there then. Now, she gathered, he did, or at any rate slept there—he and the humourless secretary who had stepped on her feet. Gosh—what a party!

She went on thinking about Lewis Brading because she didn't want to think about Charles. It had been dislike between them at first sight, and she wondered why. Most people liked her all right. Charles had loved her. Or had he? Had she ever really been the theme, or just one of the variations with which he amused himself? At any rate he hadn't married any of the others..... "For God's sake—are you priding yourself on that? The worst day's work you ever let yourself in for. Why do you want to go and rake it all up now when you've got clear of it?" Jack Constable's voice came back— "He's made a good job of the house..... Sold the family diamonds." She had a quick horrifying picture of Charles with the diamonds in his hand and the life freezing at her heart. How many times could you die?

Horrible to have it come back like that. She picked up a book which she had bought for the train and began to read aloud from it quick and low. You can think if you are reading to yourself, but you can't think if you are reading aloud. That was one of the things she had found out three years ago. She hadn't had to do it for a long time now, but she had to do it tonight. She stood there in the light breeze from the open window and heard her voice go monotonously on and on without sense or meaning. It didn't need to have sense or meaning. It was just a barrage against thought.

She put down the book at last with a deep sigh. The wind from the sea had freshened, she was cold in her thin night-gown. Her feet were like ice, and she was deadly tired. It was too dark to read any longer. The passage to the annexe was lighted from end to end. She got into bed, covered herself to her chin, and almost at once she was asleep.

She didn't know how long it was before she woke up, or what it was that waked her. One moment she was deeply, dreamlessly asleep, and the next she was up on her elbow, wide awake in the dark. She stayed like that for a moment listening, and then got out and went over to the window. The wind was cold and everything was dark. But it oughtn't to be dark. Why not? There wasn't any moon. The sky was dark, and the hill, and the trees. And the annexe was dark because it had no windows to show a light. But the passage from the annexe to the house—that ought to be lighted. Myra Constantine had talked about it—"There's only that one way in, and it's a steel door, like the door of a safe. Light's on in the passage all night, so it wouldn't be an easy proposition for a burglar." But of course she knew all that, three years ago. Lewis Brading's precautions against being robbed were public property, and the more public the better. *Burglars keep out!*

Stacy frowned at the darkness. The passage had been lighted when she turned from the window to her bed. It wasn't lighted now. And then from just beneath her there came the smallest possible sound. She thought a door had been closed, softly and carefully, but the latch had clicked. She was sure it was that sound and no other, and she was sure that it came from the door between the passage and the house. Someone had pulled it to, but the handle had slipped and the latch had gone home with a click—right there, underneath her window. Quick on that the light in the passage came on and showed it bare from end to end.

And this time Stacy wasn't sure. She wasn't quite sure. She thought the steel door to the annexe moved as the light came on. She thought it was closing too. But she wasn't sure.

CHAPTER 9

The sitting went very well next day, the morning light not too bad, and Myra Constantine in quite terrific form. The autobiography which had begun with nine people and a slum basement was carried on in a colourful manner. Sometimes Stacy listened, sometimes the words passed her by whilst she registered the play of expression on those dark ugly features, and the snapping malice, the satyric gleam, the blazing enjoyment, which looked out by turns from the big black eyes. With each change she wanted to cry, "Stay!" and felt, between enjoyment and despair, "If I could only get her just like that!"

"Pity the girls don't take after me, isn't it? When I said that to Tom Hatton he said, 'Poor little devils—why should they?' 'All right, all right, Tom,' I said. "Beauty's skin deep, and you've got your whack of it, but I'll have the better time all my life.' He drank himself to death, you know. . . . . . Oh, no, he wasn't their father. I married when I was seventeen. Constantine's my proper name. Clerk in an office, Sid was. Nicely brought-up young fellow with no money and no constitution. Just got a cold and died before I was twenty, and left me with two kids on my hands. Het's his spit and image."

Her face had fallen into heavy tragic lines. Stacy

sat waiting, and in a moment everything was changed. The lines broke up in laughter, the eyes twinkled outrageously.

"I wasn't having any more husbands after that, and if they wanted anything different, I'd laugh in their faces and tell 'em I was a respectable widow and I'd thank 'em to bear it in mind.' She cocked her head and chuckled. "It didn't stop 'em of course. Do you know who asked me to go off jaunting to Paris with him, and me never going to see fifty again? Well, maybe I'd better not tell you. But I've always had the men after me, and that's a fact."

Stacy put up a hand.

"If you could keep that expression, Mrs. Constantine—"

It broke up almost before she had spoken. The big mouth widened in a laugh.

"Well, I can't, my dear. If you could have seen your face! Did you think I meant your Charles?"

Stacy laughed too, anger just under the surface.

"He's quite free, if you want him."

"No, thank you, my dear. And as to being free— well, what do you mean by that? He's still fond of you—sticks out all over him when he looks at you."

Stacy put a little distance into her voice.

"Charles looks at everyone like that. It doesn't mean a thing. He'll tell you so himself."

"Have it your own way," said Myra Constantine. "You needn't believe me if you don't want to, but I'm never wrong about that sort of thing. I remember when Henry Minstrell began coming around I told Milly he was going to ask her, and she said he'd never think of it. 'Well, *someone* had better

60

think about it,' I said. 'He'll freeze you, and starch you, and make you over to suit his family, and it won't be what I should call a gay life, but that's your look-out, only you'd better get down to it and make up your mind if that's what you want.' So she did." She threw up her head with a jerk. "Lord—I'd have died of it in a week! But she's Sid's daughter, not mine—she likes it well enough. Only trouble she's got is there's no boy—just a couple of girls at boarding school." She smoothed all the expression out of face and voice. "'Yes, Grandmama—no, Grandmama.'" Her hands came together with a smacking clap, her shoulders rose in a shrug. "No blood in 'em, only nice pretty manners—poor Sid to the life, with a good shiny coat of Minstrell varnish! Well, as I've said more times than I can count, what's the odds so long as you're happy?"

The sitting might be considered to be going well. But which of all these fleeting expressions, these vigorous sudden changes of countenance, was Stacy going to lure to the ivory. She made a dozen sketches on paper, looked at them in despair, and made a dozen more. Myra was vastly pleased with them.

"Ugly old devil, aren't I? Hit me off to the life, these do. You just go on and you'll see it'll come, and it'll be a smasher. And now you go off and amuse yourself for the rest of the day."

Before this advice could be taken Stacy was called to the telephone. She felt a little surprised, for she could not imagine who could have tracked her here—so unless it was Charles—

It wasn't Charles. The sort of voice that suggests

61

horn-rimmed glasses and an intellectual brow enquired,

"Is that Miss Mainwaring?"

Stacy knew it at once. As a matter of fact a large portion of the English-speaking public would have known it, since it was in the habit of making announcements to them over the air, not on the most important occasions, but in what may perhaps be described as the donkey-work section.

"Tony! How on earth did you know I was here?"

Mr. Anthony Colesfoot sighed and said,

"Elementary, my dear Watson. You said you were going to Burdon. Enquiries gave me the number. The number said you had come to Warne House. So here we are."

"Where are you?"

"I have an aunt who lives at Ledstow. I've got three days off and I'm staying with her. I suggest that you dine with me tonight. There is, I believe, a place in Ledlington where the food doesn't exactly poison you." He spoke in a gentle, drawling manner and broke off to cough. "I beg your pardon, as they say on the air. I keep on doing it, which is really why I'm here. What about my calling for you at seven? I'll rake up a conveyance."

Stacy hesitated.

"Well, it's very nice of you, Tony. Look here, I'm going out in the afternoon, and I don't know when I shall get back, and I shall have to dress. I think you'd better make it half past."

"Say the quarter."

"All right."

She was just turning away, when the bell rang again. It was probably for someone else, but with just the chance that Tony might still be on the line she picked up the receiver and heard Lilias Grey say,

"Can I speak to—Miss Mainwaring?"

There was just the little significant pause before the name. With an inward feeling of having stepped back a pace Stacy said in what she could hear was a really horrid telephone voice,

"Speaking."

There was an involuntary "Oh!" And then, "It's Lilias Grey."

"How do you do, Lilias?"

"Oh, how do you do?"

Lilias was fluting, a sure sign that she was nervous. Her voice became higher and sweeter with every sentence.

"My dear, I didn't have a word with you last night. It wasn't possible at dinner, and then you disappeared. But I do so want to see you, and to show you what we have been doing to Saltings."

The "We" was a little barbed arrow that drew blood. Stacy found an arrow too.

"Yes—Charles was telling me."

"Yes? So nice we can all be friends, and such a relief, isn't it? It does simplify everything, don't you think? So much more civilized. That is why I felt I could ring up like this. I do want you to see my flat, and all we've done up here, so I wondered if you would come and have tea this afternoon."

"I'm afraid I can't this afternoon. I'm going out."

"With Charles? Of course—how stupid of me! Then what about Saturday? He won't be here, I'm afraid—some tiresome business or other. But if you can put up with just me—"

Stacy made an angry child's face at the telephone and said,

"It would be very nice."

"Then about half past four. You know where to get off the bus. There's one every twenty minutes as long as the holidays last." She rang off.

Stacy stamped her foot, looked at the receiver rather as if it were a snake in disguise, and hung it up in a despising manner. Lilias might or might not be a snake. The mere fact that she was in love with Charles didn't make her one. Adopted sister, or no adopted sister, she had always been in love with Charles. They both had flats at Saltings. And Lilias had said "We." Why on earth had she said she would go there to tea? If there was a place in the world she ought to stay away from, it was Saltings. If you've been put to the rack, you don't go and have tea in the torture chamber. Or do you? The plain fact was that she hadn't had the guts to say right out, "I never want to see the place again— or you—*or you*." Because Lilias had looked on whilst she was tortured. Kindly? Sympathetically? Regretfully? There was a question in each of these words, and it was a question to which Stacy had never been able to find an answer. It didn't matter now. What mattered was that Lilias had been there—she had seen her on the rack.

And yet—and yet—she would go to Saltings to-morrow. Lilias would show her "what we have done" with the place which was to have been her home with Charles. In the name of folly, why?

The answer came out of deep places—"Because I'm a fool—because I can't keep away."

CHAPTER 10

Stacy took the quarter past two bus to Ledstow. She wore a printed linen dress in shades of grey and blue, and nothing on her head except a good deal of really pretty brown hair. Brown hair can be very pretty indeed. Stacy's had lights in it and glints, and it curled because it was curly. It was, in fact, her one undeniable beauty. She knew as well as anyone else that she had neither Features nor a Complexion. Not in the sense in which these words constitute a claim to beauty. She had a nice skin and a pair of quite good grey eyes. Sometimes when she didn't see them herself they had rather a charming expression— something young, sensitive, aware, and rather sweet. For the rest—forehead, nose, cheeks, and chin—there wasn't very much to be said. They were there, just a forehead, a nose, two cheeks, and a chin. The mouth was red and not too small. When she smiled it showed nice white teeth. No, she had reason to be grateful about her hair.

The conclusion arrived at after an unusually prolonged study of her reflection in the not very flattering club mirror went with her to Ledstow. After that it merged into a distracted feeling that she was a fool to be going to meet Charles, and the cold bedrock conviction that she couldn't have stopped herself.

At the first halt clear of the town she got out feeling shaky about the knees. Charles must have been following the bus. He came up with her before she had walked a dozen yards, pushed open the door of his car, and said,

"Hullo, darling!"

It wasn't the old shabby car of their honeymoon, but a brand new Armstrong. Charles was doing well for himself, as Jack Constable had said last night. He looked right on the top of the wave. And all of a sudden she was there with him. They were on the top of the wave together and everything in the garden was lovely—warm sun, a breeze from the sea, and the two of them going off into the blue. It wouldn't last of course. It was just an interlude in the business of living, a breakaway from the shape and substance of reality, no more responsive to the past or future, no more substantial than a dream. What they did or said wouldn't matter, because it wouldn't really be said or done. The burden of responsibility was gone, and the burden of decision. Everything in her softened and relaxed.

Charles Forrest said,

"We can leave the car at the top and go down into Wakewell Cove. People don't go there much. The bathing's dangerous, and the path looks steeper than it is."

It was quite steep enough. They scrambled, she slipped, Charles caught her, they laughed together and he scolded her.

"You don't look where you're going."

"I do!"—indignantly.

"It's those idiotic shoes."

"But I didn't know I was coming on a beach. You said Ledlington."

Charles's arm across her shoulders, shaking her lightly, teasingly. "'Men were deceivers ever!'"

Then they were down on a beach of shell and shingle, with the sea a long way out and not a soul in sight, and Charles was saying,

"Business first, pleasure afterwards. We'll have a nice talk about alimony, and when that's given you a really good appetite we'll go and have buns at the Cat and Mouse."

Stacy sat on the fine ridged shingle. She ran her hands into it and brought up shells and small translucent stones. One of the shells was like a little cap of purple and mother-of-pearl. She frowned at it and said,

"That's nonsense. There's nothing to talk about."

Charles sounded lazy and amused.

"Think again, darling. The governing word is alimony. I think you must have missed it. There is almost no end to the avenues of conversation which it opens up."

Stacy went on looking at the pearly shell.

"I'm not interested in any of them."

He hummed under his breath,

"'No, I will not walk, no, I will not talk.
    No, I will not walk nor talk with thee.'

67

Come, come, let the blessed word alimony persuade you."

He saw the blood come up into her face. She said in a quick angry voice,

"There isn't any question of alimony! You didn't leave me—I left you."

"And you'd do it again tomorrow—a very proper spirit! You rise just like you always did. Now we laugh and start all over again. I'm doing very well out of Saltings. The flats have caught on, and people positively fight for them. All very pleasant and profitable, and a nice change from wondering where the next lot of rates and property tax were coming from. Well, that being that, and quite without prejudice, I would like you to have a look-in on it. I expect it's slipped your memory, but I did endow you with all my worldly goods."

Stacy sat up glowing.

"It seems to have slipped your memory that we've had a divorce."

She met a disturbing look.

"Think so? Well, you always go on reminding me. Now, to come down to brass tacks—I want you to take three hundred a year."

"Charles—of course I won't!"

He said in quite a serious tone,

"I'd feel a great deal more comfortable if you would."

Stacy's right hand closed on the little shell and broke it.

"I couldn't possibly! You ought to know that without being told!"

He was smiling.

"Go on—get it off the chest! There's a whole lot

more, and I know it all by heart—'I can support myself without your help! I'd rather starve than touch your money!'"

"Oh!" It was a pure breath of rage.

Charles continued to smile in a manner generally considered to be charming.

"All quite effective in melodrama, but not really up your street. For one thing it demands the flashing eye, the classic cast of feature, and either the Grecian or the Roman nose. Now with a little flub nose like yours—"

"It isn't!"

"Oh, definitely. I'm not saying anything against it, you know—I've always found it pleasant. I should never, for instance, have married a classic mark. It's what I should describe as an agreeable nose for comedy or the domestic hearth. But not calculated to carry off lines of the unhand-me-villain type."

Her mouth twitched, a dimple appeared. She broke into angry laughter.

Charles said, "That's better. It's always a pity to miscast yourself. And you might, you know, without me at hand to warn, to threaten, and command. You'll have to watch yourself."

"*Really*, Charles!"

"Definitely, my sweet. The—we won't call it alimony if you'd rather not—allowance sounds much less divorce court, doesn't it? It will be paid into your account quarterly."

"No, it won't! I'm not joking, and I can't possibly take it!"

Charles was sitting up hugging his knees. He said with a note of reproof in his voice,

"Quite right—you should never joke about money. I wouldn't dream of it. Nor would you if you knew how many midnight forms I had to fill before they'd let me get down to converting Saltings into flats. All honest-to-Ministry-of-Health toil, involving enormous mental strain. You know, the people who make out government forms are really wasted in the back rooms of the Civil Service. They ought to be drawing much larger salaries making up cross-word puzzles, then they'd be applauded and admired instead of being damned into heaps every time anyone fills up a form."

Stacy's dimple trembled in and out again.

"But I'm not going to take it, Charles."

He released his knees and with a sudden movement reached forward and took her by the wrists.

"Now you just listen to me!"

"I can listen quite well without you holding me. *Charles*—that hurts!"

"It was meant to. That money will be paid into your bank every quarter. You can go on the razzle-dazzle with it, or chuck it over Waterloo Bridge, or squander it on the undeserving poor, or you can leave it lying in the bank—I don't care a damn. But you can't stop me paying it in. I won't have you exercise your pride at the expense of my peace of mind. If miniatures boom, a miserable three hundred can be properly despised. If the bottom drops out of painting—well, I'd like to feel you had a herring and a crust."

"Charles—let go!"

He took his hands away at once, laughed, and said,

"No bruises, darling. And now let's talk about something else."

She shook her head.

"I can't stop your paying the money in—"

"Too true."

"But I shan't touch it."

"That's your affair. Let us abandon it and talk about me. Does it interest you at all to hear that I'm within measurable distance of being disinherited?"

"How—"

"Oh, not Saltings—that's round my neck for life. It's my Great Expectations. I believe Lewis to be contemplating matrimony."

"At his age!"

"Well, he's only about fifty-five, you know, and he's never been quite such a dried-up stick as he looks. He was engaged to Dossie Dale somewhere about twenty years ago. I'm told they split when he discovered that her Dossie should have been spelt with a B. One of the upper-hand-or-die brigade. Then of course there was his affair with Myra Constantine. Don't tell me you've been there nearly twenty-four hours and she hasn't told you all about it. He made strictly dishonourable proposals and suggested an unofficial honeymoon in Paris. She told him she was well over fifty, and if he was ten years younger, he was plenty old enough to know a respectable woman when he saw one. After which I believe he went the length of asking her to marry him, and she burst out laughing and said if she'd been going to marry again she could have done it twenty times a year for the past thirty years or so. They stayed good friends, and

71

that's a feather in Myra's cap. Lewis is the sort that might bear malice, but she didn't let him."

"And who is he proposing to now?"

"You saw that red-haired girl last night?"

"Of course I saw her. You don't mean to say—"

He nodded.

"Her name is Maida Robinson. Her hair, as you have observed, is red. She has a very pronounced 'Come hither' in her eye, and she has more or less got Lewis where she wants him. Up to last night the status of Robinson was in doubt, but during our third dance she confided artlessly that she had divorced him a year ago. There is therefore no just cause or impediment to her annexing Lewis."

"But they weren't taking any notice of each other last night."

"Lovers' quarrel, darling. You may have seen her look at me affectionately."

"Why should she?"

"Lewis was being shown that there were other good fish in the sea. Maida knows her stuff all right. Lewis was all ready to eat out of her hand by the time she let him have a dance. He's getting to know his place. He can adore her, and she can adore the Collection. I only hope he will have enough strength of mind to restrain her from wearing the Marsden rubies. She'll want to of course— red-haired women always hanker after crimson. And Dossie had them—someone is bound to have told her that. She wore them at the ball he gave for her when they were engaged. They are supposed to be unlucky. Some dancer was stabbed when she was wearing them—a girl called Lisa

Canaletti—in Paris under the second Empire. George Marsden bought them a dozen years later. His wife wore them for twenty years before she was killed in a carriage accident, and then her daughter had them, and she was killed in an air raid. After which the necklace sat in a bank until Lewis bought it. The middle ruby is very fine, and the story appealed to him."

"Charles, what is that Collection worth?"

He laughed.

"Quite a lot! But it won't come *our* way."

When he said *our* like that, she felt as if she had been touched upon the heart. And he didn't mean anything—he didn't mean anything at all. She heard him say,

"Just the stones themselves have a considerable market value. And then there are other morbid blokes beside Lewis who will pay a fancy price for a thing with a story pinned to it."

Something knocked at the door of Stacy's mind. She said,

"Isn't it dangerous having all that stuff?"

Charles had a fleeting frown.

"Everybody's been saying that for years, but nothing happens. Of course the stuff wasn't there during the war, but he got it back again as soon as he could. The whole annexe is really a strong-room, and the special things are in a safe over and above that. No windows, only one way in, and a light burning all night long in the passage from the house. It ought to be safe enough."

Stacy said quickly, "The light went out last night."

"Nonsense!"

73

"Charles, it did."

She told him about hearing the door click.

"I heard it, and I looked out of the window, and the passage was all dark."

"Are you sure?"

"Of course I'm sure. And then whilst I was looking the light came on again, and I'm practically certain the door of the annexe was just being shut. It was still moving."

"What time was this?"

"I don't know—late—very late—I'd been asleep a long time."

Charles broke out laughing.

"James Moberly was coming home after a night on the tiles! He would have to come through the house, because there's no other way to the annexe, and he left the light off to avoid a snooping eye."

"I haven't got a snooping eye! I was just looking out. And—Charles—he couldn't have come through the house, because the door is bolted after the last guest has gone. I know, because I asked this morning in case of dining out. I said could I have a key, and they said I could, only you have to warn in or the door would be bolted."

"Perhaps he did warn in."

"No, he didn't, because I asked if anyone was out last night, and they said no, and that everyone had gone home by twelve o'clock."

Charles looked at her curiously.

"Bit of a nosey parker, weren't you, my sweet?"

She flushed.

"It wasn't like that. I thought I'd just find out about having a key."

"In case I asked you out! How provident!"

74

"In case I wanted to go out, and—well, then everything just came along of itself. Charles, I didn't think it was anyone coming out of the house and going through the glass passage to the annexe—I didn't really."

"What did you think?"

"It's all vague, you know—just an impression. But I thought—I really did think it was someone coming from the passage into the house."

"But you said you saw the annexe door move when the light came on."

She nodded.

"Yes, I know. But I thought there was someone there with the door open, waiting for the person in the passage to get into the house and then shutting their own door and putting on the light."

Charles was looking at her hard.

"But you didn't see anyone doing those things?"

"No."

"And it might have been the other way round—someone coming out of the house, going into the annexe, and turning on the light when they got in?"

Her voice dragged and hesitated as she said,

"I suppose so."

"In which case it was probably James Moberly or Lewis himself."

"Then why was the passage dark? If there wasn't anything wrong, I mean."

"It was broad daylight when they came over to the house and they forgot to switch it on. Even Lewis is human. It doesn't switch on from the house, you know. It used to, but when Lewis turned the place over he had it changed. The

75

switches are all on the annexe side."

Stacy put her hand up to her cheek. The colour had brightened there.

"Then it was the way I said, because the light was on all right when I got into bed. It wasn't quite dark outside, but the passage was lighted from end to end. Only someone in the annexe could have turned it out after that."

Charles frowned and looked away.

"James absent without leave, I should think," he said rather shortly. Then, after a pause, "There's probably nothing in it. But I'll tell Lewis the light was off."

CHAPTER 11

It was later on when they were heading for Ledlington that Charles said in an airy voice,

"Who is the unfortunate chap?"

Stacy said, "What do you mean?"

"The object of all the staff work about the key—the current boy friend—the fellow who's going to take you out on the razzle-dazzle."

"Well, you said it was going to be you."

"Oh, no, you put in the staff work before I came along. You needn't have any inhibitions—I'm all friendly attention. Who is he?"

Stacy said,

"Why do you call him unfortunate?"

The words came tumbling out, and the moment

they were said she knew that she had let Charles score. He did it easily, lazily, with a smile for his own reflection in the driving-mirror.

"Fellow feeling, darling."

Stacy bit her lip. She ought to have bitten her tongue off before she gave him that opening.

The easy voice went on.

"Are you having him for keeps? You must let me know when you've got the day fixed. Not quite good taste for me to come to the wedding—but some little offering perhaps. I get a nice line of saucepans at wholesale rates for the flats. They're all furnished you know. Much more lucrative, and you can get rid of people if you don't like them. What about an aluminum set, with a double saucepan thrown in, and some appropriate lines on a card attached by a silver ribbon—'Thanks for the memory,' or something like that?"

She was almost too angry to speak, but she wasn't going to let him score again.

"It sounds delightful. I'll remember when it's your turn. I suppose you will be marrying almost at once?"

"I suppose so. Do you mind telling me who I am going to marry? I should rather like to know."

Stacy looked sideways. He was looking straight ahead at the Ledlington road as if he would like to murder it. Charles in a temper was Charles in a temper, a most ugly, black and exhilarating sight. Stacy felt very properly exhilarated. She said,

"Lilias, I suppose."

The car swerved right across the road. Charles swore, straightened out, and burst out laughing.

"Another crack like that and you'll have us in the ditch! Lilias—"

"It's no use your saying she's your sister, because she isn't. Your mother adopted her, which is a very different thing. The Archbishop of Canterbury would marry you tomorrow."

"I don't think so, darling. He's got views about divorce."

"Well, she isn't your sister."

"As you say. But there are about twenty million other women in England who are not my sisters either. Almost any of them would be more likely than Lilias, you know. Because when you've been brought up to the brother and sister business it gets in your bones, so to speak." He laughed again. "The fierce light that beats upon a throne is nothing to the light that beats upon a nursery. One has had all the quarrels, heard all the fibs—what would be the point of getting married?"

Under the jesting tone there was something, she didn't quite know what. She said in a hurry,

"I never told you any lies."

"You hadn't much time, darling, had you? Life's full of these wasted opportunities. Never mind, there are lots of good fish in the sea."

"I don't tell lies!"

"A neglected education. But it's never too late to mend."

He turned into the Market Square and drew up in the parking-place beneath the statue of Sir Albert Dawnish. The first of the famous Quick Cash Stores had struggled into being in one of the old houses in the direction of which he now waves a podgy hand. It has been said that he wears the worst suit of any statue in Britain. He liked an easy fit, and the sculptor has rendered it with heroic realism. But Ledlington reveres his memory, dances in the hall he built, and sends its sons to compete hopefully for the scholarships he endowed.

Charles locked the car, took Stacy by the elbow, and proceeded across the cobblestones to the Cat and Mouse. Only the name was new—a mere twenty-year-old upstart with a wrought iron sign upon which a fierce green-eyed cat curved horrid claws above a small and shrinking mouse. The house had been a mercer's shop when James I was on the throne. Great ladies of the county had bought changeable silks there, and fine Lyons velvet. It was now a tea-shop, with as many of its small rooms thrown together as was compatible with safety.

Charles had not exaggerated the gloom, but he threaded it with some assurance and arrived at the farther side of the long straggling room. Here privacy was catered for by orange curtains and palms in tubs. Each small screened cubicle contained a hard wooden settle, a table, and two chairs. Only the slim and agile could get round the table to the settle. A dim orange light lurked here and there between the black beams of the old ceiling.

Stacy achieved the settle, and was deserted. Charles had murmured, "Personal selection of buns," and disappeared. She was left to think what a fool she had been to put the idea of Lilias into his head. Perhaps she had—perhaps she hadn't. If Charles had been passionately in love with Lilias and going to marry her next minute he might have

put on just that kind of act. Carefree indifference—
that was the line. But he had swerved and very
nearly run the car off the road. Charles didn't do
that for nothing. Something had got right home—
he had very nearly lost control of the car. And then
he had laughed. She tried to remember just what
she had said.

She was still trying, when from the other side of
a bristly palm and some dusty orange curtains a
voice said,

"Oh, yes, Charles will play if I want him to."
There was a pretty, enraging laugh.

If Stacy had been in a more normal frame of mind
she would have reflected that Charles is one of the
commoner English names. She didn't reflect at
all—she jumped to a conclusion. The voice was
one of those low, husky ones rendered popular by
the films, and she thought there was a red-haired
sound about it. The conclusion to which she
jumped was that only a cheap orange curtain and
a leaf or two of palm separated her from Maida
Robinson, and that Maida was talking about
Charles Forrest. She thought about coughing, she
thought about moving the table, but she didn't do
either. There was the indistinguishable murmur of
a male voice, and then the woman again.

"It'll be all right. You needn't worry—he'll
play—" There was just about half of some other
word, interrupted by an exclamation. "Gosh—
here he comes! What do we do?"

This time the man's reply was audible.

"We're only having tea. Even Lewis—"

She said, "Shut up! We'll go. We've finished anyway."

Stacy sat where she was and saw them emerge. She had been perfectly right. Maida Robinson it was, in white linen, her hair glinting copper under the orange lights. And the man was Jack Constable. Encountering Charles midway amongst the little tables, they greeted him gaily, fleetingly, and were gone.

Charles came on and set a plate of buns on the table. Stacy wondered what it was all about and held her tongue.

She had plenty of time to dress before Tony Colesfoot came to call for her. He was, in fact, a little late, and more than a little sorry for himself. Long before they reached Ledlington it was evident that the evening was not going to be a success. Arrived at the Crown and Sceptre, he complained about the draught from the tall dining-room windows, which were all open at the top and could only be shut by the united efforts of three waiters. After changing their table twice he hunched his shoulders and shivered ostentatiously.

The dinner wasn't good, but it wasn't bad. Tony shuddered some more, and began to tell her all about the influenza he had had last winter, and just where it differed from the influenza he thought he was getting now, drawing the gloomy conclusion that he was in for a much worse go. He ate nothing, drank three cups of black coffee, and at twenty past eight announced that he thought he had better go home to bed.

"My aunt said I wasn't fit to come out."

Stacy found herself agreeing with Miss Colesfoot. She wasn't quite prepared to find herself cast as the vamp who had lured poor Tony from his

81

bed, but one glance at the angry solicitous lady who opened the door to them was enough to tell her that this was, in fact, her role.

"He should never have gone! I told him so, but he said he must keep his appointment. Most thoughtless, I must say. No, there isn't anything you can do, Miss Mainwaring. Straight to bed, Tony! I have the kettle on, and you shall have a boiling drink and two hot-water bottles."

There was really nothing to be said or done. Tony was coughing his head off, and Miss Colesfoot, stout and formidable, would have been glad to fry her in boiling oil. Thankful to find that the taxi had waited, Stacy climbed back into it and was driven to Warne House.

CHAPTER 12

She meant to go straight to bed, but as she came into the hall there were quite a lot of people there. They were apparently coming out of the drawing-room and moving in the direction of the annexe, shepherded by Lewis Brading. He wore an air of importance. Even before Lady Minstrell slipped a hand inside her arm and spoke, Stacy guessed that the Collection was on view.

"I don't know if you've ever seen it, but it's well worth while. Lovely things—most of them with stories attached. And models of all the really famous jewels."

Before Stacy could answer, she was calling to Lewis.

"Miss Mainwaring has just come in. May I bring her too?"

He turned, and Stacy met his cold, disliking eyes—even colder and more disliking than they had been when she was Charles's wife. He inclined his head in the slightest of bows, said, "Certainly," in that rather grating voice, and they were all moving down the passage. She did murmur something about going up to bed, only to hear Myra Constantine say, "Nonsense!" just behind her.

She looked round and saw her, quite square in crimson brocade, with Jack Constable on one side of her, and her daughter Hester on the other. Myra said heartily,

"You've seen 'em before, and so have I, but I can always do with seeing them again. Gives me something to covet. It's as good as a tonic."

The door at this end of the glass passage was like any garden door at the side of a house, the upper half of it glass, so that the whole length of the passage beyond could be seen from the hall of the house. It was not lighted yet, because it was still broad daylight, but Stacy could hear Lewis explaining.

"I take my precautions, you see. At sunset we light the passage up. . . . . We? Oh, Moberly or I. I have a sitting-room over on this side in the house. . . . . Yes, this door on my right. It was my study, and I've kept it. But Moberly and I both sleep in the annexe. . . . . No, there aren't any windows, but it's all air-conditioned."

They were in the passage now. A fine steel chain

83

swung from his hand. He fitted the key to which it was attached and opened a door at the far end. It was very different from the one through which they had just come—a metal door painted green— not a house door at all, the door of a safe. There was a small lobby, and then a second door equally strong.

Lewis went on explaining.

"The whole building is guaranteed burglar-proof. This is the only way in. The glass passage was my idea. Anyone having a shot at these doors would be a bit conspicuous. And the light is projected from inside this building—it can't be tampered with. Quite ingenious, I think."

The second door swung in. He touched a switch, and they came into a brightly lighted room, long and narrow in shape and hung from ceiling to floor with curtains of black velvet. Round the sides there were glass-topped show-cases, and in the middle, set about with chairs, a long narrow table like an old-fashioned trestle table covered by a black velvet cloth. The effect was macabre. The change from the brightness of the summer evening, where the blue of sea and sky were shot through with golden light, was so great as to produce a mental shock. It was bright enough in this strange room, but there was no life in the brightness. The impression made upon Stacy three years ago was repeated. Now, as then, a shiver went down her spine and she had a childish impulse to run away. A breath stirred her hair. Charles's voice murmured at her ear,

"The mortuary chamber—"

She very nearly screamed. She hadn't heard him come in, she didn't know there was anyone behind her. She stopped the scream, but she hadn't time to stop her body jerking with the start she gave.

Charles's hand came down on her shoulder. He said in the same murmuring way as before,

"Stupid little thing—you needn't jump right out of your skin."

His hand felt warm through the thin silk of her dress. He left it there for a moment, and for that moment everything in her rocked. Whatever Charles was, or whatever he had done, he had only to touch her and the past was back again. The thought was there, and gone. She wrenched from looking after it.

Lewis Brading was continuing the personally conducted tour.

"Those two doors on the left as we came in lead to Moberly's bedroom and the bathroom. The one on the long side of the room gives on to a passage which serves my bedroom and the laboratory. Now here—" he led the way to the show-cases—"here is a very interesting part of the Collection—models of famous stones." He paused and quoted, as he always did at this point, " 'Too dear for my possessing.' " The self-conscious note in his voice robbed the words of their poetry and made a pun of them.

Everyone crowded forward to look where he was pointing.

"They are only models, of course, without the fire and brilliance of the originals. The Star of the South, found in eighteen-fifty-three in the mines of Bogagan by a poor Negress. It weighed two hundred and fifty-four-and-a-half carats before cutting. It is, as you see, faintly tinted with rose, and must be one of the most beautiful diamonds in the world. . . . . The Koh-i-noor weighed seven hundred and eighty-seven-and-a-half carats before cutting according to Tavernier who saw it at the court of Aurangzeb. It has, of course, been re-cut, and can be seen in the Queen's crown at the Tower. . . . . Here is a model of the famous Rajah of Mattan's diamond. It was found in Borneo, and weighs three hundred and eighteen carats. It is, as you see, shaped like a pear and without facets."

He continued to enumerate diamonds. The Nizam. The Regent, carried by the first Napoleon on the hilt of his state sword. The Sancy, lost on the battlefield by Charles the Bold, found by a Swiss soldier and sold for two francs, recovered from the dead body of a faithful servant who had swallowed it to prevent it falling into the hands of thieves. The Pigott. The Orloff, shaped like half an egg, and once the eye of a famous idol. The triangular Nassac. The famous Hope diamond, blue as a sapphire.

All this information was being punctuated by questions and cries of admiration. Myra Constantine's deep voice commented on the Sancy.

"Well, I shouldn't fancy wearing a thing that had come out of a dead body—not myself, I wouldn't. Anyhow I've never been all that struck on jewelry. Never had the face nor the figure for it—perhaps that's why. What's going to happen to all these pretty things, Lewis?"

He said without a smile,

"I have left this part of my Collection to the Ledlington museum. It is, of course, of great interest, but of no particular monetary value."

His grey face had no expression. Without further comment he passed on to the next show-case and began to discourse on rubies. From there to the sapphire, the emerald, the topaz, the amethyst, to famous engraved stones.

Stacy had heard it all before. It brought a horrid feeling that there had been a kind of time-slip— that they had been caught back again, she and Charles, to where they were three years ago. It was, of course, sheer nonsense. The one thing no-body could do to you was to make you live the past over again. She turned and said to Charles,

"I want to get out."

His eyes smiled into hers.

"Too, too reminiscent?"

"No. There's no air."

He laughed a little.

"Lewis will be mortally offended—he's fright-fully proud of his air-conditioning. And you know you'd like to see the real stuff. He'll be getting round to it any time now."

"I don't—want to—"

"Darling, I promise to catch you if you faint."

She could not have looked less like fainting. Her cheeks burned. She moved abruptly away from him as Lewis passed behind one of the velvet cur-tains and disappeared from view. James Moberly followed him. After a moment or two they could hear an unseen door swing back, and then the two men came out again, carrying between them a long tray covered with black velvet and heaped with jewels.

This was the moment which Lewis Brading par-ticularly enjoyed. He liked to hear his guests draw in their breath, he liked to watch awe and greed come up in the women's eyes. The whole thing was, of course, very carefully stage-managed. These necklaces, bracelets, pendants, and rings had each its own place on the shelves of his inner safe, but when he was going to show his Collection it pleased him to produce this Arabian Nights effect.

Stacy found Charles at her elbow again.

"Nubian slaves are indicated, don't you think? I always feel that James and Lewis strike a jarring note. But there's going to be a Sultan all right. Just watch!"

Her eyes followed his. James and Lewis had set down the glittering tray just at the centre of the long table. Maida Robinson faced them across the narrow black velvet strip which covered it. Everyone had moved that way, but it was she who held the eye. Her black dress melted into the background. Her arms, her neck, and her dazzling copper hair stood out against it. She was leaning forward, her two hands on the table, her eyes on all those shining stones. For a moment Stacy had a flash of recognition. The hazel eyes had gone green. They had a slitted look. She thought of a cat watching a bird. It was gone in a moment, but it was horrid while it lasted.

Maida broke into a low laugh, lifted her hands from the table, and clapped them softly.

"Ooh—how lovely! And now you must tell us all about them."

Lewis was more than ready to oblige.

"Well, if you'll sit down first—I think there are

enough chairs—then everyone will be able to see without crowding."

Maida sank gracefully into the chair behind her, pulled it up close, and leaned forward across the table, her arms bare to the shoulder without the least stain of sunburn to spoil their milky beauty. Some red-haired women tan easily, and freckle too, but there are others upon whom the sun has no effect. Maida was one of them. She could bask the whole summer through upon the beach without acquiring a single freckle or the least shade of brown. Since sunburn was the rage, she sometimes applied it artificially, but for the past few weeks she had left her skin to nature and been rewarded by Lewis Brading's approbation. Certainly against all this black velvet and under the bright overhead lights she made a very dazzling effect. Charles appeared to think so. He said lightly, "Breath-taking, isn't she?" and went to take the place beside her. She had glanced round for a moment. Perhaps the look had beckoned him.

Stacy sat down at the end of the table. She had Hester Constantine on her right. There were some people called Brown beyond her, of the sort of young middle age that is by way of keeping up with all the things their children do; then Charles, Maida, Jack Constable, Lilias Grey, Myra Constantine, and Lady Minstrell. All this brilliance was not becoming to Lilias. The jewels, Maida's glowing vitality, gave her a drained, colourless look. Ugly old Myra came out of it better than she did.

Myra said in her deep voice,

"Come along, Lewis, get a move on! Ring up the curtain!"

She didn't exactly sing the last words, but the sound of the *Pagliacci* tune came through.

Lewis turned and made her an odd stiff little bow.

"But you have heard it all before," he said in a deprecating voice.

She laughed enjoyably, crinkling up her eyes.

"Nothing new under the sun, they say. But I don't get tired of the old things—old songs, old friends, old times—so stop being modest and get the goods out from under the counter!"

Lewis came back with, "Hardly *under* the counter, my dear Myra," and dipping into the glittering heap before him, he brought up a ring. The square emerald caught the light between flashing diamond shoulders.

Maida stretched out her hands and said, "Ooh!", and before half a dozen pairs of envious eyes Lewis dropped it into her palm.

"Put it on and let's see what it looks like."

She slipped it on to the third finger of her left hand. It looked magnificent. Lewis nodded his approval.

"Women with your colouring should always wear emeralds—it brings out the green in their eyes."

She lifted her long dark lashes.

"But my eyes aren't green. They're supposed to be hazel."

They might have been alone. He said,

"I have seen them look green. If you were to wear emeralds—"

"I haven't any." Her eyes went again to the ring.

Lewis raised his voice from the low confidential tone which it had taken.

"Now that is a very fine stone, and it has an interesting history. You remember the Greystairs murder? You will, Myra."

Myra Constantine nodded.

"The girl asked for it," she said. "Nineteen-seventeen, wasn't it? Johnny Greystairs got a spot of leave and came home to find his wife carrying on with another chap. Shot them both, and jumped out of a fifth-floor window as the police broke in. I used to know Johnny—not a ha'p'orth of vice in him till she drove him crazy. You don't mean to say—"

Lewis Brading smiled.

"Yes, it was her engagement ring. My latest purchase. So there's something you haven't seen!" He leaned across the table and drew the ring from Maida's finger. "Now, this bracelet—" he lifted a solid gold band about two inches wide encrusted with diamonds and rubies—"this went down with the *Birkenhead*. I bought it twenty-five years ago from the granddaughter of the woman who was wearing it. And this—no, it's not beautiful or valuable. It's just a little hair brooch with a pearl border, but it was worn on the scaffold by Mrs. Manning the poisoner. She was hanged in black satin, and no one would wear it for a generation."

Hester Constantine, drooping beside Stacy, said in a quivering voice,

"I wouldn't wear any of those things if you were to pay me."

Stacy couldn't have agreed with her more. Every one of the things which Lewis displayed with so much pride had a story, and every story was heavy with blood and tears. Not that he gave them in a

91

dramatic manner. Murder, retribution, jealousy, hatred, revenge—his dry voice brought them all down to the common-place, and in a way that made it more dreadful, because it is in the commonplace that we all live and move. The great, the devastating passions are all very well on the other side of the footlights in the never-never land of drama and romance, but when murder comes down off the stage, sits beside you in the gallery or the stalls, and walks back with you into your own respectable suburb, then it has a bare, stripped terror to chill the heart.

As Lewis went on with his recital, Stacy felt her heart being chilled. This necklet had belonged to quite an ordinary girl from a safe and pleasant home. She had shot a man because he was leaving her for another woman. . . . . This scintillating buckle had clasped the cloak of a famous courtesan of Victorian times. She had started life as a poor girl in a milliner's workroom. She ended it on the filthy straw of a debtors' prison. At some point between these two places she had dazzled the eyes and wrung the hearts of countless fellow women.

"I hate them," said Hester Constantine in that shaking voice. Lewis Brading must have heard what she said. He looked sideways at her with a cold resentment which was very unpleasant. Hester hardly seemed to notice it, but Stacy felt a shiver go over her. There was something about Lewis Brading—

He had picked up a glittering brooch.

"Very few women could hate this," he said. "Of course diamonds do not suit everyone." His glance touched Hester cruelly and came back to the jewelled brooch. "Beautiful—isn't it? The Marziali brooch—five perfectly matched brilliants of four carats set on a bar. A wedding-present from her husband to Guilia Marziali in 1817. She was wearing it when he stabbed her and her lover three years later. The affair made a great sensation in Rome, but as the Count committed suicide he was never brought to justice. She was a great beauty, of a noble Sardinian family. Strange to think that these bright stones were drowned in her blood."

Hester Constantine said, "Don't!"

The Browns beyond her, without going so far, opined that they wouldn't really care about having things like that.

"Very handsome, and must have cost a lot of money," said Mr. Brown in his hearty voice. "But I wouldn't care to give my wife anything with such unpleasant associations." To which Mrs. Brown responded with a shudder, "And I wouldn't wear it, Tommy, if you did."

Maida looked round at her for a moment.

"Wouldn't you?" she said. Then, with a darting glance at Lewis, "Are you going to take her at her word? You'd better not—she might think again. And I warn you, don't count on me to refuse anything because someone got murdered in it. I *adore* these lovely things." Her voice made the word really sound like adoration. Her hands went out to the necklace he was picking up. "Oh, Lewis, let me put it on—*please*—just for a moment!"

He let her take it and snap the clasp. Diamonds in a light linked tracery of roses, the flowers flat and formal, each with an emerald at its heart. Stacy

93

looked at them, and couldn't look away. She heard Lewis say,

"Well, no one was murdered in this. It belonged to my several times great-grandmother, Damaris Forrest, who was a lady-in-waiting at the court of Queen Anne. She was beautiful, she was virtuous, she lived to a ripe old age, and died lamented by a numerous family. All the Forrest women have been goodlooking and good."

Lewis had his showman's patter by heart. It was word for word what he had said three years ago when he had brought out the necklace to show her and Charles had fastened it about her neck. She couldn't flatter herself that it had looked as well there as it did on Maida Robinson, but she had run to the long plain mirror at the end of the room and admired herself in her white dress with the diamonds and emeralds making little rainbows under the light. Her eyes had been bright above the stones, and her cheeks rosy with happiness, and Charles had looked as if he loved her with all his heart. The picture came back as Maida sprang up and ran, just as Stacy had run, to the mirror which hung between two of the velvet curtains. And then it was blotted out by that other picture, the one she could never forget—two nights later, and Charles in his pyjamas standing with his back to her in front of the bureau in his dressing-room. Just the one light on overhead, and Charles standing there with the necklace in his hand. Midnight and no one stirring, her nightdress falling away from one shoulder, her bare feet cold on the carpet. And Charles with Damaris Forrest's necklace in his hand.

She came back with the feeling that everything

was sliding from under her feet. Because the necklace was here. Lewis Brading had it again. It was flashing from Maida's reflection in the mirror at the end of the room.

Maida turned. They heard her take a long sighing breath. She came to her seat again with a floating step, a lovely, vital creature, her eyes as green as the emeralds. She put up reluctant hands to the clasp, held the necklace dangling, her eyes caressing it, and with an impulsive gesture thrust it across the table to Lewis Brading.

"Oh, take it, take it! And you'd better be quick, or I shan't be able to bring myself to give it up."

He met the extravagance with the faintest of smiles.

"Well, it suits you," he said.

Stacy saw their glances meet. She thought, "It won't be very long before she has it for keeps."

Lewis delivered the rest of his lecture. But Stacy never got past the Forrest necklace. She was back to three years ago, and she was wondering what she had done.

CHAPTER 13

It was strange to come out into the daylight. They had only been in the annexe for an hour, and there was still sunlight on the sea. Charles found himself taking Maida home. It was just one of those things. He certainly hadn't planned it, but it was happening. Jack Constable had been neatly paired off with Lilias, and Charles manoeuvred into handing over his car to them. It had all been very smoothly done by way of "Charles darling, if I don't have some fresh air I shall pass out. And, *honestly*, if somebody doesn't positively march me home, I shall come back to those emeralds like a moth and be found all battered and smashed against that horrible steel door. Too paralysing for poor Lewis. And of course there isn't any need for me to break up the party. Lilias, Jack—all the rest of you—it's just that I simply can't take in any more. It's been too wonderful. I feel like the Queen of Sheba—just completely gone down the drain with looking at so many marvellous things." She ran back to where Lewis stood on the threshold of the annexe, both her hands stretched out, her voice low and husky. Snatches of what she said drifted to Stacy—"You do understand what I feel, don't you?" Then a murmur, and then, "A good opportunity really. I'll break it gently. You stay here and put your heavenly things away." There was a final murmur before she broke away to link arms with Charles and cry,

"Let's get out into the air! It looks too lovely!"

They went off together.

Lewis stepped back and shut his door. Stacy went up to her room.

The cliff path to Saltings runs just as Stacy had seen it in her dream, only without the high wall she had imagined. It twists and turns along the cliff, with a drop to the beach which is sometimes quite sheer and giddy. When the tide is in you look down upon the water, when it is out there are rocks, but on the landward side there is only a bank which seldom rises more than a dozen feet. Here and there the bank hollows into a bay, and there is a seat. A pleasant walk for a summer evening.

Charles was wondering why he had been cut out and carried off. Not to make Lewis jealous, since Maida had been at some pains to soothe him. He thought he would leave her to play the game her own way.

He was telling her what had always been considered a good story, when she waved it away and said,

"Charles, I want to talk to you."

Drama? Well, it was her game. He would have preferred. . . . . He had no time to pursue the theme, for she came out plump with,

"Lewis has asked me to marry him."

He nodded gravely.

"Which of you do I congratulate?"

"I haven't said I will—not yet."

"Then perhaps I congratulate him."

She flared.

"How can you be such a beast? But you won't make me lose my temper!"

"An admirable resolution. Let me help you out—I will congratulate you both."

"For what?"

His crooked eyebrows rose.

"For your hesitation, reluctance, or whatever it is."

"Charles, you *are* a beast!"

"For suggesting that you will probably make each other damned unhappy?"

"Why should we?"

He looked at her with a hint of mockery.

"You can't live on emeralds—or can you?"

"They'd go quite a long way," said Maida Robinson.

"In that case it's your funeral."

As if the word had rung a bell, she said almost eagerly,

"He has made a will in my favour."

Charles allowed himself to smile.

"This time I really do congratulate you."

She changed colour vividly.

"I didn't plan it—it was all on the spur of the moment. I was going to make a will myself—I had one of those will-form things. I asked if he would witness it, but when he found I was leaving him something—"

"A most artistic touch!"

She met him with bravado.

"Yes, it was, wasn't it? Anyhow he said he couldn't, as he was an interested party, and—and—well it ended in his asking me to marry him. And he took the will-form and he filled it in, leaving everything to me, and he said he would get two people to see him sign it—somewhere outside the club, so as not to make talk."

Charles gave her an enigmatic look.

"But it isn't signed yet. I'm surprised you didn't strike while the iron was hot."

There was a brilliant triumph in her eyes.

"Oh, he'll sign it all right. He's mad about me. Anyhow it's really only a gesture. He'll make a proper real will next week when he goes up to see his lawyers—settlements, you know, and all that sort of thing. This is just—well, what I said, a gesture, and in case of getting run over by a bus, or anything like that. It's as well to be on the safe side, isn't it?" She tilted her head and looked up at him. "Well?"

"Well, what?"

"Haven't you got anything to say? Don't you *care*? Aren't you going to do anything about it?"

He gave her his charming smile.

"I could push you over the cliff of course—that would be one way out."

Her voice softened, her eyes held his.

"There might be another way—"

Charles cursed all red-haired women with green eyes. *"Les yeux verts vont à l'enfer."* He said lightly, "I can't think of one." Then, with a complete change of manner, "Look here, Maida, this is your show, and I don't want to butt in. Lewis can marry anyone he pleases, and he can leave his money and that damned Collection to anyone he likes. If you're fond of him, go ahead and marry him. You'll look very well in the emeralds. If you're not fond of him, I should advise you to think again. I've known Lewis for a good many years, and you won't change him. When the first effervescence is over you'll take second place to the Collection. That's what he's really married to, you know—any woman is just a temporary diversion. He's had flutters before, but he always comes back to what he really loves. I can tell you quite honestly, I don't believe he's capable of love for anything else. He'll go on living in that mausoleum with his ghoulish gewgaws, and you'll be just another acolyte. He's got James Moberly, poor devil. But James can't wear the jewels—you can. One acolyte to tend the stuff, another to show it off. I seem to remember that the women captives in a Roman triumph used to be loaded with jewels. Well, that would be more or less your place in Lewis's scheme of things."

She kept her eyes on his. They really were very beautiful eyes, large and full of light, neither grey nor brown nor altogether green. They had the shoaling play of colour that water has in a green place. She said,

"*Charles—*"

He dragged his eyes away. A light sweat broke on his temples.

"Well," he said, "you have been warned."

They had been standing. The sun was very low. A little cool breeze came in from the sea. It was grateful. He began to walk on again, and she fell into step.

After a moment she said in the voice of an angry child,

"What's the good of warning me? I've got to have *something*. You don't suggest anything else."

"I'm only the looker-on. He sees most of the game, you know."

"But he doesn't play?" Her voice made the words an invitation and a caress.

Charles said, "Oh, no, he doesn't play. He has his own game, you see. It wouldn't do to mix them."

She broke into odd angry laughter.

"Then I'll just have to be a cousin to you, darling!"

CHAPTER 14

Stacy went up to her room and locked the door.
When she had done that she stood irresolute. Time
went by. Presently she went over to the window
and sat there. The window looked to the annexe
and to the hill against which it was built. Very little
air came in. She would have liked to feel the breeze,
but it didn't come this way.

All at once she knew that she was cold. She
would have liked to feel the air, but she was cold.
She got a coat and pulled it close about her, but
there was a cold shaking inside her which went on.
She had broken her marriage because of Damaris
Forrest's necklace. Because Charles had stolen it.
Because she couldn't be married to a thief. But now
Lewis Brading had it back. Charles must have given
it back. Perhaps Charles had put it back, and Lewis
had never known. That didn't make any difference.
It was what she knew herself that mattered—it was
what she knew about Charles. And Charles was a
thief. Slowly, painfully, straining, she could listen
to Lilias saying, "He's always done it, but it's never
been found out. We've managed—we've put
things back. It broke his mother's heart—it's breaking mine. That's why I wouldn't marry him. He
oughtn't to have married anyone. I hoped you'd
never know." She had to strain to catch the words
because they came on such low, broken breath. She

had had to strain—there, in the half light, three years ago, with Lilias turned away from her and saying, "He's always done it."

Looking back at that young, crude Stacy was like looking at someone else. You didn't live with a thief. Charles was a thief—she couldn't go on living with Charles. She couldn't see him—she couldn't tell him—she couldn't talk about it ever. Even to think about it made her hot with shame. She must get away—she must get away at once. The thing that wanted to stay was her body. You could make your body do what you told it to do. She could make her hand take a piece of paper and write on it, "I've made a dreadful mistake. I oughtn't to have married you. I can't talk about it. Don't try to make me come back. I *can't*."

He had tried all the same. First an angry, "What's all this nonsense?", and so on through, "At least let us meet and talk it out," to the last, "Very well—just as you like. I won't ask you again. We have to wait three years for a divorce."

She had hidden herself and she hadn't answered any of the letters—not really answered them, because all she had done was to write those first lines over again and say, "I can't ever come back." She had always known that she couldn't hold out if she and Charles were face to face. If he looked at her, if he touched her, she would give way—and despise herself and him forever. You can't live with a thief.

She sat there and looked at herself, and Charles, and Lilias. There was something in each of them that was a kind of bedrock self, the thing which couldn't be changed. She supposed that everyone had a bedrock self. When you lived with people you found out what it was. Suppose, when you got down to it, there was no rock but only shifting sand. That was what had happened with Charles. . . . . Lilias? She wasn't sure. . . . . Perhaps *her* bedrock was the way she felt about Charles, because she had always known he was a thief, and she went on loving him. Stacy couldn't do that. All at once she felt mean and small.

What was the use of thinking about it? It was all over now. She wouldn't have stayed here five minutes if it hadn't been all quite over. Stop thinking, stop analysing. It's all past, it's all gone, it's all dead. Charles's face rose before her so vividly that she very nearly cried out. His eyes smiled . . . . .

She sat a long time after that. Presently, as the room darkened, her thoughts tangled, drifted a little way and came back, drifted farther and took her into a dream. She didn't know what it was, or how long it held her, but she woke from it with a startled sense of fear. For a moment she did not know where she was. The room was dark, and she was cold. She shivered in her coat. She had fallen asleep by the window, and she had had a frightening dream, but she couldn't remember what it was. Fear had come back with her, but not memory.

She stood up and went to look out of the window, and just as she got there, the light came on in the glass passage below. She stood staring at it. It hadn't been on when she waked. Everything was quite dark. If the light had been on, she would have seen the reflection here in her room. She stepped to the chair from which she had risen. The glow from the passage followed her. It threw the pattern of the window across the floor, it touched her breast, her hands, her feet. It hadn't been there when she woke up.

With the thought in her mind that someone had come from the annexe to the house, she made her way to the door. It was not a reasoning thought, but it took hold of her. She opened the door, and saw the dark passage run towards a dimly lighted landing. Without stopping to think she went in the direction of the light. If anyone came from the annexe, he must pass along the passage under this one. He must come out into the hall—unless he turned into the billiard-room or into Lewis Brading's study.

She was on the landing before she thought about the study, and all at once she felt she was making a fool of herself. Anyone coming from the annexe would be Lewis, or James Moberly. Either of them could have business in the study. She frowned, standing with her hand on the rail which guarded the landing and looking down over it into the hall. A light burned there too. The stairs came up in an easy curve. If James Moberly or Lewis Brading had business in the house, why should the light in the glass passage be turned off and then on again? There was only one answer to that, because there was only one reason for turning off the light—the person using the passage didn't want to be seen. But only Lewis or James could turn the light off, and turn it on again.

She had got as far as that, when she heard a sound from below. Someone was walking along the passage from the glass door. She looked down over the railing and saw Hester Constantine come into the hall. Just for a moment Stacy did not recognize her. She was in her nightdress, with her bare feet in slippers and her hair loose on her shoulders. She held a gorgeous embroidered shawl about her. The colours of bright birds and flowers threw back the light, a scarlet fringe dripped to the floor.

Stacy stared incredulously. The shawl, of course, was Myra's. But this woman with the loosened hair and the dreaming face, was she really Hester? She was at any rate ten years younger, and twenty years better looking. She had a slow smile, and the air of a woman who is content.

Stacy ran back to her room in a hurry and shut the door.

CHAPTER 15

The morning came up clear and fine—a blue sky, a blue sea, and the promise of heat. There was nothing to show that the day would be any different from any other day—an August Friday with the weather set fair and a warm week-end to follow. The club was going to be full. The bathing would be perfect, there would be tennis on the hard courts—all the normal routine of a holiday place in the height of a holiday season.

Stacy lay between sleeping and waking, with an idle wash of thoughts that came and went like drifting seaweed. Emeralds and Maida's red hair. Lilias with the pinched look she had last night. Charles going over to sit by Maida—walking home with her. Lewis like something grey that had come from under a stone—she didn't like Lewis Brading any more than he liked her. Hester Constantine wrapped close in Myra's brilliant shawl. . . . .

She roused herself with an effort, sat up, pushed back her hair, and began to think about the miniature. Myra would give her a sitting at ten. Yesterday's sitting seemed a long time ago. She had to fight against the feeling that the miniature didn't matter as much as it had mattered yesterday. It had been crowded out, pushed into the background, swamped by all these people and what they were thinking and feeling. For three years she had pushed people out of her life. She had shut herself up from them, not cared what they said or did, and turned all her thoughts, her interests, her energies into the channel of work. And now all the things she had shut out were flooding back again. They mattered again. The cold indifferent feeling was for her work, which no longer seemed to matter at all.

But everything which happened at Warne House on that Friday was going to matter. Every single smallest thing, every detail; the exact moment at which everyone came and went; what they did, said, wore; whether they spoke to anyone; whether they wrote or received a letter; whether they telephoned—it was all to matter, down to the last shade of expression, down to the last turn of the head and tone of the voice. But Stacy wasn't to know that. Perhaps none of them knew it yet, though even that was to be in doubt.

It was not to be in dispute that Lewis Brading walked down to the entrance gate and took the nine-thirty bus which goes to Ledstow and then on for the seven straight miles into Ledlington. At a quarter past ten he entered his bank, asked to see the manager, and in his presence and that of a clerk put his signature to the will-form which left Maida Robinson his sole legatee. He was very pleasant and smiling over the business—laughed, and said he might soon be asking for congratulations.

"But at the moment it is all confidential. This is just a stop-gap will in case of accidents." He laughed again. "I shall be going up to see my solicitors. The museum will still get part of my Collection. It is just that—well, one never knows what is going to happen."

The manager was genial, the whole affair very pleasant indeed.

Lewis Brading took the next bus back. At half past eleven he was in his study with James Moberly. Part of their conversation was overheard. At five minutes past twelve he went over to the annexe and put through a couple of calls. At one o'clock he came into the dining-room for lunch, and about half an hour later returned to the annexe, stopping for a moment by the table at which James Moberly was lunching alone to say, "You'd better take the afternoon off. I shan't want you." This was overheard by half a dozen people, but nobody seems to have heard Mr. Moberly's reply. He may not have considered that there was anything to say. He was observed to be looking tired and pale, and it was noticed that he hardly touched his lunch.

At about half past one he returned to the annexe, following Lewis Brading after an interval of only a few minutes. There is no means of knowing whether they met, or what, if anything, passed between them there. James Moberly was to state on oath that they did not meet, that he only went back to the annexe to fetch a book, and that he returned without delay to the club and went into the study, where he spent the rest of the afternoon.

When lunch had been cleared at Warne House the staff are, for the most part, off duty, though there is always someone in the office and a waiter can be summoned. That afternoon was hot. Miss Snagge, in the office, wouldn't have minded changing places with Mrs. Constantine who, as everybody knew, just went to bed after lunch and slept like a baby. Good thing she did too, as far as the daughters were concerned. Only chance they ever got. Lady Minstrell went off with a book into the garden. It would be nice in that old summer-house up the hill. Her favourite place, that was. You could see over the sea for miles, and a nice cool breeze off the water. The white dress with its large black spots went out of the shaded hall and took the bright glare of the sun outside. Very good clothes Lady Minstrell had—kind of quiet but with a sort of look about them you never got unless you paid the earth.

Edna Snagge had a nice amiable disposition. She didn't envy other people, but she would have liked to be going to meet her boy friend tonight in a dress like that—only perhaps the spots navy blue, because you're only young once and black is a bit dull when you are twenty-two and nobody's dead.

108

Mr. and Mrs. Brown went through the hall carrying towels and bathing things. Miss Snagge could have done with a dip herself—not too soon after lunch, but round about half past three. Mrs. Brown waved and said, "Wouldn't you like to be coming too?" which was rubbing it in. Not meant of course—nothing catty about Mrs. Brown, everyone knew that. It was just her way, like wearing clothes too young for her and a bit on the tight side. Even on a girl that pink linen would be rather too much of a good thing. Funny how the wrong people always went for those strong pinks. Now a nice navy—

Her thought was broken off by the entrance of Mrs. Robinson and that Major Constable who was staying at Saltings. The red hair dazzled in the sun which left the smooth, creamy skin untouched. Maida came into the hall looking as cool and fresh as if she had just stepped in from a shady garden instead of having walked along the hot cliff path from Saltings. It was Major Constable who showed the heat—regularly flushed with it, he was. It made his eyes look ever so blue. Miss Snagge admired him. Nice friendly way with him. No airs, but he didn't get fresh either like some did.

Maida Robinson came up to the open front of the office.

"I'm just going through to the annexe to see Mr. Brading. Be an angel and give him a ring on the house-telephone. I don't want to stand and cook in that glass passage whilst he comes to open the door. Mr. Moberly's out, isn't he?"

Edna Snagge said,

"I didn't see him go."

"Oh, well, just give Mr. Brading a ring." She turned to Major Constable. "What will you do, Jack? I shan't be long. I don't know what Lewis wanted to see me about."

Jack Constable laughed.

"Doesn't he always want to see you?"

She made a face at him.

"Don't be silly! Anyhow I shall tell him we're going to play tennis and then bathe. He doesn't do either, so he can't complain. I'll run in and find out what he wants and be back again. I can tell him I'll dine with him—that will keep him quiet."

They spoke with a careless indifference to Edna Snagge. She might have been a chair, or a table, or a fly on the wall. Bad manners, she called it. If hers hadn't been any better, she'd have tossed her head as she picked up the house-telephone and rang the annexe.

Maida Robinson said, "Well, so long," and went off round the corner in her white dress.

Mr. Brading answered the telephone. That meant Mr. Moberly was off somewhere. Mr. Brading wouldn't bother if his secretary was there. She said,

"I'm speaking from the office, Mr. Brading. Mrs. Robinson asked me to give you a ring. She's just going through to the annexe."

She hung up and looked out into the hall. Major Constable had picked up a paper and was standing there reading it. She thought if she was Maida Robinson, money or no money, she would let Mr. Brading go when there were chaps like that about. Served in the Commandos someone said. Horrible what they went through, getting themselves

110

dropped out of planes and all. Even just to think of it made you feel as if you hadn't got any inside. Major Constable must be ever so brave. And of course Major Forrest was too. A shame about him being divorced like that—she didn't know how any girl could. There was something about him made you feel you'd do anything he asked you. Funny, her coming down here and calling herself Miss Mainwaring again, and their seeming quite friendly. Well, you never could tell with these divorces, could you? There was always something that didn't come out.

Major Constable put down his paper, walked along the hall to where he could see right past the study door into the glass passage, and then walked back again. This time he came up to the office window and said in a laughing voice,

"When you say you won't be a moment, how long do you generally mean?"

Miss Snagge said demurely,

"It would all depend."

"On what?"

"On who I was talking to."

He laughed again.

"Well, suppose you were talking to Mr. Brading."

She put a little distance into her voice.

"Mr. Brading doesn't talk to the staff."

He glanced up at the office clock, one of those big old wall-clocks which keep such excellent time.

"Well, she's been gone seven minutes. That's long enough to say you're going to play tennis and come away again, isn't it?"

As he spoke, Maida came round the corner of

the passage. She looked down at her wrist and said,

"Oh, Jack, I've left my bag. Run back and get it! I'll ring Lewis and tell him you're coming."

He laughed, humped a shoulder, and went off saying,

"Why do women always leave their bags?"

Maida laughed too.

"We do, don't we?" she said to Edna Snagge. "But then we don't have all the pockets that men do. If I was plastered all over with the things like they are, I wouldn't have to have a bag." She gave her husky laugh. "Oh, well, I suppose I should. I couldn't very well tuck away a bathing-dress, could I? It would spoil the figure a bit, to say nothing of being damned wet."

As she spoke she came through into the office.

"I just want to speak to Mr. Brading. Is this the house-telephone? What do I do? Oh, I think I know. It's this way, isn't it? . . . . . Hullo, hullo!. . . . . I say, have I really got it right? Nothing's happening. . . . . Oh, yes, here he comes. . . . . Hullo, hullo! Is that you, Lewis?. . . . . Look, darling, I left my bag. . . . . Yes—on the table. Jack is on his way to get it. Just go and let him in. . . . . Oh, has he? Did I? How *awful* of me! Don't be too angry—I won't do it again. . . . . Now, Lewis—*really!* . . . . No, I don't think you ought to talk to me like that. Anyone might make a mistake—I expect you've done it yourself. . . . . No, I suppose you wouldn't, but when you were my age. . . . . Oh, Lewis, *don't!* I didn't mean that. Is Jack there? Because I don't think it's very nice of you to scold me if he's listening. . . . . Oh, he's started back? Then I'd better

112

hang up. Well, so long, darling. Be good. See you tonight."

She hung up the receiver and turned to Edna with a face of mock horror. "He didn't have to let him in, because I'd left the door open! I let myself out because Lewis was busy, and I suppose I didn't bang the wretched thing hard enough or didn't bang it in the right way. My gosh—I hope he's forgotten about it by this evening! It's the world's worst crime, you know. Could you hear what he said? Did you think he sounded really angry? We shall have a merry evening if he is!"

Edna Snagge shook her head.

"I couldn't hear any words, only the voice."

Maida laughed and shrugged.

"What's the odds?" she said. "Men get angry a lot more than we do—no idea of hiding it either. Anyhow I don't think Lewis was really angry. He just wants me to be properly impressed with the sacredness of the Collection. Have you seen it?"

"No, Mrs. Robinson."

Maida said in a meditative voice,

"There are some lovely things. Emeralds—I do adore emeralds. What is your favorite stone?"

Edna Snagge considered.

"I don't know—you have to think what you're going to do—I mean, there are times and places and what's suitable—"

Maida caught up the word with a laugh.

"*Suitable!* Gosh—how dull that sounds!"

As she spoke, Major Constable came lounging up with a big white plastic bag dangling from his hand.

"That right?" he said.

Maida burst out laughing.

"Darling! It wouldn't be Lewis's, or James Moberly's, would it? It's got my bathing things in it. Come along!"

Edna watched them go out into the sunlight, stopping a moment to retrieve their tennis racquets from the porch. She began to think what sort of ring she would have if she really got engaged to Bill Morden. It was all very well for Mrs. Robinson to laugh like that, but if you were engaged you would be wearing the ring all the time, and you did have to think of what it was going to look like with your other things. Most of the time she wore blue. She looked down at her neat linen with the large white buttons. Navy, or butcher, or one of those nice grey-blues—they always did look good style, and a sapphire would go with them all. If she got engaged to Bill, she thought she would have a sapphire ring.

CHAPTER 16

At a little before three Lilias Grey walked up the porch steps and came into the hall. She wore a blue dress and a pair of dark sun-glasses with white rims. Her hair caught the light as she paused to put down the sun-umbrella she was carrying. Edna Snagge, looking up, was confirmed in her opinion that pale blue was tricky. "Makes you look like a chocolate-box when you're young enough to wear it, and too much like mutton dressed lamb when you're getting on." Everyone knew that Miss Grey must be getting on a bit. Pretty of course, but getting on. Glasses always made you look older too.

Lilias stood just inside the hall and took them off. It made a lot of difference—showed the colour in her cheeks—restored her almost to the chocolate-box stage. When she had put the glasses away in her bag she came up to the office window and said,

"Good afternoon, Miss Snagge. I'm just going over to the annexe. Mr. Brading is expecting me."

Then she went on and turned into the passage.

The office was on the left-hand side as you came in. It was just a slice of the hall, with a counter across the front and some match-boarding run up all around. Fortunately it took in one of the windows which flanked the hall door, so that you did get some light and air. The passage turned off on the opposite side of the hall, but much farther along. As soon as Miss Grey turned the corner she was out of sight.

Edna Snagge went back to thinking about Bill Morden. He wasn't getting bad money, but nor was she. Once you'd had your own money, how was it going to feel having to ask someone else for every penny? Of course she could go on working, but she didn't really plan to do that when she married. She planned to have a home and kiddies—a couple anyhow, boy and girl. Not too quick of course, but it didn't do to wait too long either—you wanted to have them whilst you were still young enough for it to be fun. She began to think about names. Bill would want to choose for the boy, but a girl had a right to something pretty. Not too fancy, but something a little bit different. Denise now, or Celia. Celia Morden—very good style that sounded. She liked it better than Denise—or did she? She began to toy with the idea of twin girls.

It was ten minutes past three when Lilias Grey came back through the hall. She had put on her glasses again. She went right through, picked up her sun-umbrella in the porch, and down the steps with the light catching her hair again.

As Edna turned back from seeing her go, Miss Hester Constantine was on the stairs. She had on the new dress she had bought in Ledlington, a flowered silk, not very suitable and a bit too bright for her with all those colours. She'd always be difficult to dress. You'd have to make her hold herself up a bit better before anything would have a chance of looking right. She hadn't bad hair if someone would show her how to do it. She came down the stairs poking her head and looking worried to death, and off round the corner and down the passage. She might be going to the billiard-room, or the study, or the annexe. Wherever she was going, she looked worried to death, and she didn't come back again.

It was about ten minutes later that Charles Forrest ran up the steps and said,

"Hullo, Edna! How's everything?"

Edna Snagge came back from planning her kitchen. She wanted one of those cabinets. . . . everything right up to date. . . . and a fridge. She gave a little start and said,

"Oh, you made me jump!"

He laughed.

"Asleep—or only dreaming? Look here, is Mr. Brading in?"

"So far as I know. He's quite popular this afternoon—people in and out to see him all the time."

"Anyone there now?"

"Not unless it's Miss Constantine—but she'd be more likely—" She broke off, her colour rising.

Charles laughed and said,

"Hush—not a word!" And then, "Unfortunate James!"

"Major Forrest, I never said a thing!"

"Nor did I—wash it out! One man's poison is another man's meat. Well, well, it's a sad world, and we needn't make it any sadder. How's Bill? Going out with him tonight?"

"I might."

"He's one of the lucky ones. Tell him I said so. Be good!"

He went off whistling.

The breeze that had been coming in through the window had dropped. Edna got out her compact and powdered her nose. She wished that she had done it before Major Forrest came through. Definitely shiny, that's what it was, and would be again before you could turn round if everything went on getting hotter every minute the way it was doing.

Down in Ledstow it was a good five degrees hotter than it was on the hill. The heat was coming down out of the sky and up off the pavement without so much as a breath to stir it. The police station looking due south got all its share and a bit more. The brick with which it was faced was as hot as an oven door, and inside—well you could carry out the simile for yourself. Constable Taylor didn't know when he had been hotter. He was a large young man with a rosy face, and his uniform was tighter than it had been six months ago. He undid a button or two, laid down his pen, and leaned back in his chair. He had no intention of dropping off. He would not have admitted that he had done so. It was a hot afternoon, and he might have closed his eyes. He was thinking about his marrows. No doubt of it, they'd beaten Jim Holloway's to blazes. And a much handsomer marrow. And still growing. And likely to.

In that moment when his eyes were shut the marrows all had faces on them. The biggest had a ginger moustache like the Super. Regular fierce expression too. There was a little dark green one with a gimlet eye for all the world like old Ma Stevens. She'd got a hand-bell in her skinny old hand and ringing it something wicked—fair went through your head. His eyes came open with a jerk, and the marrows weren't there any more. The room was a bit swimmy, but no marrows and no Ma Stevens, only the bell was still ringing. After a couple of blinks he got that straight. It was the telephone-bell, and it was fair ringing its head off. He picked up the receiver, subdued a yawn, and said, "'Ullo!"

A familiar voice said, "That Ledstow police station?"

Constable Taylor's jaw ached with his effort not to yawn again. "Ledstow police station"—that's what he ought to have said first go off when he lifted the receiver. He said it now with the feeling that it sounded flat. The voice that had seemed familiar became Major Forrest's voice. He couldn't think why he hadn't known it at once after all the cricket they'd played.

The slow-moving thought was cut sharply across.

"Major Forrest speaking from the Warne House Annexe. There's been an accident here—to Mr. Lewis Brading. I'm ringing Dr. Elliot, but I'm afraid it's no use—he's dead."

Constable Taylor found his voice.

"What kind of an accident, sir?"

Charles Forrest said, "He's been shot," and slammed down the receiver.

CHAPTER 17

It was Miss Silver's practice to open her letters before she looked at the morning papers. There had been times during the war when she had departed from her usual custom, but except under the pressure of a national emergency she would deal with her correspondence before she so much as scanned the headlines. On this Saturday morning London was even hotter than Ledstow. The thermometer in her bedroom already registered 75°, and would certainly pass the 80° mark by midday.

She took up her letters and sorted them through—one from her niece Ethel Burkett; one from Ethel's sister Gladys, a selfish young woman for whom she had no great affection; a third in a handwriting which she had seen before but could not immediately identify, the postmark Ledstow. Her brows drew together in a slight frown. The writing was that of Mr. Lewis Brading. He had made an appointment and paid her a visit about a fortnight ago, and she had not been favourably impressed—oh, not at all.

She put his letter aside and opened Ethel Burkett's.

"Dearest Aunt Maud,
          The scarf is just lovely....."

Miss Silver's eyes rested fondly upon the page. Dear Ethel—always so affectionate, so grateful. And the scarf was really nothing at all—just made up out of the odds and ends she had left from Ethel's last two jumpers and one or two of the frocks she had knitted for little Josephine. Such a pretty, healthy little girl, and so good in spite of having three brothers to spoil her.

Returning to the letter, she read with concern that Josephine had had a cold—"so trying in this weather," and with relief that "it has now, I am glad to say, completely disappeared and she is getting her colour back." The boys were enjoying their holidays—Ethel's husband was the manager of a bank in a Midlands country town—but, "we are hoping to get a fortnight at the sea in September. Mary Loftus has offered to exchange houses. She has that tiresome business of her Uncle James's furniture to go into. And, dearest Auntie, you must keep the time clear and come to us September 2nd–17th. With love from us all, Ethel."

Miss Silver gave a slight pleasurable cough. A

fortnight by the sea with dear Ethel and the children—how really delightful. She must do her best to keep the time clear.

She turned to Gladys's letter with a good deal less warmth. Gladys never wrote unless she wanted something, and she thought of no one but herself. All through the war she had managed to preserve this attitude. She had married a well-to-do man of middle age because she disliked having to earn her own living. At first the advantages had outweighed the disadvantages. Now that income tax was so heavy, the cost of living so high, and domestic help almost unobtainable, Gladys was having to work again—to cook, to clean, to polish. The advantages had disappeared, and the disadvantages remained. The elderly husband was ten years older than when she married him, and she was feeling very badly treated. "It isn't as if I couldn't get a job, and a good one. I'm sure the money some of these girls get makes you open your eyes. And it wouldn't be cooking and cleaning and that sort of thing either. Really I'm nothing but an unpaid *servant*. . . . ."

Miss Silver read to the end with deep disapproval. Not the letter of a gentlewoman. And the postscript! Piling Ossa on Pelron, Gladys had written, "Next time you go away, do give me a ring. I could come up and look after the flat and do some theatres. Andrew is so sticky about my being out at night."

Miss Silver pressed her lips together as she laid the letter down.

She opened Lewis Brading's envelope with a feeling of distaste. She had not liked him—oh, not at all. "Self-interest—there is no stronger motive"—a really shocking statement! And his treatment of that unfortunate secretary. Very dangerous, and really not very far off blackmail. She unfolded his letter and read:

Dear Madam,
    I am writing to ask you to reconsider your decision. There have been developments. The matter is confidential, and I do not wish to go to the police—at present. This is a pleasant country club. I have reserved a room for you, and must beg you to come down immediately. You may name your own fee. If you will ring me up and let me know by what train you will be arriving, I will see that you are met at Ledstow.
                                    Yours truly,
                                    Lewis Brading

Miss Silver sat and looked at the page. Curious writing, formal and precise. But the lines sloped upwards and the signature was blotted. The letter had been written in a hurry and under some strong impulse. "You may name your own fee—" Something had happened, or he was afraid that something was going to happen. Her mind became engaged with the possibilities. They might be—would be interesting. But she did not like Mr. Brading.

She put the letter down and opened her morning paper. The name which had been in her mind stood out at the top of the page in a bold headline:

She said, "Dear me!" and began to read what the paper had to say about it. There was quite a lot, but it did not amount to very much. The story overflowed into two columns, but there was really more about the Brading Collection than about Mr. Brading's sudden death. His cousin Major Forrest, coming to see him by appointment, had found him shot dead in his laboratory. He had fallen across the table at which he was sitting. A revolver lay beside him on the floor. Major Forrest had at once rung up the Ledstow police station and sent for a doctor, but life was extinct. There was a lot about it and about the Collection, but that was what it amounted to.

After a short interval for reflection Miss Silver dialled Trunks and gave the private number of the Chief Constable of Ledshire. At this hour of the morning it would, she hoped, be possible to get through without delay. Actually, she hardly had to wait at all before a familiar voice said, "Hullo!"

"Miss Silver speaking, Randal."

At the other end of the line Randal March pursed up his lips in a soundless whistle. After which he said,

"Well, here I am. What can I do for you?"

"You are all well? Rietta? And the baby?"

"Blooming. Well—what is it?"

"The Brading case."

"And where do you come in on that?"

She would never have allowed such an expression in her schoolroom. Her cough reproved him.

"My dear Randal!"

"Well, well, what is it?"

"I had been approached a fortnight ago—"

"By whom?"

"By Mr. Brading."

"Why?"

"He was uneasy. He wanted me to come down to Warne. I refused."

"Again why?"

This time the cough was of a deprecatory nature.

"The case did not attract me."

"Well?"

"That is not all, Randal."

He gave a short laugh.

"I didn't think it was."

"No. I had a letter from him this morning."

"What!"

"The postmark is Ledstow, two-thirty, so you see—"

"What did he say?"

"That there had been developments. That he had taken a room for me at Warne House. That any train I might come down by today would be met. And that I might name my fee."

This time March whistled aloud.

"And what is your reaction to that?"

She said in a thoughtful voice,

"I have not made up my mind. I believe that Major Forrest is his cousin's executor."

"Did Brading tell you that?"

"Yes, Randal."

"During a first interview—when you were refusing the case?"

"Yes."

"Did it occur to you that he was anticipating—how shall I put it—what has just happened?"

She coughed.

"I could not put it quite as strongly as that. He had made certain arrangements."

There was a pause. Randal March was frowning. He said,

"I'd like to see you."

There was another of those faint coughs.

"I thought perhaps I should ring Major Forrest up. If he wishes me to do so, I could come down to Warne House for the week-end. Without his endorsement Mr. Brading's commission lapses—I have no status."

March said,

"Yes, I see. Let me know if you are coming down. I think I should see you."

Miss Silver's call found Charles Forrest in his cousin's study at Warne House. She had decided that she was more likely to find him there than at his own address, which she would in any case be obliged to ascertain, whereas Mr. Brading's number was embossed upon his notepaper.

When she got as far as the exchange a voice said,

"That is Mr. Brading's number. We are putting all calls through to the club."

Miss Silver said, "Thank you," and waited.

She got Edna Snagge next.

"Major Forrest? Yes, he's here. I'll put you through."

In the study Charles Forrest lifted the receiver. A prim pleasant voice repeated his name in an enquiring manner. He said,

"Speaking."

There was a faint cough.

"My name is Miss Maud Silver. I do not know whether it conveys anything to you."

Charles's expression of weary indifference changed to one of attention. He said,

"Yes, it does."

"May I ask in what connection?"

"My cousin left a letter—I suppose you've heard?"

"I have seen the morning papers."

"He wished you to be called in—if anything happened. He went to see you about a fortnight ago?"

"Yes."

"He wanted you to come down then. You refused. He seems to have been impressed. He says you warned him that he was upon a dangerous course."

Miss Silver coughed.

"I fear that he disregarded my warning."

"He came home and wrote me a letter which has just been found. He said that in the event of matters passing beyond his control he would wish you to be called into consultation."

Miss Silver said, "Dear me!" And then, "I received a letter from Mr. Brading by this morning's post. He pressed me to come down to Warne. He said he had reserved a room for me, and that he would meet any train which I might find convenient."

"Today?"

"Yes, Major Forrest."

Charles's frown deepened in intensity. What on earth had Lewis been up to, and where did a private detective who sounded like an old-fashioned governess come in? He would have to see her, of course, and if Lewis had booked a room for her she might just as well come down. The mess was so bad that one elderly lady more or less would be neither here nor there. She might even provide a much needed red herring or two. He didn't see how she could possibly make matters worse than they were. With these things in mind he said,

"I should be very glad if you would come down for the week-end, Miss Silver. What train would suit you?"

CHAPTER 18

Miss Silver arrived by the train which had brought Stacy to Ledstow three days before. Charles Forrest, on the platform, saw her alight with incredulity. There was no one else who could possibly be the person he had come to meet, but he found Miss Silver incredible. That is to say, incredible in this year of grace, upon Ledstow platform, coming down to investigate Lewis Brading's death. In his nursery days the moral maxim, "A place for everything, and everything in its place," had been all too frequently instilled. Miss Silver's place was in a photograph album of about forty years ago. The rather flat, crushed-looking hat was the spit and image of one worn by Lewis's mother in a wedding group of that date. It was of black straw with some ribbon bows at the back and a small bunch of mignonette and pansies on the left-hand side. The high boned net front was of the same date, but the dress of grey artificial silk with its smudged pattern of mauve and black departed from the type to the extent of having a much more comfortable waistline and being at least six inches off the ground. The black lisle thread stockings thus revealed and the black laced shoes were, however, well within the period. A string of bog-oak beads circled her neck twice. A pair of eyeglasses were fastened to the left-hand side of her dress by a gold bar brooch set with seed pearls. There was also a bog-oak brooch in the form of a rose with an Irish pearl at its heart.

All these details presented themselves to Charles as part of the incredible whole. He couldn't believe in her outside a family album, but there she was, stepping down from the train with a small well-worn suitcase in one hand, and a handbag and a flowered knitting-bag in the other.

The day was even hotter than yesterday. It was a relief to leave the streets behind and come out upon a country road. Then, and not till then, did Miss Silver give her slight premonitory cough and say,

"What have you to tell me about Mr. Brading's death?"

Charles drove on for about a hundred yards, turned into a lane which ran inland, and drew up under a large shady oak. Then he said,

"If we're going to talk we might as well be cool. You want to know about Lewis's death. He rang up yesterday morning round about half past twelve and asked me to come and see him—just that and nothing more. He suggested half past three. As a matter of fact I got there rather earlier. The girl in the office said he was alone, so I went through—" He paused, looked round at her, and said, "I don't know what you know about the layout."

"Mr. Brading explained it, I think, quite clearly."

"Then you understand that everyone going to the annexe or coming away would go through the hall of the club and past the office—that is, unless they got through a window in the billiard-room or the study."

"That would be possible?"

"I suppose so. Anyhow the girl in the office said he was alone, and I went through. There's a glazed passage to the annexe with a very strong steel door at the end of it which is always kept locked. I take it you know about the Collection."

"Oh, yes."

"Well, the first thing that struck me was that the steel door wasn't shut—it was standing ajar. You go in, and there's a small lobby and a second very strong door. The second door was wide open. I went into the big room where he shows off his Collection and called. Nobody answered. There's a door opposite the entrance which leads into a passage. There are three rooms there—Lewis's bedroom, a bathroom, and a laboratory. I called again. The laboratory door was open."

Miss Silver coughed.

"Ajar—or wide open?"

"Standing at right angles to the jamb. I went through, and saw Lewis. There's a table he uses for making notes—about his experiments, you know. It's an old knee-hole table with drawers on either side. It's on the right-hand side of the door as you come in, facing towards it. As soon as I came in I saw Lewis. He was sitting at the table, and he had fallen forward across it. I came over to him, and saw that he had been shot through the head a little behind the right temple. His right arm was hanging down. There was a revolver lying as if it had dropped from his hand. The second right-hand drawer was open. I knew he kept a revolver there. I thought he had committed suicide, and I thought he had sent for me and left the doors open because he wanted me to find him. One of the less agreeable duties of an executor!"

At this point he met a gaze of singular intensity and intelligence. Miss Silver coughed.

"You say you *thought* that Mr. Brading had committed suicide."

Charles Forrest said,

"The police don't think so."

"Could you tell me why?"

They continued to look at one another. Charles said in a voice that matched his frown,

"I could. But can you give me any reason why I should?"

Both frown and voice appeared to Miss Silver to denote concentration rather than resentment. Had it been otherwise, she would scarcely have answered as she did.

"You do not know me."

"No."

"You have therefore no reason to trust me."

He paused on that.

"My cousin apparently did so. He wasn't much

130

given to trusting people. In his letter he quotes Randal March as saying that you can be trusted."

Miss Silver inclined her head.

"I must tell you, Major Forrest, that I refused this case a fortnight ago because I could not approve of Mr. Brading's line of conduct. It appeared to me to be dangerous in its possibilities, and indefensible on moral grounds."

One of Charles's dark eyebrows rose.

"Poor old James?"

"He imparted some information about his secretary, Mr. James Moberly."

Charles said quickly,

"James wouldn't hurt a fly—you can take that from me. He got into shady company when he was a boy—got had for a mug, and Lewis has been holding it over him for years. He's worked like a black and not been able to call his soul his own. He isn't capable of standing up for himself—that, I imagine, is how he got let in to start with—and he certainly isn't capable of violence."

A smile just touched Miss Silver's lips. Then she looked grave again.

"Mr. Brading spoke of information with regard to Mr. Moberly which would come into your hands in such a contingency as this. From what you say I understand that this information has reached you."

Charles took a moment. Then,

"I told you he wasn't much given to trusting people. Poor old James—a complete dossier, I suppose. No, it hasn't reached me yet. The solicitors will have it, I expect. And if the police get wind of it, there'll be the devil to pay."

Miss Silver coughed.

"But you knew—"

"Lewis dropped more than half a hint, and James told me the rest. Look here, what I've got to know is, how do you stand with regard to the police? If they go on thinking that it isn't suicide, there's going to be quite a lot of suspicion flying about. I'd like to know where I am. Do I talk to you in confidence, or does everything I say get handed on? I want to know where I am."

Miss Silver looked at him.

"I am glad that you should have raised the point. I could not, in a murder case, be a party to concealing any material evidence from the police. I could not come into a murder case to serve any private interest. I have been engaged in many such cases and have worked in harmony with the police, but it is not my practice to work for the police. In a murder case, as in any other, I can have only one object, the bringing to light of the truth. It is only the guilty who have to fear this, the innocent are protected."

There was again that characteristic lift of the eyebrow. He said,

"You find it as simple as that?"

"Fundamentally, yes. What appears to obscure the fact is that so many people have something to hide, and an enquiry in a murder case has this in common with the day of judgment, that the secrets of all hearts are apt to be revealed. It is not everyone who can contemplate this with equanimity. It is not only the murderer who tries desperately to conceal his thoughts and actions. And now, Major Forrest, are you going to tell me why the police

132

think that this may be a case of murder?"

Still frowning, Charles said,

"Yes, I'll tell you."

He had been sitting easily, his hand on the wheel. He leaned back now into the angle between the driving-seat and the door. Something had been happening in his mind. The dowdy little governess out of a family photograph-album sat there in the opposite corner, her hair very neat, her old-fashioned hat a little crooked, her hands in their black thread gloves folded primly upon a shabby bag with a tarnished clasp. There she was, and that was what she looked like. Yet he was feeling the impact of an intelligence which commanded respect. If that had been all, he would have found it surprising enough. But it was by no means all. He was conscious of an integrity, a kindness, a sort of benignant authority. He couldn't get nearer to it than that. It wouldn't go into words, but it was there. A good many of Miss Silver's clients in the past had had a similar experience. But he was not to know that. He only knew it would be a relief to talk, to formulate his thoughts, to look at them through the focus of someone else's eyes.

She had been waiting, now she gave him an encouraging smile.

He said, "Lewis hadn't any reason for suicide—I'm putting it the way it looks to the police. He had quite a lot of money, he wasn't ill, and he was thinking about getting married. You didn't know that?"

"No."

"Nor did he a fortnight ago. You wouldn't have thought he was the sort to go in off the deep end, but it just goes to show that you never can tell. She's a goodlooking red-head, about twenty-five, with a divorced husband in the background and a flat in my house, Saltings. I've been cutting it up and letting it off—about the only thing you can do with big houses nowadays. Her name is Maida Robinson. On the day before his death—that is, the day before yesterday—Lewis asked her to marry him."

Miss Silver coughed.

"Did he tell you that?"

"No, she did. He was showing his Collection to a whole party from the club. I walked home with her afterwards and she told me. She also told me that he had made a will in her favour."

Miss Silver said, "Dear me!" And then, "Has this will been found?"

"It has, and it hasn't. He went into Ledlington yesterday and signed a will such as Maida described. She said it was made out on a will-form. It was witnessed by his bank manager and a clerk, and something was said about his asking for congratulations before long. But no actual statement about the contents of the will, which is not to be found, unless you can count some burnt paper on an ash-tray. There was just one corner left unburned, but no writing. The paper corresponds with the will-forms sold by a Ledlington stationer. Maida bought one there—she says for herself. She asked Lewis's advice about it, and it ended in his using it instead."

Charles's voice was non-committal in the extreme, but Miss Silver received some impressions. He continued in a less careful tone.

134

"I gather the police have a theory that the destruction of the will could be a fairly strong motive for murder."

Miss Silver said crisply,

"It might equally be argued that Mr. Brading had destroyed the will and then committed suicide owing to some disappointment connected with his projected marriage."

Charles said, "I don't think that cuts a lot of ice with the police. Frankly, I don't see Lewis shooting himself over a woman—no one who knew him would. He wasn't such a stick as he looked. He'd had affairs before this, you know. I don't say he hadn't fallen pretty hard for Maida, but I just can't see him shooting himself. And that's giving you my confidence to a fairly marked degree, because if it's murder, I'm naturally pretty high up among the suspects. I found him, and I had the best of motives for destroying this new will, since under the old one I'm the principal legatee. The police love that sort of motive—all nice and clear and crude. And they're pretty well sure it's murder because of the fingerprints on the revolver. They're Lewis's, but they're not in the right places. They think they were made after death. It's an old trick to fake a suicide by closing a dead man's hand on the revolver, but it's a ticklish business for the murderer. If you've just shot someone, your own hand is probably not too steady, and you're in the devil of a hurry." His voice cooled and hardened. "I can imagine that it might be quite a job to get the prints in exactly the right places—they might easily slip. The police say that these particular prints have slipped. That is why they're sure it's murder."

CHAPTER 19

As if he had said all that he meant to say for the moment, Charles Forrest swung round, started up the car, and backed out of the lane. He did not speak for the rest of the way, nor did Miss Silver. She had, indeed, a good deal to occupy her thoughts.

As they passed through the hall of Warne House, Stacy was coming down the stairs. Reaching the bottom step as Charles approached, it was natural that he should pause and speak—any casual acquaintance might have done the same. But Miss Silver was instantly aware of a change in the atmosphere. The words which passed were few and simple. Charles Forrest's rather sombre gaze rested momentarily on the girl in white. She was pale. She carried a green-lined sun-umbrella, which he recognized as belonging to Myra Constantine.

He said, "Going out?"

Stacy said, "Yes." And then, "Lilias asked me to tea. She wants me to go."

There was nothing in the words, but voice and manner were those of intimates. The whole encounter was so brief that it hardly halted either of them. Stacy went on and out, putting up her green umbrella in the porch.

Miss Silver went up to the room which Lewis Brading had booked for her.

When she came down ten minutes later Charles was waiting. He took her down the passage to the study and gave her tea. It was between the first and second cups that she asked him about Stacy.

"A very charming girl—very graceful. She is staying here?"

Charles had been wondering why kettles took so long to boil and tea so long to cool. At her question the mouthful which he had just swallowed appeared to be even more scalding than he had thought it at the time. Oh, well, if he had nothing worse to explain than Stacy—He explained her with a careful poise.

"She is Stacy Mainwaring, the miniaturist. She is painting our local celebrity, the rather famous Myra Constantine. We were once married, but are now divorced—for nothing worse than desertion—and we are quite good friends. Myra is worth painting, you know. She will be a feather in Stacy's cap."

He told stories about Myra and gave an entertaining account of the other people in the club until she had finished her tea. Then he took her out to the annexe and showed her over it.

"The police have finished here. You can go anywhere, touch anything, and ask as many questions as you like."

She asked a great many—just how he had come in—where he had stood—what he had seen.

Charles went through it all, as he had done so many times already. If he wasn't word-perfect by now he never would be. With each repetition the thing became less real.

When he had finished she said,

"You arrived just before half past three?"

"About twenty past."

"And you came straight through?"

"Straight through."

"And he was dead when you found him. How long had he been dead?"

"I'm not a doctor."

"You served in the war. How long had he been dead?"

"I don't know."

"But you could hazard a guess."

He shook his head.

"I'm not fool enough to rush in."

She was looking at him all the time, standing there beside the table at which Lewis Brading had died, one hand resting upon it. A bright overhead light beat down upon the laboratory and its equipment, striking sparkles from glass and metal, making every object just a little clearer and more distinct than it would have been by daylight. She gave her little cough and said,

"At what time did the police arrive?"

"I think it was a quarter to four. But they are not experts either, you know. The doctor I rang up was out, and the police surgeon didn't get here till four. He isn't going to swear within half an hour as to how long Lewis had been dead when he saw him. It was a very hot day."

"Exactly."

She walked round the table and stood in front of it. Lewis Brading's chair had been drawn back. The table was orderly—blotting-pad, pen-tray, scribbling-pad, a rack for writing-paper and envelopes, a large flat metal ash-tray a good deal dis-

138

coloured, a box of matches. The knee-hole aperture was flanked by drawers on either side. On the deep green leather of the table top there was the one dark stain. She said,

"Will you show me just how he was when you found him?"

The thought went through his mind, "This is ghastly." She noticed that his dark skin showed a change of colour. Without speaking he did as she had asked, sitting down in the chair, leaning forward until his head rested over that ominous stain, letting his right arm hang down until the hand was only a few inches from the floor. When it was over she broke the silence in which this dumb show had been acted.

"Where was the weapon?"

He said shortly,

"Just under where his hand was. As if he had dropped it."

"It was his own revolver?"

"Well—yes—"

There was enough hesitation to make her press the point.

"That has an ambiguous sound, Major Forrest."

He lifted a hand and let it fall again.

"You don't miss much. It's this way. I had two—a pair. I let Lewis have one of them."

"How long ago?"

"Some time last year. He had something pretty antiquated. I saw it one day when he had that drawer open, and told him he'd better have something a little more up to date. That's how it happened."

"And he kept it—in which drawer?"

He said, "The second on the right." Then, as she pulled it out, "It isn't there now. The police have got it."

She coughed.

"How many people knew that Mr. Brading kept a revolver in this drawer?"

He gave a short laugh.

"I did, James did—anyone might have done. He was rather proud of it, you know—made a bit of a flourish about being armed. He still had his own museum-piece in his bedroom."

She pushed the drawer in, took another look at the table, and said,

"That metal ash-tray—is that where the will-form was burned?"

He nodded, and said, "Yes."

"Just where was it when you found Mr. Brading dead?"

He moved to indicate the far side of the table.

"Over here, at the edge, a few inches from this corner."

"Out of Mr. Brading's reach?"

"As he sat at the table, yes. At least, I suppose he could have touched it if he had leaned forward. But he wouldn't have burned a paper that way."

"And the matches—where were they?"

"Just clear of the ash-tray."

"To the left, or right?"

He was facing her across the table now.

"To your left—to my right."

She said soberly,

"You do not need me to underline that, do you? Whoever burned that will-form was standing at the back of the table as you are standing now. If it was Mr. Brading, it seems difficult to find a reason for this. It is quite certain that it was not done by him whilst he was sitting at the table in his normal position."

Charles said, "No."

There was a little pause. Then she seated herself, drawing up the chair until it was comfortably placed, taking the scribbling-block, selecting a pencil. Having done all this, she turned a bright enquiring glance upon Charles and said very composedly,

"Will you not sit down, Major Forrest? I should like to take a few notes. You say Mr. Brading appeared at lunch, and then returned to the annexe. Did anyone see him alive after that?"

Charles had reached for a high wooden stool. He leaned rather than sat on it, his long legs stretched out before him, his manner as casual as his attitude.

"Oh, quite a number. According to Edna Snagge—that's the girl in the office—Lewis had a procession of visitors. They all had to come through the hall, as I told you."

"Can you tell me who they were, and at what time they came?"

He fished in his pocket.

"Here you are, straight from the horse's mouth—Edna is very methodical. Lewis came off here after lunch at half past one, and James Moberly followed him a few minutes later. Now James says he only came over to fetch a book, and he went straight back to the study and stayed there. Lewis had given him the afternoon off. That, I gather, is not in dispute—people in the dining-room heard Lewis tell him he wouldn't be wanting him again. Well, that's James. Then at half past two Maida Robinson, Lewis's red-head, came along with a chap called Constable. He served in the Commandos with me, and he blew in the other day for a long week-end. He and Maida were going to play tennis and then bathe. I gather Maida wanted to see Lewis and break it to him that she was off for the afternoon with another boy friend, but of course she would be dining with him and he mustn't think that she would ever love anyone else." He smiled engagingly. "I'm just giving you the gist of what Maida handed me, you know. I'm not going bail for anything a red-head says, but it all seems quite likely. Now listen. Maida goes off to see Lewis alone while Constable kicks his heels in the hall. In about ten minutes Maida comes back. She says she's left her bag out here and sends Constable for it. And whilst he's gone she steps into the office and rather annoys Edna by using the house-telephone to tell Lewis that Jack Constable is on his way. Edna can hear them talking, but she can't hear what Lewis says, only his voice. But it seems he was annoyed because Maida hadn't shut the steel door when she went out and Jack Constable had just walked in. Now that's important, because someone else could have slipped in that way—from the billiard-room for instance. It's not very likely, but it's possible."

Miss Silver coughed.

"You say from the billiard-room? Not from the study?"

Charles let his eyes meet hers directly.

"James Moberly was in the study, and he

142

wouldn't need to slip in that way—he had his key."

She inclined her head.

"Pray continue."

"Constable wasn't away five minutes. He came back with the bag, and he and Maida went off. They didn't play tennis, because they decided it was too hot, but they went down and bathed. That brings us to a quarter to three. A little before three o'clock Lilias Grey arrived to see Lewis. She is my adopted sister. My father and mother adopted her when she was four years old because they hadn't any children. And then I arrived—what you might call bad timing. She isn't married, she has a flat at Saltings. She says she wanted to consult Lewis on a matter of business. Well, this is her story, and you'll see how it narrows things down. She says she went along to the annexe, and like Jack Constable she says she found the steel door open. Now Jack swears he shut it—he'd be likely to, you know, after Lewis cutting up rough over Maida leaving it open. But ten minutes later Lilias finds it open again. She says she thought Lewis had left it ajar for her, and I suppose he had, because he doesn't seem to have said anything about it when she walked in. She says they talked for about ten minutes about business. Some shares my mother left her were falling in, and she wanted to know what Lewis thought about re-investment. He told her to stick to government securities, and she said she'd think about it, and came away. She can't remember whether she shut the door or not—she's rather a vague person. She was out of the club by ten minutes past three, and just as she was leaving, Hester

Constantine came down the stairs and went along the passage in this direction. She is Myra's unmarried daughter, a gawky female in the late thirties, and no one has been able to think of any reason why she should want to murder Lewis. She says she went along to the study. James was there like he says, and she stayed talking. About ten minutes later I came on the scene and found Lewis dead."

Miss Silver looked down at the scribbling-pad with her neat writing.

"Your friend—is he—Major Constable?"

Charles nodded.

"He and Mrs. Robinson left the club at a quarter to three. At twenty past three you found Mr. Brading dead. You will not give an opinion as to how long he had been dead, though I think that you must have formed such an opinion. Miss Grey says that he was alive when she left him. If that is the case, he could not, when you found him, have been dead for more than a few minutes. The murderer would naturally have allowed Miss Grey to get away before risking the use of firearms. Did anyone hear the shot?"

Charles shook his head.

"They wouldn't. The place is sound-proof—especially this room, which is built into the hill."

Miss Silver coughed.

"Then, Major Forrest, there are these possibilities. If everyone is telling the truth, Mr. Brading was shot between the time of Miss Grey's departure and your arrival—a bare ten minutes. During that time nobody came through the hall except Miss Constantine. She would have had time to

144

reach this room, shoot Mr. Brading, and return to the study. What is Mr. Moberly's evidence upon this point?"

"He says she came to the study at ten past three, and was there till I gave the alarm."

Miss Silver looked at him very directly.

"And what does she say?"

"Oh, she says they were there together. They both say that."

Miss Silver coughed.

"Are they friends?"

He hesitated.

"Hester doesn't run to friends much. Myra keeps her family busy."

"The clever, brilliant mother and the repressed daughter. A not uncommon situation, and one with dangerous possibilities."

Charles gave a short laugh.

"Well, I can't think up any reason why Hester should have it in for Lewis, and nor can anyone else."

Miss Silver glanced at the scribbling-block.

"Leaving Miss Constantine on one side, and still assuming that everyone has told the truth—a circumstance very unusual in a murder case—the most striking evidence is that which concerns the annexe door. It was not, I imagine, Mr. Brading's habit to leave it open."

"The inner door might be open if he was there. The outer door never."

"I received that impression from the way he spoke of it on the occasion of his visit a fortnight ago."

Charles nodded.

"There were only two keys. He had one, and James had the other. If anything happened to Lewis, James was going to be in the soup, so James could be trusted with a key. Nobody else was. In my opinion Lewis would no more have left that door open than he would have flown."

"Yet it was left open."

"By Maida, coming away in a hurry for her bathe."

Miss Silver coughed.

"That is the first evidence we have of its being left open, but it is not the last. After Mrs. Robinson came out Major Constable went back to fetch her bag. He says he left the steel door shut at a quarter to three, but Miss Grey found it open ten minutes later. You say that she cannot be depended on to have shut it when she came away at ten minutes past three, and you yourself found it open when you arrived at twenty past. The door is therefore known to have been open for a minute or two between Mrs. Robinson leaving the annexe and Major Constable arriving there to fetch her bag. No one passed through the hall at that time except Major Constable himself, but it would have been just possible for someone to reach the annexe from the billiard-room and conceal himself there—in Mr. Moberly's room, the bathroom, or one of the other rooms. A far more likely time for someone to have concealed himself on the premises would be during one of the later periods when we know that the door was open. Miss Grey found it open just before three, and you found it open at three-twenty. We do not know who opened it, which

146

means that we do not know how long it was open. Major Constable may be mistaken in thinking that he had shut it. It closes, I notice, with a spring. He was in a hurry. It may have stood open for the whole ten minutes before Miss Grey arrived, and then for a further ten minutes between her departure and your own arrival. We have no means of knowing. All we do know is that no one passed through the hall during either of those times except Miss Constantine."

Charles frowned.

"There could have been someone in the billiard-room—"

"Could there, Major Forrest? When we passed the door just now I tried it, and it was locked."

Charles said nothing for a moment. His face hardened. His lids came down until they almost covered his eyes. All at once he stood up, drove his hands deep into his pockets, and said abruptly,

"That puts the lid on."

Miss Silver looked at him, her head a little tilted on one side, her expression that of an inconspicuous but intelligent bird which has just perceived a worm.

"The door was locked yesterday?"

He said, not looking at her,

"The room is being done up. There's a hitch about some of the materials—a hang-up over the week-end. The men had left their stuff there."

"Then the windows would have been shut and the door locked yesterday?"

"They may have been."

147

"It is a point which can be verified."

She tore off the sheet upon which she had made her notes, laid the pencil back in the tray, straightened the blotting-pad, and rose to her feet.

"Thank you, Major Forrest."

CHAPTER 20

Stacy took the bus to the Saltings corner. She had really only a step to go from there, but the sun beat upon the shadeless road, and she was glad of the umbrella which Myra Constantine had pressed upon her—a big, old-fashioned thing, dust-coloured, with a bright green lining.

The trees about Saltings came into view. She turned in at the gate. Rather like being a ghost this coming back. Ghost stories always took the wrong point of view. It was all how dreadful for the living to be haunted, how the flesh crept and the hair rose and the courage failed. But what about the poor haunting disembodied thing come back to walk where it had loved and been loved, and now was no more than a shuddering and an amazement? She felt very much like a ghost as she came out in front of the big house and walked up the steps.

The front door stood wide. The hall had been stripped, altered. The rugs were gone from the floor, the display of arms from the chimney-breast. There was a lift running up through the well of the stairs, rather cleverly fitted in. Some of the old portraits remained to gloom upon the scene.

She looked about her. Charles had one of the ground-floor flats. She found his name, and then came back in a hurry to climb the stairs. The lift was an automatic one, and she didn't like them very much. Besides, she was in no hurry to arrive. She had three years to bridge over. This was to have been her home—no, Stacy Forrest's home. And she wasn't Stacy Forrest any more. She was Stacy Mainwaring again. It made her feel a little giddy—as if time had been telescoped—as if she was in two places at once—as if today wasn't today but something strange and out of time.

She came to the top of the stairs and found a door with Lilias Grey's name on it. She was lifting her hand to the bell, when it opened, and Lilias was saying,

"But you're late. Do come in. It's terribly hot, isn't it?"

Stacy had wondered what she would say, and what Lilias would say, but it was all quite easy. She didn't have to say anything—unless you count the sort of things you say when somebody else hardly stops to take a breath. Lilias wanted to show her the flat, to talk about the flat, to say how clever Charles had been, how clever the architect had been.

"You see, this was my mother's bedroom—divided to make bedroom and sitting-room. And quite big enough. I don't care about very big rooms—do you? It was such a huge room before—but of course you remember it. And I get the view over the sea from both these windows. Then, through here, the dressing-room has been divided to make a kitchenette and a bathroom. I'm sure you wouldn't recognize it, would you?"

No, she wouldn't have recognized it. In the room which was Lilias's sitting-room she and Charles had slept. Out here in the chopped-up dressing-room there was a kitchen sink where his bureau had been. She had watched in the night and seen him stand there with Damaris Forrest's necklace in his hand. She felt an intolerable revulsion. Tragedy with the kitchen sink imposed upon it!

"It's nice, isn't it?" said Lilias Grey.

This kind of conversation continued whilst Lilias made tea, offered cucumber sandwiches, and played the charming hostess. Stacy could only tell herself that she had asked for it. It was her own fault, she should never have come, but now that she was here she had no choice but to appear the willing guest. As she set herself to the task, it did just cross her mind to wonder why Lilias had asked her, and just what lay behind this almost febrile flow of talk. There was too much of it—too much nervous energy. It was overdone, in the same way that Lilias Grey's make-up had been overdone. The blue eyes were brilliant, there was colour in the cheeks, the lipstick was deftly applied, but it was all just a little too much of a good thing, and in spite of it Lilias looked her age.

That was the first thing that made Stacy think. The second was that after nearly half an hour there had still been no mention of Lewis Brading. In the end when she had put down her cup and said, "No, thank you," to a quick, "Won't you have some more tea?" she brought in the name herself.

She wasn't going to sit here and let Lilias get away with pretending that nothing had happened. She waited for the first momentary pause and said,

"It's a dreadful thing about Lewis."

Lilias lost colour. The rouge stood out upon a suddenly whitened skin. She said with a shudder,

"Don't let's talk about it. You don't know what it's been like—having to see the police—and make a statement!"

She had said, "Don't let's talk about it," but now all that nervous energy flowed into the new channel. Her hands twisted in her lap. Her fair hair shone like a nimbus.

"I always said something dreadful would happen. All that jewelry was too valuable."

"But was anything taken?" Stacy's surprise showed in her voice.

"Oh, I don't know. The police don't tell you anything. They just go on asking their stupid questions. And I was hardly there any time at all. I just walked in—the door was open, you know. I was going to ask Lewis about investing some money my mother left me. It was a mortgage that had been paid off, and I thought that he might know of something good. But all he would say was, 'Put it into government securities.' You know, he was like that. He was really almost disagreeable, and I wished I hadn't come, so I didn't stay any time at all." Her hands twisted. "Just because he's dead it's no use pretending he was all the things we know he *wasn't*. I really came away feeling quite upset."

Stacy was wondering why on earth Lilias should have thought of consulting Lewis Brading. He was

151

not the sort of person to invite that kind of thing, especially from an adopted relation whom he didn't very much like. She didn't put this into words, but she went quite near to it by saying,

"Why didn't you consult Charles?"

Lilias made a jerky gesture. She said quickly,

"Oh, I couldn't—not about *money*."

Stacy felt the colour rise and burn in her cheeks. It was just as if she had taken an incautious step and felt the ground give way and the smell of burning come up through the broken crust. She hadn't meant—she hadn't ever meant to touch that ground again. The burning came up into her face.

Lilias leaned forward and said in a low, horrified voice,

"I'm so frightened—"

Stacy's nails dug into her palm.

"Why?"

Lilias began to tremble.

Stacy said, "Why?" again. She had drunk two cups of tea, but her lips were dry and parched.

The big blue eyes between the darkened lashes stared into hers. Lilias said,

"About Charles."

"Why?" She didn't seem to be able to get past that word.

The blue eyes were afraid. You could see the fear brimming up in them, brimming over. Words came in a whisper.

"If he did it—"

Something right down inside Stacy said, "Nonsense!" It was a very comforting reaction. She tried what it would be like if she said it aloud. Her voice came out firm and strong, and it sounded good.

"Nonsense!"

Lilias shuddered. She went on in that silly creepy whisper.

"Oh, Stacy, I'm so frightened. That's why I had to see you—only when you came it didn't seem as if I could talk about it. But I must talk to someone. I shall go mad if I don't."

Stacy was being surprised by her own feelings. The thing that had said "Nonsense!" went on saying it. She looked at Lilias, and felt a lot older and more competent than the Stacy of three years ago. She thought, quite dispassionately, that one of those old-fashioned bedroom jugs full of cold water tipped right over the fair hair, the eyelashes, the make-up, and all the rest of it would probably be a good plan. Lilias was making her own flesh creep—perhaps. She wasn't going to make Stacy's flesh creep any more. Three years ago, yes, but not today. Not any more. She sat up straight and said in the coolest voice she could manage,

"You really are talking nonsense, Lilias. I think you'd better stop."

Lilias shut her eyes. The long dark lashes were wet. She said in an exhausted voice,

"It's only to you—I must talk to someone—it doesn't matter if it's only to you."

It was no use thinking of tipping jugs of water over people if there weren't jugs of water to tip. She did the best she could with her voice,

"What is all this? If you've got anything to say, go on and say it!"

The lashes flew up.

"Oh, Stacy—I didn't think—"

153

"You'd better. It doesn't do to say that sort of thing—to anyone."

"I wouldn't to anyone else. It's just—*Charles*. He's everything to me, you know—he always has been. It doesn't matter what he's done, he's *everything*."

Stacy said, "Lilias—"

"I *must* talk to someone—isn't it better that I should talk to you? Because even now—even *now* you wouldn't want to do him any harm."

Stacy said, "No—I wouldn't want to do him any harm."

"Then let me talk to you. I didn't sleep last night. I could only go on thinking, 'Suppose it was Charles, or suppose they think it was.'"

"Why?"

With a rush of nervous energy, Lilias told her why.

"Don't you see—you usen't to be stupid—I came away at ten minutes past three, and Lewis was alive. He was sitting at his table and he was *alive*. Charles came only ten minutes later, and he says he found him dead. If Lewis didn't kill himself, who killed him? Charles says that the police don't believe it was suicide. I don't understand all the reasons why, but they don't believe it. Then who killed him? And why? There wasn't anything stolen, or any attempt made to break into the strong-room—besides, who would in the middle of the afternoon, with people coming and going all the time? I went at ten past, Charles came at twenty past—there simply wasn't time. And if he wasn't killed for that wretched Collection, why was he killed?"

Stacy put up a hand. It was curious to feel how

154

cold it was as she lifted it.

"Look here, Lilias—stop! You can't have it both ways. You started off by saying you always thought something dreadful would happen—because of the Collection. And now you say nobody tried to steal anything, and they wouldn't in the middle of the afternoon anyhow. Then you finish up with, 'If he wasn't killed for that wretched Collection, why was he killed?' You're arguing from both ends and getting a head-on collision in the middle. You'd better make up your mind which way you do want to have it and stick to that."

Lilias beat her hands together.

"It's not like that at all! Of course that's what we must *say*—the bit about the Collection, I mean. We must all say it, and stick to it, that someone was hiding, and went in when the door was open. Maida and Jack Constable must have left it open— they *must*. And we must say that a thief got in and hid, and shot Lewis, and then hid again when Charles came." Her eyes widened and stared. "Oh—it might have happened like that, mightn't it? If we go on saying so *hard*—"

"Then why don't you? You started off that way, and then you swung right over and said nobody would try to steal the Collection in the middle of the afternoon. Why did you say that?"

Lilias's eyes brimmed over.

"Because it's true—because I was just talking to you. The first bit was only—only what we've got to say because of Charles. Lewis wasn't killed for the Collection."

"Do you know why he was killed?"

"Anyone will know if they stop to think. He was

going to marry Maida. He had made a will in her favour—on one of those stupid will-forms. I tell you I saw it when I was there—it was lying there on the table. He saw me looking at it, and he said in his most disagreeable voice, 'You seem interested. That's my new will. I'm afraid Charles won't like it.'"

"Did he tell you he was going to marry Maida, and what was in the will?"

"Of course he did—and in the most horrid sneering way! That's why I didn't stay. Don't you see what must have happened? If he spoke to Charles like that—and he *would*—well, there was the revolver in the drawer."

"You knew where it was?"

"Everyone knew where it was. Lewis wanted everyone to know—he used to leave that drawer open on purpose. Now don't you see how it must have happened? Charles saw the will—and the revolver—"

Stacy said, "I think you're talking nonsense."

Lilias had colour enough now. It came up bright under the rouge and drowned it. Her eyes shone. She said in a high, clear voice,

"Then who burned the will? It didn't matter to anyone but Charles, but it mattered to him. Why should anyone else burn it?"

"Was it burned?"

"Of course it was! Didn't Charles tell you that?"

"I haven't seen him. He hasn't told me anything."

"He wouldn't tell you that—he wouldn't tell anyone. The police told me. The will was all burned to ashes on a metal tray. They wanted to know if

I'd seen it—whether it was burned when I was there. And it wasn't—it *wasn't*. Who burned it?"

Stacy said soberly,

"I don't know. But I do know that you're talking nonsense, and if you care for Charles you'll stop. I suppose you don't want to put ideas into people's heads?"

All the colour and fire went out of Lilias. With a quick nervous shudder she twisted round, laid her arms across the back of the chair, and bent her head upon them. Her shoulders heaved. A difficult, slow sobbing began.

It might be well over eighty in the shade, but Stacy had never felt colder. Some of the cold was fear. She banged the door on that with the blessed word, "Nonsense!" Some of it was anger—there is a cold anger more potent than the hot. Some of it was just a chill revulsion from all this hysteria. After a moment or two she said,

"For God's sake pull yourself together! If you have any real feeling for Charles you will."

Lilias continued to sob, but she managed to find words as well. Nothing would ever prevent Lilias from finding words.

"I'd do anything for Charles—you know that. I wouldn't hurt him for the world. Haven't I helped to cover everything up all these years? Oh, you don't know what it's been like, or you wouldn't be so unkind!"

This was the sort of thing which could go on for ever. Theme with variations—and the variations were infinite. When it had all got a little past endurance Stacy went through to the bathroom and came back with a dry towel and a wet face-cloth.

Lilias was induced to sit up and dab her eyes in a delicate, half-hearted manner. The ravages were not so very dreadful, and it sufficed. The sobbing died down to a catch in the breath, and the tumbled words gave way to a sighing,

"Oh, I'm so sorry—but you understand, don't you? I couldn't bear it alone any more, and you're *safe*. Oh, I must go and tidy up!"

Stacy had perforce to wait. Her "I'll go now" was waved away with an "I won't be a moment."

The moment lengthened to a good many minutes before Lilias came back, a little pale, a little sad, but quite under control. She told Stacy that she had done her good.

"One exaggerates things, sitting here all alone with nothing to do but think. You won't speak of it to anyone—you won't tell Charles?"

"I'm not very likely to be seeing him."

Lilias sighed quite gently.

"You might. He goes to the club quite a lot."

The cold anger in Stacy looked round the door behind which she had shut it in.

"And I should be likely to walk up to him and say, 'Lilias has just been telling me she thinks you shot Lewis and burned his will!'"

The blue eyes filled with tears.

"Oh, Stacy!"

Stacy pushed the anger back and shut the door on it again. She had had all the scenes she could stand. The one remaining thing to do was to get away. She said,

"Sorry, Lilias, but you did rather ask for it. I'm not the one who's been saying things, you know. Goodbye."

CHAPTER 21

Stacy came down into the hall. Well, it was over.
And it had been her own fault for coming. She
needn't have come. She had just let Saltings draw
her like a magnet, and she deserved every bit of
what she had got. It was all over now, and she
needn't think about it again. A horrid niggling
whisper said, "You're going to have to think about
it quite a lot."

She came out on to the steps, and felt the sun.
It was still very hot. She stood for a moment wondering if she would put up Myra Constantine's
umbrella. She didn't like the glare, but she was still
cold inside. As she hesitated, a car turned in at the
gate and came up between the trees. Her heart
jumped. Charles was the last person on earth she
wanted to see. Or was he?

Before she could make up her mind he was out
of the car and running up the steps. No smile, no
greeting, nothing but a hand on her arm and a
quick, "I hoped I'd catch you."

"I'm just going."

"You can't. I want to talk to you. Come along—
you haven't seen my flat. I've got the billiard-room,
the butler's pantry, and some of the things house-
agents call offices—all very commodious. Adams
did a very good job of work, I think. Come along!"

She was being taken through the hall again.

159

Charles opened a door, they went in, and it shut behind them. She had no time to consider the competency of Mr. Adams. There was a sort of lobby, a bit of passage, another door, and a section of the billiard-room with two windows to the garden. It wasn't until they were there that she managed to say,

"I really ought to go back."

Charles said, "No." He walked to the window and looked out. As he stood there with his back to her, Stacy was aware of currents, feelings, emotions. She had a panic-stricken desire to run away, but her legs wouldn't move. Her tongue wouldn't move either. She just stood.

Then the moment passed. Charles turned round and said,

"This is all rather a mess. I'm sorry you've been let in for it, but there it is."

Legs and tongue became normal again. It was a great relief. She said,

"If there's anything I can do—"

Charles had his frowning look. Not the kind he had when he was angry, but the kind that meant he was thinking. He said,

"Well, there is. You saw the woman who was with me when I came into the club just as you were starting out?"

"The little governessy person?"

"Yes. Don't laugh. She's a private detective. Sit down, and I'll tell you. Lewis went to see her a fortnight ago."

As they sat down side by side upon the sofa, Stacy was aware that she couldn't have stood for another minute. Her head felt quite empty.

She said, "*Lewis*—" and stuck.

Charles said, "I know—it's incredible, and she's incredible. But it's happened—she's happened. Lewis went to see her because he was uneasy. He wanted her to come down. She didn't like him, and she wouldn't. This morning she got a letter from him saying there had been a development, and asking her all over again. She put down the letter, took up her morning paper, and read the headlines. Meanwhile I had a letter from Lewis too. It was in the top drawer of his desk. It said Miss Silver was to be called in if anything happened."

"Charles!"

He nodded.

"He was uneasy—he had his presentiments? I don't know, you don't know, nobody knows. He had heard about Miss Silver from Randal March who is our Chief Constable. She used to be his governess."

"That's what she looks like."

"I know. But she impressed Lewis. She does impress one—somehow. She showed me his letter, and, believe it or not, she had impressed him to such an extent that he told her she could name her own fee. How's that?"

Stacy's face expressed the incredulity he expected.

"Lewis said that?"

"He did."

The fact that Lewis Brading had seldom been known to spend a penny upon any object not connected with his Collection rose imposingly between them. There was a pause while they contemplated it. Then Charles said,

161

"So you see! And there's something about her. After giving her tea and taking her over the annexe I'm rather sitting at her feet myself. Now what I'm leading up to is this. I want you to tell her what you told me—about waking up and hearing things in the night."

Stacy looked horrified.

"Charles, I couldn't!"

"Why?"

"Because it couldn't have anything to do with Lewis being shot."

"Why couldn't it? It's just what he told Miss Silver when he went to see her. He said he slept— too heavily—and woke with the feeling that there had been someone in the annexe—all vague like that, but he thought he had been drugged. It fits in."

Stacy's horrified look had changed to one of distress. She said,

"Yes, but—Charles, I think it's something quite different. There's something I can't tell you. I don't think it would be fair."

"All right, darling, go on being beautifully, perfectly fair. *Fais ce que dois, advienne que pourra*, and all the rest of it. Let the murderer get away with it because you couldn't possibly repeat something you weren't supposed to know! You'll come and see me in the condemned cell, won't you? Or don't divorced wives count? We shall have to find out."

"Don't!"

He raised his eyebrows.

"I'd much rather not have to. But there it is—if you've overlooked the fact that I'm the natural, first-class, A-1 suspect, the police haven't. They're

162

only in the early stages at the moment, and they're being quite polite, but they think I did it. So if you know anything, and don't particularly want to score me off—"

She said, "*Charles*—" in an agitated voice.

His manner changed.

"Here's something Miss Silver said. It struck me rather. She said that most people have something to hide. And that when it came to a murder case, it wasn't only the murderer who was trying to cover up. Well, you can see for yourself how that complicates things. If there's something you know—something you didn't tell me—"

"It hadn't happened then. Look here, I'll tell you what it was, then you'll see for yourself it couldn't have anything to do with Lewis being shot."

"Yes, you'd better tell me."

She sat up straight in the sofa corner with her hands in her lap. No rings on them. She had taken off her wedding-ring. His glance just flicked the bare third finger. She said rather quick and low,

"Yes, I'll tell you. It was quite a different sort of thing. I found out what it was after I'd spoken to you. I heard the sound again—at least I woke up out of rather a frightening dream—I think it waked me. I got up and looked out of the window. The light came on outside in the glass passage. It wasn't on when I woke up, then it came on—suddenly. I thought someone—Charles, it sounds like nonsense, but all along, both times, I thought someone had come from the annexe into the house."

He shook his head.

"The light can only be turned on and off from the annexe."

"I know. I'm not arguing about that. I'm only telling you what I thought at the time, because that's what made me go and look down over the stairs."

"Well?"

"I saw Hester Constantine—"

"My poor child! You must still have been dreaming. No wonder you said it was a frightening dream!"

"Charles, I'm serious."

"You really mean you saw Hester Constantine come from the annexe?"

"I don't know whether she came from the annexe, or whether James Moberly did—they might have been in the study. It must have been he who turned the light on and off—unless you can possibly imagine it was Lewis."

"*Honi soit qui mal y pense*—I can't. Hester Constantine! I think not!"

"Then it was James Moberly. She looked quite different, poor thing—all lighted up and happy. And she had one of Myra's shawls, a bright embroidered thing. She—Charles, you can't mistake it when anyone looks like that. It's—it's frightfully pathetic—those two poor things. Myra says Lewis has always treated him like dirt and he couldn't call his soul his own. She didn't see that Hester couldn't either. If they sort of clung on to one another and tried to get a little happiness—" She put out her hands to him. "Charles, don't you see how—how savage it would be if we were to throw them to the police?"

He said, "Poor old James!" And then, "We won't throw him to the police if we can help it. But I think we'll have to have a showdown. There's more to it than you know, and if James has been snapping lights on and off, and letting people into the annexe at night—to say nothing of drugging his employer—well, I think he'll just have to explain what it was all about, and he can begin by explaining privately to Miss Silver and me."

Stacy said, "I feel awful."

He took her hands, held them for a moment lightly, and let them go again.

"Nice womanly sentiment, darling. But I'm not prepared to be led away with gyves upon my wrists because of being too delicate to ask James a few straight questions."

Stacy's mind swung back. She had said, "Nonsense!" to Lilias, and she felt like saying "Nonsense!" again, but there was the cold breath of fear blowing. She didn't know how serious he was, but if he was serious at all—

Charles said, "I don't actually want to be arrested for murder if I can help it." Then, before she could say anything, "Being a little morbid, aren't we? How did the visit to Lilias go off?"

"All right."

He laughed.

"As bad as that! My poor sweet, I thought you looked a bit jaded."

CHAPTER 22

At about the same time that Charles and Stacy were talking at Saltings, Randal March got out of his car, walked into the hall at Warne House, and enquired for Miss Maud Silver. Edna Snagge thought him a very goodlooking man. She could admire Charles Forrest with his dark ugly charm, and she could admire as different a type as Randal March with his fair hair burned brown, his steady blue eyes, his look of health. She thought Miss Silver no end lucky to have the two of them coming to see her one after the other and nothing to bring them so far as she knew. She went to find Miss Silver, and received a gracious word of explanation.

"Mr. March? Oh, yes—certainly. He is an old pupil of mine. So kind and attentive of him to call."

Edna said, "I've put him in the little writing-room. You won't be disturbed there."

She received a beaming smile.

The little writing-room was on the shady side of the house. On cold, dull days it had been stig-matized as a gloomy hole. On a hot evening like this it had its points, but it was never a popular resort. Miss Silver reflected that their conversation was not likely to be disturbed.

She found the Chief Constable standing with his back to a funerary mantelpiece carried out in black marble. The clock matched it, but was relieved by little gold turrets. A shadowy engraving of what was probably some famous battle picture was hardly to be distinguished from the surrounding wall-paper.

Greetings of the most affectionate nature passed, to be followed by enquiries for his mother—"I was so concerned to hear about her having a cold"— and about his sisters, Margaret and Isabel.

Difficult as it was to believe now, Randal March had been a delicate little boy, and it was for this reason that he had shared his sisters' schoolroom. He had also been very much spoilt. Having successfully routed two governesses, he had regarded Miss Silver's arrival as the provision of more cannon-fodder. The local doctor had opined that it would do him harm to be thwarted. Miss Silver, after listening sympathetically to all Mrs. March had to say, dismissed it from her mind and proceeded to establish the cheerful discipline which she was accustomed to maintain in her schoolroom. Randal found his energies provided with a more interesting outlet than naughtiness. He conceived a high respect for his teacher which remained in full force down to the present moment. For her part, though she had never allowed herself to have favourites and was always scrupulous in her enquiries for his sisters, it was an unadmitted fact that her affectionate feeling for Randal was of a more spontaneous character.

Preliminaries over, she seated herself, took out her knitting, and revealed the inch-wide strip of soft pale pink wool which indicated that a baby's vest was in process of construction.

Randal March sat down opposite to her and said, "Well?"

She gave a little cough.

"Well, Randal?"

He laughed.

"All right, I'll deal. I'd like to see Brading's letter."

She produced it—from the knitting-bag, a circumstance which struck him as characteristic.

Leaning forward to take it from her, he scanned the few lines:

Dear Madam,

I am writing to ask you to reconsider your decision. There have been developments. The matter is confidential, and I do not wish to go to the police—at present. This is a pleasant country club. I have reserved a room for you, and must beg you to come down immediately. You may name your own fee. If you will ring me up and let me know by what train by you will be arriving, I will see that you are met at Ledstow.

Yours truly,
Lewis Brading

March looked up and said,

"What did he mean by developments?"

"I have no idea."

He sat frowning at the letter for a moment. Then he said,

"You only saw him once?"

"That is all."

"Will you tell me what he said?"

She was knitting rapidly. The strip of pale pink wool revolved. There was a moment before she answered him.

"Yes, I think I must."

With the verbal accuracy which he knew was to be trusted she gave him Lewis Brading's words and her own. When she had finished he said coolly,

"Well, he seems to have asked for it. You know, this looks very bad for Moberly. It fits in too. Look here, perhaps you'd like to take some notes. Here's a timetable of what happened yesterday up to the shooting." He reached sideways to pick up a pencil and paper from the small writing-table at his elbow.

The knitting was laid down, the pencil poised. He produced a sheaf of papers from the case beside him, detached one of them, and said,

"Here we are. Brading took the nine-thirty bus to Ledlington. At ten-fifteen he went into the Southern Bank, asked to see the manager, and signed a will-form which was duly witnessed by him and a clerk. He said something about asking for congratulations before long. A lady called Maida Robinson says he had asked her to marry him on the previous evening."

Miss Silver inclined her head.

"Major Forrest has told me about Mrs. Robinson. He has also given me a timetable showing Mr. Brading's visitors during yesterday afternoon."

"Well, that clears the ground—I need only give you the morning. Brading got back here at eleven-thirty. He went to his study—you've seen it, I suppose?"

"Yes."

"He was there for about half an hour. James Moberly was with him. One of the waiters overheard part of their conversation. He dresses it up—says he was taking Brading some letters which had come in by the second post and couldn't make up his mind whether to go in or not, because they were quarrelling. Of course there isn't the slightest doubt that he heard the raised voices and listened deliberately. He may even have loosened the catch a bit—it slips rather easily. Anyhow, he's prepared to swear that he heard Moberly say, 'I can't and won't stand it any longer.' He says Brading laughed in a nasty way and said, 'I'm afraid you'll have to.' Moberly said, 'I won't, and that's flat!' Brading laughed again and asked him what he was going to do about it, and Moberly said, 'You'll see.' After which this man, Owen, appears to have thought he had stood there long enough, so he knocked and went in. He says Brading was sitting at the table and Moberly was standing looking out of the window. Moberly admits there was a disagreement." March put down the paper from which he had been reading and took up another. "Here's his statement—all very watered down and innocuous, as you will see. He says:

'I was in the study at eleven-thirty, when Mr. Brading came in. I took the opportunity of telling him that I would like to resign my post. This was not on account of any personal disagreement or any dissatisfaction on either side, but because I found my health was suffering from having to live under the unnatural conditions which he considered necessary. A good deal of my work has to be done in the annexe, and I have to sleep there. The absence of air and light were affecting my health. Mr. Brading was angry and said he would not let me go. What Owen says he overheard is substantially correct, but we were not quarrelling. He was annoyed at my giving notice, and I was sticking to my point. At five minutes to twelve Mr. Brading went over to the annexe. I let a minute or two go by, and then I followed him. I had my own key, so I was able to let myself in. I could hear his voice coming from his bedroom. He was telephoning, so I stayed where I was—that is, in the passage from which his bedroom and the laboratory open. I kept at the far end of the passage, so I did not hear what was said. When he rang off I was going to go to him, but he asked for another number. I could not distinguish what number it was, only the tone of the voice. I thought it sounded as if he was angry. Just at the end of the call I heard him say, 'You'd better.' Those words were said most emphatically. Then he rang off, and I went to him and told him that I could not withdraw my notice, but that I would of course remain until he was suited. I then returned to the study, and from there went in to lunch. When he had finished his own lunch he came over to my table and stopped for a moment to say that I might have the afternoon off, as he would not be wanting me.'"

March looked up for a moment.

"They apparently had all their meals over here in the club. I asked him if they usually ate at separate tables, and he said yes, their hours were different and they both preferred to be independent. I may say that the staff confirm this. Well, I'll go on now. There isn't much more."

171

He went back to James Moberly's statement.

"'I left the dining-room a little later and went over to my room in the annexe to fetch a book. The steel door was locked as usual, and I used my key to open it. When I came back to the club a few minutes later I made sure that it was shut behind me, as I always do. It locks itself when it is shut, and I am quite sure that I left it locked. I went to the study and spent the afternoon there reading. I heard the clock strike three. About ten minutes later Miss Constantine opened the door. When she saw that I was alone she came in. We sat there talking until Major Forrest gave the alarm. We were together the whole time. Neither of us left the room.'"

Miss Silver coughed.

"The study window looks towards the annexe. Did you enquire whether Mr. Moberly was in a position to see the glass passage, and whether he noticed any of Mr. Brading's visitors?"

"Yes, I asked him that, but it doesn't get us any farther. He says people were coming and going, but he was reading and didn't take any particular notice. The only person he saw was Major Constable. He says he heard someone running, looked up, and saw him in the glass passage. He was running from the annexe, and he had something white in his hand."

Miss Silver was knitting briskly.

"Was Mrs. Robinson's bag white?"

"Yes—a big white plastic affair. She had her bathing things in it. I think it's quite clear that Constable was coming back from fetching it when Moberly saw him. You say Forrest gave you all

172

those comings and goings?''

"Yes, he was most helpful."

"Well, Moberly says he didn't see anyone else until Miss Constantine came in, and after that they were talking."

"What does Miss Constantine say?"

"That she was with her mother until three o'clock, went to her room to tidy, came downstairs just as Lilias Grey left the club, went along to the study, and spent the time there talking to Moberly, just as he says."

Miss Silver's needles clicked.

"When I asked Major Forrest if they were friends he replied that he did not think Miss Constantine 'ran to friends much.' The study was Mr. Brading's room. Unless she had previous knowledge, she could not have expected to find Mr. Moberly there alone. Did she know that he would be there alone? Was her visit to him, or was she looking for Mr. Brading? It was his study."

March made an impatient movement.

"Does it matter?"

She looked at him mildly.

"It might, Randal."

"They both say that they were together between three-ten and three-thirty. It is, of course, possible that one or both of them are not telling the truth. In fact I'll go so far as to say that things don't look too good for Moberly. In which case Miss Constantine may be lying to protect him, or she may simply have been muddled about the times. She impressed me as rather a vague sort of person."

Miss Silver said in a considering voice,

"That would not be so easy. The time of Miss

173

Grey's departure is fixed by Miss Snagge in the office, also the time of Major Forrest's arrival ten minutes later. It would be difficult for Miss Constantine to be muddled as to whether Mr. Moberly was in the study when she got there and for the next ten minutes. You are, I suppose, drawing my attention to the fact that it was during this time that Mr. Moberly would have had the opportunity of going over to the annexe to shoot Mr. Brading?"

March nodded.

"According to Miss Grey, Brading was alive at three-ten. According to Forrest, he was dead at three-twenty. According to Miss Constantine and James Moberly, they were together in the study during the intervening ten minutes. According to Edna Snagge, no one came through the hall. Since you always know everything, I suppose you know that the only other room opening on to that short length of passage, the billiard-room, was locked up all day."

Miss Silver coughed.

"Yes—Major Forrest very kindly verified that."

"Miss Peto, the manageress, says there is only one key, and she had it. The room keys are not interchangeable. I've had them all tried, and there isn't one that fits the billiard-room door. So we get this situation. Lewis Brading is alive at three-ten, and dead at three-twenty. In that intervening time one of six people killed him—Miss Grey, James Moberly, Miss Constantine, Charles Forrest, Edna Snagge, or Brading himself. Some of these are too improbable to be considered at all seriously. I'll take Brading himself first. The death was meant to look like suicide, but Crisp was suspicious from

174

the beginning—Inspector Crisp from Ledlington—
you'll remember him at the Catherine-Wheel, I expect.* He's as sharp as a terrier after rats, and as
soon as they got the fingerprints on the revolver
he said they were all wrong. It's the most difficult
thing in the world to get a natural print from a
dead hand. The murderer had had a try, and he
hadn't brought it off."

Miss Silver said, "Dear me!"

March gave his half laugh.

"Dear me it is. And that rules out Lewis Brading.
Now we'll take one of the improbables, Edna
Snagge. All the times depend on her observation
and statement. She could have walked down the
passage, and, provided the steel door was left open
by Miss Grey, she could have entered the annexe,
gone through to the laboratory, and shot Lewis
Brading. Only there's no earthly reason why she
should. I don't really think we need consider her.
She is a perfectly good, respectable girl on the brink
of becoming engaged to a perfectly good, respectable young man. She wasn't a legatee under Brading's will, and she had no more to do with him
than with anyone else about the place. In fact she
had no conceivable motive, and I only mentioned
her because it was physically possible for her to
have done it."

Miss Silver's needles clicked. Miss Silver said,
"Quite so."

"Then we have Miss Grey, who also seems to
have no motive. We have been in communication
with Brading's solicitors, and she had no interest

*The Catherine-Wheel

under his will. Charles Forrest's mother adopted her at a time when she had no children of her own. Brading's mother was a Forrest, so I suppose she ranks as a cousin, but you know how those sort of things work out. She and Brading have lived practically next door to each other for about thirty years in one of those semi-detached relationships in which there is neither intimacy nor disagreement— perhaps never enough intimacy to lead to disagreement. One sees the sort of thing every day. They've always known each other, and never cared enough to quarrel."

Miss Silver coughed.

"An excellent description."

He smiled.

"Praise from Sir Hubert Stanley! Well, so much for Miss Grey." He leaned forward, a slight change in his manner, and said, "Then there's Forrest. Crisp is rather hot on Forrest. Very zealous fellow Crisp. He points out that Forrest has a most indubitable motive. The Forrest finances have been as embarrassed as those of most other landed proprietors. Charles has managed to keep his head above water and pay his rates by cutting his house up into flats and letting it piecemeal. Brading's father made a pile in commerce. Some of it's locked up in the Collection, but there's quite a lot left, and under the original will Charles Forrest scoops the lot. Brading's projected marriage and Brading's new will would undoubtedly be a nasty jar. Crisp points out the obvious with a good deal of triumph—Brading was shot as soon as he became engaged to be married and altered his will. And the new will was destroyed. He thinks that conclusive. I don't go so far as that, but—well, there are some suspicious circumstances. And then, out of the blue, comes this business of Moberly's past. That gives him a motive too. Crisp won't like it of course—the money motive is such an obvious and easy one."

Miss Silver quoted from her favourite Lord Tennyson.

"'And lust of gain in the spirit of Cain,' Randal."

"Quite. But we are not all Cains. The normal man doesn't get knocked off his balance and do murder because a cousin contemplates matrimony. I must confess to thinking that Moberly had a much stronger motive. To all intents and purposes Brading was blackmailing him. He had had years of wanting to get away and being forced to stay. Not so good to be chained to one's past, and under the eye of someone who knows all about it and doesn't scruple to use his knowledge. It's a strong motive. Whether it would be strong enough depends on things like Moberly's temperament, character, and what incentive he had to break away and make a fresh start. I must tell you candidly that I think it lies between him and Forrest, with the probabilities rather evenly balanced."

Miss Silver coughed.

"Major Forrest asserts with a good deal of warmth that Mr. Moberly would not 'hurt a fly'—I use his own words. He was aware of the fact that Mr. Brading was holding something over him, and he knew what that something was, but he would not, I believe, have said anything about it if I had not told him what Mr. Brading had said to me on the subject. He is, I think, really convinced that

177

Mr. Moberly had nothing to do with his cousin's death."

March gave a short half laugh.

"He would be if he had shot him himself. And he might have shot him, and yet not wish to see an innocent man hang. I still think that the balance is fairly equal between the two of them. But there is a thing which may tip it down on Forrest's side."

She looked at him across her knitting.

"The destruction of the will?"

He nodded.

"Forrest had the most interest in that—in fact the only obvious interest. But if we are to consider subtleties, Moberly may have had some reason of his own for burning the will. He may, for instance, have hoped for some help or provision from Forrest who had been friendly to him, whereas he couldn't expect anything from Maida Robinson. It's not much of a theory, I admit, but a wealthy Charles Forrest might have done something for him, you know."

"That is true."

"That's five out of my six people. The last one is Miss Constantine. I hardly think she could be a principal. She may be screening Moberly. At present there doesn't seem to be any motive for her doing so, but of course you never can tell. If she is really speaking the truth when she says that she and Moberly were together in the study for that all-important ten minutes between Miss Grey's departure and Forrest's arrival, well then, Moberly is out of it and we are left with Charles Forrest. We must just go on digging and see what turns up."

"There is nothing missing from the Collection?"

"No. Everything is catalogued in Brading's own hand. We have had a check over with Moberly and Forrest. There is nothing missing." He paused for a moment, and then went on again in a slower tone. "There was a diamond brooch in the open second drawer of the writing-table—a very handsome one—five big diamonds in a row. Can you make anything of that?"

"Any prints on it?"

"No. Not much surface, you know."

She had her considering look.

"If he had just become engaged to Mrs. Robinson, it might have been intended as a present."

His expression changed to one of distaste.

"Rather an odd one, but Brading was an odd sort of person. The brooch is valuable, but it has unpleasant associations. One would hardly have thought—" He gave a slight shrug. "It's down in the Catalogue as, 'The Marziali brooch—five brilliants of four carats each,' and then, 'Guilia Marziali was wearing it when her husband stabbed her and her lover, August 8th, 1820.'"

Miss Silver coughed.

"Mr. Brading's tastes were morbid in the extreme."

Her needles clicked. The pink strip had lengthened considerably. She said, "I suppose you will have had a report on fingerprints. Does it suggest anything of interest?"

"Did you expect that it would?"

"Frankly, no, Randal."

He laughed.

"Well, you would have been right. Brading threw a party on the previous night to show his

179

Collection. Present Myra Constantine and her two daughters, Charles Forrest, Lilias Grey, Major Constable, Maida Robinson, a Mr. and Mrs. Brown—innocuous people with no interest in Brading and perfect alibis for the time of the murder—Brading himself, Moberly, and a girl who used to be married to Charles Forrest and now calls herself Stacy Mainwaring. I suppose you've heard about her?"

"I have met her."

"Seems a nice girl. There doesn't seem to have been any scandal about the divorce—they just separated, and are now quite good friends."

"So Major Forrest tells me."

"She seems to have been one of the party. And of course everybody's fingerprints are all over everything."

"Not, I suppose, in the laboratory."

"No. But most of them touched the steel door coming or going, and the table and chairs in the big room have all the prints. You can tell where everyone was sitting. But we knew that already. Brading got out his stuff and had them all round the table watching him show it off."

Miss Silver coughed.

"What about the other rooms? What about the laboratory?"

He answered the first question first.

"Nothing in the other rooms except Brading's own prints, Moberly's, and those of the woman who used to come in and clean. In the laboratory, Brading's and Moberly's all over the place, Constable's on the back of a chair in which Maida Robinson says she had been sitting. It was across the table from Brading, and it would have been quite a natural place for her to be. She says she left her bag there, and if it was on that side of the table, Constable would be quite likely to take hold of the chair as he leaned over to get the bag. That's his only print. There are none of hers, and none of Lilias Grey's. Forrest has the print of his right hand on the top of the table at the back. He says he stood there and leaned across when he first came in, to make sure that Brading was dead before he went round and touched him. There's a print of his left hand on the back of Brading's chair, and some impressions of his right upon the corner of the table near where Brading's head was lying. And that's all."

"No prints on the door?"

"Brading's and Moberly's."

"Not Mrs. Robinson's?"

"No."

"Then it must have been open when she came."

"That's likely enough. He was expecting her, and Edna Snagge rang through from the office to let him know she had arrived. He came and opened the steel door for her and took her through to the laboratory."

"I see. Were there no prints upon the ash-tray where the will had been burned?"

"Forrest told you about that? No, there were no prints on it."

"Or on the handle of the drawer in which he kept the revolver?"

"Only his own."

"And the prints on the revolver, you say?"

"Were made after death."

CHAPTER 23

It was not very long after Randal March had taken his leave that Charles Forrest's car drew up in front of Warne House. He got out, and Stacy Mainwaring got out. All very interesting for Edna Snagge, who was just going off duty. She wondered what it would be like to marry someone and leave him, and then come down and meet him again as if none of it had ever happened.

Charles put Stacy in the study and went off to get Miss Silver, whom he found in the writing-room sitting by the window, enjoying a cool breeze and considering her late conversation with the Chief Constable. He came in and said,

"Stacy wants to see you. At least that's putting it rather high—there's something I think she ought to tell you."

He was impressed by the fact that she asked no questions, merely said, "I shall be very pleased to hear anything Miss Mainwaring has to say," and accompanied him to the study without more ado.

Stacy, over by the window, was reminded of interviews with a headmistress. There was the same dampness on the palms of the hands, the same feeling of being quite hollow and empty. And then Miss Silver smiled at her and everything felt quite different. Charles had disappeared, which somehow made things easier, and by the time they were sitting down and Miss Silver had got out her knitting the study felt really almost cosy. Stacy found herself saying,

"There's something—Charles thinks I ought to tell you about—but I don't know—"

Miss Silver produced a ball of pale pink wool and unwound a length of it so as to avoid any drag upon the needles. She said,

"You are afraid of hurting someone?"

Stacy gave her a grateful look.

"Yes." Then, after a pause, "It might hurt them—dreadfully."

Miss Silver coughed.

"What you have to tell is connected with Mr. Brading's death?"

"I don't know—it might be—Charles thinks—"

Miss Silver looked at her kindly.

"In a murder case private feelings and reticences very often have to be sacrificed. If you know something, I think that you should speak. What is unconnected with the murder need go no farther. But you are, perhaps, not in a position to judge what is, or might be, important evidence—and to withhold evidence may involve an innocent person."

Stacy said, "Charles—" and then stopped. She looked from the clicking needles to Miss Silver's face. An extraordinary feeling of reassurance and relief came to her. She began to tell Miss Silver about seeing the light in the glass passage turned on, hearing the click of the door, and watching Hester Constantine come through the hall wrapped in her mother's bright shawl.

Miss Silver knitted and listened. At the end she said,

"Major Forrest is right. You could not have kept this back."

Stacy said, "I'm so sorry for them. I don't think they've ever had anything."

Miss Silver coughed.

"Pray do not distress yourself. If what you saw has no connection with Mr. Brading's death, it is, and can remain, their private affair. And now, perhaps, you would like to slip away. Major Forrest said he would give us a few minutes and then bring Mr. Moberly here. You will not, perhaps, wish—"

Stacy said, "Oh, *no*," and fled.

James Moberly came in a little later with Charles Forrest behind him. Miss Silver's position having been explained, he showed no surprise at her presence. Everything had become so disturbing, so complicated, so fraught with unpleasant possibilities, that he no longer had any expectation of comfort or security. Police, or private detectives, Inspector Crisp barking at him, or an elderly lady knitting up pale pink wool—it really no longer seemed to matter, since there appeared to be nothing but stark ruin ahead.

Charles said, "Sit down, James. I think you've met Miss Silver," and he sat down, though he would rather have remained standing. Now they were all sitting, and no one had said anything yet— not anything that mattered. Presently they would begin. He supposed it would be the same thing over again. He sat there in a dull misery and waited.

Charles turned a frowning face upon him.

"Look here, James, I hope you don't mind—for all our sakes we've got to do what we can to get

184

to the bottom of this business. As I told you, Miss Silver is here because she is a private detective. Lewis went to see her a fortnight ago."

James Moberly said, "You didn't tell me that."

"No."

"Why did Mr. Brading go to a private detective?"

Miss Silver said in precise tones,

"He was uneasy. He said that on more than one occasion he had slept more heavily than was natural, and on waking he received a definite impression that there had been someone in the annexe."

James Moberly could not have looked paler or more harassed. His face showed no change.

Charles said, "You understand the implication?"

He gave a slight hopeless shrug.

"That I drugged him? Oh, yes. Why am I supposed to have done that?"

"He did not say. He was uneasy. He wished me to come down and investigate. I refused. This morning I received a letter from him urging me to reconsider my decision. The postmark was Ledstow, two-thirty p.m. Immediately after reading it I read of his death in my morning paper. Major Forrest afterwards asked me to come down here."

There was a pause. Then Charles said,

"It's all damned unpleasant—better get on with it."

He had a reproving glance from Miss Silver. She said,

"Mr. Brading suspected that someone was being admitted to the annexe at night. I must tell you that his suspicion is borne out by certain facts. On two occasions the light in the glass passage, which, I understand, is supposed to burn all night, was for a time switched off. Someone looking out of a window noticed that the passage was dark, and saw the light switched on again. This person had been wakened by the click of a latch. The second occasion on which this happened was the night before Mr. Brading's death. Miss Hester Constantine was observed to come from the direction of the passage."

James Moberly said nothing. He stared before him.

Miss Silver said,

"The person who saw Miss Constantine was able to describe every detail of her appearance. She was wearing an embroidered shawl of her mother's—"

James Moberly said, "Stop!" But when the silence fell he had no more to say until Miss Silver spoke his name.

"Mr. Moberly—"

He broke out then.

"What are you implying? What is all this about? What have I got to do with Miss Constantine?"

"That is for you to say. The implication is, of course, quite clear. Perhaps we should ask Miss Constantine to join us."

He said, "No!" in a dreadful voice. And then, "Not that!"

From staring at Miss Silver, he swung away to fix his eyes on Charles.

"Forrest—"

"Look here, James, this has gone far enough. Don't you think you'd better make a clean breast of it? The plain fact is, we've none of us got any private affairs any longer. If you and Miss Con-

stantine have been meeting here or in the annexe—
well, in the ordinary way it would be no concern
of mine, but—don't you see, man, don't you see,
if you were fool enough to have her into the annexe—"

James Moberly lifted his head.

"She is my wife."

Miss Silver said, "Dear me!"

He repeated the words defiantly. He had not
known that it would be such a relief to say them.

"She is my wife. We were married in Ledlington
a month ago. There wasn't any way we could meet.
We could hardly see each other. You know how it
was, Forrest. Mr. Brading wouldn't let me go. But
you mustn't say I drugged him—I wouldn't do
that. He had his own sleeping tablets. I wouldn't
drug him."

Charles laughed.

"My dear James! So you put one of his own sleeping tablets into that revolting drink which he always took the last thing, I suppose—some awful
malt and cocoa compound. And that wasn't drugging him!"

Moberly went on staring in a tired, obstinate
way.

"It was only one of his own tablets. I wouldn't
drug him."

Charles lifted a hand and let it fall again. He said,
"Well, well—" And then, "Everyone isn't going
to make such a nice distinction. March won't, I'm
afraid."

The look of fatigue deepened.

"Are you going to tell—the police?"

"My dear James, what are we to do—you—I—

187

any of us? Suppose we hush all this up and they nose it out. After all, you can't get married without quite a number of people knowing about it. How did you do it? . . . . Registrar's office in Ledlington? Well, then, there you are. Before this happened it wasn't anybody's business, but now—why, it's simply bound to come out, and it's going to look a whole lot better for you if you come forward with the information yourself. After all, it's got to come out some day."

Moberly said,

"You don't understand. If they know that Hester and I are married, it puts us both under suspicion. We say we were together here in the study between the time that Miss Grey left the hotel and the time you arrived. It happens to be true. We were here. I was telling her what I had said to Mr. Brading before lunch, and what he had answered. She knew that I was making a very strong effort to induce him to let me go. I had to tell her that I had failed. That is the truth. But the police won't believe it. Because we are husband and wife they will think I could have gone into the annexe and shot Mr. Brading, and Hester would say I hadn't left her. They might even say that she—" He broke off with a groan.

Miss Silver had been watching them in an interested manner, her hands busy with her knitting, her eyes noting every shade of expression. She now gave a gentle cough and said,

"It is true, Mr. Moberly, that your alibi for the time of the murder will not appear quite so strong once it is known that Miss Constantine is your wife. But it is also true, as Major Forrest says, that this

188

fact is bound to emerge, and that any further attempt at concealment cannot fail to have a prejudicial effect. If you speak the plain truth, it will, I believe, carry conviction."

He shook his head, and said without looking at her,

"You don't know—"

Charles Forrest said,

"Yes, she does. Lewis told her when he went up to see her a fortnight ago. He spilled the whole thing—told her all the back history, and that I was his executor and would get his instructions to hand the dossier on to the police if anything happened to him."

James Moberly dropped his head in his hands.

"That finishes it." After a pause he spoke again. "Have you handed it on?"

"The dossier hasn't reached me yet. He didn't keep it knocking about, you know. It was in his solicitor's safe. Someone will be coming down on Monday, and I expect I'll get it then. As to whether it goes any farther or not, I never intended that it should. But it's a bit out of my hands now—Lewis took it out of them when he went to see Miss Silver."

Moberly looked up, his face dull and wretched.

"Miss Silver—he told you?"

"Yes, Mr. Moberly."

"What? What did he tell you?"

"Mr. Brading informed me that he had a hold over you. He informed me of the nature of that hold."

"Who else—knows?"

"The Chief Constable."

James Moberly put his head in his hands again. He remained like that, bent forward over his knees, the long thin fingers running up into his hair—dark hair falling over the temples, fingers stained from the laboratory where Lewis Brading had died. All at once he made some sort of impatient sound, pushed back his hair, and got up. He turned to Charles.

"I've got to think. I must have time—I can't take a decision like that all in a minute—it affects my wife. Nobody's ever considered her, but she's going to be considered now. I don't want to let anyone down, but I've got to have time to think—you must understand that."

Charles eyed him curiously.

"No one's trying to hustle you."

Moberly did not seem to hear this. He said again, and more vehemently,

"I must have time! It isn't as if I'd only got myself to consider. You've been my friend. If it was only myself—but it isn't—it can't be. I'm bound to think about Hester. I can't let her down without putting up a fight. You must see that."

Charles nodded. He said, "Take all the time you want," and saw him go over to the door and jerk it open.

He stood there a moment, half turning back as if he had something more to say, but in the end he went out, leaving the door standing. Charles went over and shut it. Then he came back and sat on the corner of the writing-table.

"He's gone out to the annexe. That door into the glass passage clicks just like Stacy said. Did you notice it?"

"Yes, Major Forrest."

He beat a tattoo with his fingers on the table and said,

"Poor devil! They'll make up a case against him. He has a Past. He has a Motive. He drugs his employer—I'm afraid the gendarmerie will call it drugging. He gets married in a very clandestine manner. And his alibi is now on the flimsy side. All the same he didn't kill Lewis, you know."

Miss Silver gazed at him with mild enquiry.

"Why do you say that, Major Forrest?"

Charles gave his charming smile.

"Because I rather gather that he thinks I did."

CHAPTER 24

Next day being Sunday, Miss Silver attended morning service at the little church which stood in the middle of Warne village, very small, crouched, and old, with its graveyard round it. It had stood there for seven hundred years, and some of the headstones were so old that they would have crumbled long ago if moss and lichen had not held them together. Inside, a little girl worked the bellows for the old-fashioned organ, and an older girl stumbled through the chants and hymns under the eyes of a congregation which had seen her grow up and knew that she was substituting for the schoolmistress who was on holiday. The girl was plump, nervous, and not above seventeen. She got hotter and redder every moment. No kindly curtains intervened to prevent any worshipper from being aware of the fact, but on the whole the verdict would be that Doris hadn't done too bad.

Miss Silver found the service very restful. The simple faith and Norman blood mentioned in a famous poem by her admired Lord Tennyson appeared to be happily conjoined in this archaic edifice. No one in Warne had a voice, but everyone sang heartily. The sermon was delivered in a conversational undertone by an old man who allowed long, dreamy pauses to punctuate his discourse, during which he gazed kindly upon his congregation, not a few of whom had dropped into a gentle Sabbath doze. It was all worlds and worlds away from murder. Yet as everyone came out into the August sunshine the Brading case was there, to be discussed, deplored, and whispered about. "They do say"—"My Annie says"—"There's a London detective come down"—"I'd nothing against Mr. Brading myself"—"Well, I always did stick to it that Collection of his wasn't any better than the Chamber of Horrors.". . . .

Miss Silver's hearing was very acute. She caught these and similar snatches of talk as she walked down the cobbled pathway to the lych-gate which opened upon the village street. She was in its shadow, when a quick footstep came up behind her and a brisk voice said,

"Are you Charles Forrest's detective?"

Miss Silver turned with some dignity. She was not tall, but she had an air of authority—she could impress.

She failed to impress Theodosia Dale, who stood

under the melting sun in her thick, laced shoes, her iron-grey tweed, her black felt hat, and repeated the question.

"Are you Charles Forrest's detective?"

"My name is Maud Silver. I am a private enquiry agent."

Theodosia nodded.

"I thought so. You are staying at Warne House. We can walk up together. I am lunching there."

They passed out into the street. It was extremely hot, but Miss Dale's skin showed no sign of moisture. Lewis Brading had been murdered, but she showed no sign of being affected by that either. If there were interested glances turned her way they could detect no change in her. She was Miss Dossie, and she never looked any different winter or summer. She didn't look any different now. She walked beside Miss Silver and said,

"You are enquiring into Lewis Brading's death? I should have thought the police could do that. But no matter—I daresay they are very incompetent—men usually are. I hear it wasn't suicide. No one would ever have got me to believe it was. Lewis wasn't that sort. If he wanted anything he went on till he got it, and once he got it he held on to it. He would never have taken his own life. What do you think about it all?"

Miss Silver coughed.

"I could not offer any opinion," she said mildly.

Theodosia nodded.

"The name is Dale—Miss Dale—Theodosia. My friends call me Dossie. I've lived here all my life, and I'm a nosey old maid. I could be useful to you, you know. There was a time when Lewis and I were going to be married. Somebody else would tell you if I didn't myself. It gives me a point of view."

Miss Silver said, "Yes—" Her tone was a thoughtful one. Miss Dale interested her a good deal. She would certainly know things which might be useful—or confusing. If they were to walk to the club together, it would do no harm to let her talk. It would probably be extremely difficult to prevent her doing so.

It appeared that Miss Dale had very decided opinions.

"I always told Lewis that Collection of his would be the death of him—a nasty morbid idea, and one he ought to have been ashamed of. I had a lucky escape when I had the sense to break off my engagement. Everybody thought I was mad, but I knew what I was doing. Who killed him?"

"Who do you think killed him, Miss Dale? I am sure you have an opinion."

Theodosia shook her head in an impatient manner.

"I wish I had, but I haven't. I can tell you who didn't—Charles Forrest."

"Why do you say that?"

"Not his line of country. I've known Charles ever since he was born. He's got a good disposition. And something else. He's clannish—strong sense of family. He didn't like Lewis, but he'd a family feeling for him. He'd have gone to any amount of trouble to rally round in an emergency. Same with Lilias Grey. Extraordinarily tiresome woman, but because his mother adopted her Charles will go on giving her a flat and seeing that she's got an income exactly as if she was his sister—and that's more than a great many brothers would do. Take that depressed secretary of Lewis's—nobody would have bothered about him or treated him as a human being if it hadn't been for Charles. See what I mean—that sort of person doesn't turn killer. But I shouldn't wonder if that odious Ledlington Inspector didn't try and cook up a case against him. I wouldn't put it past him. He and Charles had words about a speed limit. Charles was run in and fined. Too bad. Crisp is a regular jack-in-office. Look here, there's a thing you can tell me—about the revolver. Lewis was shot with a revolver, wasn't he? Do you know if it was the one Charles gave him?"

"I believe so."

"Well, they can make quite sure about that, you know. That's one of the things I wanted to say to you. They needn't think they can drag Charles into it on account of the revolver being his, because he had a pair, and when he gave one of them to Lewis about six months ago he scratched his initials on it—L. B. Lewis showed them to me—I can swear to that. So, you see, they can't drag Charles in over the revolver."

Miss Silver said,

"Thank you, Miss Dale. That is very interesting."

They turned in at the gate of Warne House.

195

CHAPTER 25

It appeared that Miss Dale was lunching with Myra
Constantine and her daughters. In her character of
a private gentlewoman Miss Silver would certainly
not have consented to being included in the party
by someone who was herself only a guest, but as
a detective she made no resistance when Theodosia
introduced her to Myra, to Lady Minstrell, to Hester Constantine, following up these introductions
with a downright, "Ask her to come and sit with
us for lunch, Myra. Too depressing, eating alone
after what has happened."

Miss Silver found herself placed between Mrs.
Constantine, vast in a dress brightly flowered with
poppies and cornflowers, and a pale, reluctant
Hester, who gave her the sort of glance a nervous
horse gives when he is about to shy, and then
looked down at her plate.

James Moberly sat alone, as he always did, at
the small table by the door. He and Hester never
looked at one another. Each felt the drag of the
other's misery, the other's fear. The room was almost empty. Mr. and Mrs. Brown had left in a
hurry. The golfing men had gone off for the day.
Guests who had been coming for the week-end had
cancelled their bookings.

Miss Silver accepted cold salmon, and found herself engaged in conversation by Myra Constantine.

"Shocking thing this, and I hope you'll find out who's done it before it wrecks the club. Lewis had a share in it, you know, and so have I. Ridiculous, people giving it the cold shoulder. It's not even as if it had happened in the club. I always did tell Lewis that Collection of his ought to be in a museum, but he wasn't one to listen—" She broke off to call the waiter. "André—some of that mayonnaise sauce!"

"Madame—"

A silver sauce-boat was proffered. Myra went on talking.

"Stingy with it, aren't you? And everybody ought to know better by now. What's the good of salmon if you don't have plenty of sauce?" She helped herself lavishly and turned back to Miss Silver. "That goes for everything, doesn't it? Salmon, or life, it's all the same—it's the sauce that counts, and I like plenty." She called across the table. "Now, Miss Mainwaring, you'll just take a proper help and eat it! No poking it away under your fork. I don't want Charles to say we got you down here and starved you. No one's going to make anything better by going off their food, and what I said to Miss Mainwaring—oh, bother, I can't go on Missing you, my dear, it'll have to be Stacy and be done with it. What I said to you goes for Hester too—she doesn't eat enough to keep a fly. And what good it's going to do anyone starving and making yourself ill passes me. No matter what happens, we've got to eat, and if you don't fancy fish, Het, there's cold ham and salad, but one or the other you'll take, and no nonsense about it! André—get Miss Constantine some ham!"

Hester Constantine said nothing at all. A little dull colour came up in her face and went away again. When the ham was brought she cut it up into very small bits and pushed them under the salad.

Miss Silver observed in a conversational voice that many people had very little appetite on such a very hot day. Myra speared a slice of cucumber, added lettuce, potato, and watercress, imposed the whole on a good-sized piece of salmon, and conveyed it skilfully to her mouth.

"Thank God, I've always been able to take my food," she said. "Makes a lot of difference, you know. I didn't have enough when I was a growing girl. You wouldn't believe how hungry I used to be, and have to see the other girls go off to supper with their young men. Nobody'd look at me—I was too ugly. And then—" she lifted a glass of shandygaff and drank hugely—"well, then I went on being ugly, but they started looking, and I went out to supper with the best."

Lady Minstrell broke off her conversation with Theodosia Dale to say, "Mama dear!"

Myra chuckled.

"You go on with your talk, Milly, my dear, ever so nice and refined, and I'll go on with mine. I'm not refined, and never shall be. Never went in for it, or I daresay I'd have got there just as well as Lottie Loring that's so high-toned and classy now that she wouldn't walk the same side of the road with what she was when she got her first kick-off. André—more shandy!"

She turned back to Miss Silver.

"If you're made one way, you get some kind of

a nasty twist if you start turning yourself round to look like something else—does something to you—like those contortionists. I know, because I had a go at it. Poor Sid now—that was my husband—he was refined. Didn't want to fall in love with me, but couldn't help it, if you know what I mean, and once we were married, the way I dropped my aitches, well it fairly shook him. So I had a go at it. When Milly was born he wanted a nice refined name, so we took Millicent—nice and easy to say, and Milly handy when you weren't feeling grand. And then there was Hester, and he wanted an aitch to her name so I'd have plenty of practice. It was his idea, you see, that if I'd got to say a name with an aitch in it every few minutes all round the clock, it'd break me in properly. So I sat down and thought. Hermione was what he wanted, but I said, 'No you don't, Sid Constantine—not if I know it, you don't! I'm not going to be made a holy show of every time I call my own kid, so you needn't think it! If you want an aitch, you can have an aitch, but I'm choosing one I can dodge with. The name's Hester, and if the aitch slips off any time I'm not thinking, well, Ester's a good name too—in the Bible and all, and you can't say different.'" She gave her deep laugh. "He was vexed, but he hadn't a word to say—I saw to that. And it was good practice for me. I got my aitches that steady I was able to start calling her Het before she was two years old, only by that time poor Sid was gone, so it didn't really matter." She took an enormous helping of trifle and called across the table to Stacy,

"Charles coming over this afternoon?"

Stacy said, "I don't know." She was not pleased to feel her colour rise under the eye of Theodosia Dale.

"Well, he and that Major Constable have got to get their lunch somewhere, I suppose. They might just as well have come here and all among friends—unless they're lunching up at Saltings with Lilias. Or with Mrs. Robinson. I don't suppose she wants to be left on her own any more than most of us do when things go wrong. Funny idea that, leaving people alone because they're in trouble."

Miss Silver coughed mildly.

"Some people really prefer it, Mrs. Constantine."

Myra shook her head.

"Can't understand it myself. When things go wrong you want your friends. And that's where you find out just what friends you've got. When poor Sid died and I was left with two kids and not enough money to give him a proper funeral, do you suppose I didn't want my friends? *Or* find out which was the real thing, and which wasn't? There was a man I hadn't thought anything about—one of the la-di-da up-stage kind—twenty pounds he sent me, and didn't want anything for it either, which is more than you can say for some."

It was a little after this that Miss Silver was called to the telephone. Randal March's voice came to her.

"I'm sorry to trouble you—"

"It is no trouble, Randal."

"That's very nice of you. Is Forrest in the club?"

"I believe not."

There was a vexed sound from the other end of the line, and then,

"I rather want to see him. He's not at Saltings."

"I believe he does not take his meals there. There are no facilities. He may not have wished to meet everyone here today. It is rather like a big family party."

"Quite."

Miss Silver coughed.

"He will, I think, be coming in. He happened to mention that he would be busy with Mr. Brading's papers."

March said, "Thank you. I'll look in on the chance. There's just a small point I'd like to ask him about." He rang off.

Charles Forrest came into the club at about three o'clock. He went straight to the study and sat down at the writing-table.

He had not been there for more than five minutes, when Miss Silver came in, prim and cool in her grey artificial silk with its pattern of black dots and small mauve flowers. She wore her bog-oak brooch in the form of a rose, and the matching string of small carved black beads. Since the weather was so warm, her stockings were of black lisle thread instead of wool. Her shoes were a new pair of glacé kid with flat Petersham bows.

"I hope, Major Forrest, that I do not intrude."

Charles said, "Oh, no," in the tone which means, "Oh, yes."

"I will not keep you."

He had risen to his feet politely, and now saw to his dismay that she proposed to sit down. When she had done so he did not resume his own chair, but remained half sitting, half leaning against the table. It is the kind of attitude which suggests that no prolonged conversation is expected. Miss Silver's knitting-bag was upon her arm. He derived some encouragement from the fact that it remained there. No knitting-needles appeared, no pink wool. She said,

"I merely looked in to inform you that the Chief Constable rang me up shortly after lunch. He wanted to know if you were in the club. When I told him that you would be here later he said that he would come round on the chance of seeing you."

Charles frowned.

"What does he want?"

"He said some small point had arisen. He had tried to get you at Saltings."

The frown deepened.

"I took Jack Constable over to Ledbury. It's a rotten week-end for him, poor chap. Oh, well—" His voice implied, "Is that all?"

Miss Silver answered the implication.

"There is something which I should just like to mention. I walked up from church with a Miss Dale—Theodosia Dale."

"Our Dossie! Then I don't suppose there's anything left for me to tell you. She knows all the answers."

Miss Silver permitted herself to smile.

"She was quite informative, and, I think, a good friend of yours. She gave me a number of reasons why it would be absurd that any suspicion should be attached to you."

His eyelids came down, narrowing the iris and

pupil until they were just a dark glint between the lashes.

"Does it have to be such a very good friend to believe that I didn't murder Lewis?"

Miss Silver coughed.

"That is a very imprudent way to talk. I think Miss Dale is really a good friend. The fact that she is also extremely indiscreet is largely discounted by her friends being so accustomed to her way of talking that they no longer attach much importance to what she says."

Charles relaxed into an ironic smile.

"What a hope! She's practically the local yellow press. If she goes round telling everyone I didn't shoot Lewis, in twenty-four hours there won't be a soul who doesn't believe I did. Is that all she says?"

"By no means. She made a statement about the weapon. Or perhaps I should say she asked me a question about it."

"Yes?"

"She wanted to know whether the revolver found by Mr. Brading's body was the one which you had given him."

"It was. I told you that—I told Crisp—I told the Chief Constable. You, I presume, told Dossie. And Dossie can go and tell the world!"

Miss Silver gave a faintly reproving cough.

"Miss Dale appeared to think that this might involve you in some suspicion. She said she could bear witness that you had given him the revolver, and that there was a still further proof in the fact that when you did so you scratched upon it the initials, L.B."

Charles nodded.

"And what is that supposed to prove? Everyone knows I gave him the revolver—everyone knows he kept it in that drawer. When I found him the drawer was open and the revolver lying on the floor beside him. I don't see what my having given it to him over six months before is supposed to prove."

Miss Silver said,

"I do not think that Miss Dale is a very clear thinker."

As she spoke, the door opened and Randal March came in. He said,

"How do you do, Miss Silver?" And then, "Hullo, Forrest! I've been chasing you. I hope I'm not disturbing anything."

Charles said, "Oh, no." He had risen to his feet. When March had seated himself he returned to his former careless attitude, half on, half off the table.

The window stood wide to the outside air, but no breeze entered. The book-lined walls darkened the room in a manner not unpleasant on so hot a day. They gave out a faint aroma of old paper, old leather, quite perceptible when you first came in, but soon ceasing to attract attention. It passed through March's mind that Brading had been addicted to singularly gloomy surroundings. He himself liked plenty of light and air. He looked directly at Charles and said,

"There's a point that's come up about the revolver—I don't know if you can help us at all. You say you gave it to him. Do you happen to know whether he had a licence for it?"

Charles lifted a shoulder and let it drop again.

"I haven't an idea. Your guess is as good as mine. But if you want me to guess, I should say it was most unlikely."

"Can you tell me why?"

"Just the way his mind worked. Some people are sticklers over what you might call the minor points of the law. Lewis was just the opposite. Regulations annoyed him—he liked dodging them. My guess is he'd have argued that he'd a perfect right to keep a private revolver on his private premises to protect his private property."

"In fact you don't think there was a licence?"

"Oh, I don't get as far as an opinion."

"Well, we can't trace one. If there had been a licence, we could, of course, have identified the weapon positively. Can you tell me if it had any distinguishing marks?"

Miss Silver was sitting with her hands quietly folded in her lap. She had not opened her knitting-bag. She watched the faces of both men closely. Randal had not come here on a Sunday afternoon to ask Charles Forrest whether his cousin had taken out a licence for his revolver. She concluded that she was not the only person to whom Miss Dale had talked. She thought that Charles stiffened a little as he said,

"What do you mean by distinguishing marks?"

"Just what I said. For instance, initials."

Charles said carelessly,

"Oh, yes."

"What initials?"

"Oh, his own—L. B."

"Engraved?"

"No. I scratched them on the butt when I gave him the revolver."

"Are you quite sure of that?"

"Quite sure."

"Anyone know about it?"

"I don't know. Anyone might have known. I can't say if anyone did—except—"

"Except whom?"

"I was thinking of James Moberly—but that's just another guess. May I ask what all this is getting at?"

"In a minute. You say you put Brading's initials on the revolver you gave him. It was one of a pair. Did you put your own initials on the other?"

"No. I should like to know what all this is about."

"You're quite sure you put Brading's initials on the revolver you gave him?"

Charles stood up.

"Is this the moment where I say I won't answer any more questions unless my solicitor is present?"

March said gravely,

"You are not bound to answer."

Charles walked to the window, turned there, and came back again.

"Oh, I'll answer. Of course I'm sure. If you show me the revolver, I'll show you where I put the initials."

March said in a completely non-committal voice,

"There are no initials on the revolver with which Brading was shot."

Miss Silver said, "Dear me!"

CHAPTER 26

Stacy was waiting in the hall. She wanted to see Charles—she wanted to see him dreadfully. There was something going on, she didn't quite know what. Nobody told her anything, but she could feel all the things they were thinking, and it seemed to her that these things were becoming more frightening with every hour that passed. It was like being down below in a ship overtaken by a storm—you couldn't see anything, you didn't know what was happening, but you felt the shock of the waves, and you could hear the wind rising. Things had been happening. Myra's voice had risen and risen behind her closed door, and then fallen suddenly silent. Hester had come out of the room looking like a trampled ghost. Then Lady Minstrell had gone in, and the voice had begun all over again until the walls shook and echoed with it. Across the way in her own room, with two doors and a passage between, Stacy felt as exposed as a leaf in a high wind. And then when the gong sounded for lunch Myra had emerged without a sign of storm or earthquake, her hair curling violently, her eyes sparkling with vitality, her air buoyant, her voice rolling with warm affection as she called to Stacy,

"Bit of a turn-up we've been having. I expect you heard it. Always did have a carrying voice. I remember Mosscrop saying I could fill the Albert Hall, and a pity I'd never get the chance. But there it is—it's given me an appetite for my lunch. Nobody need think they're going to get me down. Het—you go back and put on a bit of colour! You're not the corpse, and no need to dress the part. Milly—you see she does it! I'm walking fine today, and Miss Mainwaring will give me a hand if I want one. I'm going to see this thing through, and those that think they can down me—well, there've been others that thought that way before, and they've had to think again!"

All through lunch she had continued in this dominant mood, and at intervals she had enquired of Lady Minstrell, of the silent Hester, of the two waiters, the manageress Miss Peto, of Miss Silver, of Stacy herself, whether Charles Forrest was expected at the club, and if he wasn't, why wasn't he, and what was he doing? The telephone had been employed to wring this information from Saltings, but without success. When, at about three o'clock, Charles entered the club there was a severe explosion of wrath at the intelligence that he was closeted with Miss Silver and the Chief Constable in the study.

Stacy, most unwillingly present, had been glad enough to seize the chance of escape.

"I'll run down into the hall, Mrs. Constantine, and catch him as soon as they come out."

So here she was. And how long was it going to be before Myra lost patience and came down herself? She was perfectly capable of surging into the study and cutting Charles out under the nose of an entire police force.

There were chairs in the hall, two or three in a clump, set about little bright tables. Stacy sat down where she could watch the study door. The short length of passage lay open to her view, with the billiard-room on the left, the study on the right, and, straight ahead, the French door leading to the glass passage. She would see Charles the moment he came out, and if he stayed behind when the others came away, it wouldn't take her a moment to reach him. She saw herself running down the passage, opening the study door, and going in. She couldn't see any farther than that.

The moments dragged. They were like raindrops on a windowpane, moving imperceptibly, haltingly, sluggishly, joining with other drops to go sliding down the glass and never come back.

When Stacy had sat there for what seemed a long time, the girl in the office called to her. Edna Snagge was off duty. This was a pale, plump girl. Stacy did not know her name, but the girl knew hers. She called across the office counter,

"There's a call for you, Miss Mainwaring. You know where the box is—at the back of the hall."

Stacy got up and went to it.

When she was in the box she could no longer see the study door. If Charles came out of the passage, she would see him, but not if he went into the annexe. She lifted the receiver and said in rather a breathless voice, "Hullo!"

The woman who answered didn't sound very friendly. Her tone suggested words like bombazine and buckram. Stacy didn't really know what bombazine was, but the tone suggested it. It said,

"Miss Colesfoot speaking. Is that Miss Mainwaring?"

Still a little breathless, Stacy said, "Yes." Just for a moment she wasn't there. Then light broke. Tony was Tony Colesfoot. Miss Colesfoot was Tony's aunt—the one she had left him having influenza with on Thursday night.

The voice went on being stiff.

"I am calling up for Anthony. You will, I am sure, be glad to hear that his temperature is ninety-nine point eight."

"Oh, yes."

"The doctor says he is satisfied, and I can only hope that he is not too sanguine. He says that Anthony may be allowed a quiet visitor. If you will come down after tea—"

Stacy's blood began to boil a little. Tony seemed to belong to some remote period of history, and Miss Colesfoot didn't belong at all.

"I am so sorry, but I am afraid I can't manage it—" She got as far as that, and then her heart smote her, because Tony always thought he was going to die if he had a fingerache. She said hastily, "I'll see what I can manage tomorrow. May I give you a ring?" and hung up.

Miss Silver and the Chief Constable were just coming out of the passage. Suppose she hadn't heard them—suppose Miss Colesfoot had made her miss Charles—The thought hurt so much that she wondered what had happened to her. Only four days ago she was all armour-plated and not caring what happened to herself or anyone else, and now she hadn't any shelter at all. Everything hurt.

She ran along the passage and opened the study door. Charles was over by the window looking out. Even from the back of his head she could tell that he was frowning. She wondered if he was cursing the annexe and Lewis Brading's Collection. He had that sort of look.

She shut the door very softly behind her and came over to stand beside him and slip her hand inside his arm. He hadn't heard her come in. He had the kind of face you wear when you are alone. Stacy saw it for a moment before she touched him. She had been wrong about the frown. He wasn't frowning. He looked open, unguarded, young. When she touched him his face closed up again. He looked down at her and said,

"What is it, my sweet?"

Silly of her heart to race. Charles didn't mean anything when he said things like that. She ought to give him Myra's message. Instead she said in a frightened voice,

"What is it?"

"Nothing you can help, darling."

"Charles—*what* is it?"

He put his arm round her.

"Just one of those things."

"Tell me."

"Lewis wasn't shot with his own revolver."

She said in a bewildered voice,

"How do they know?"

"I scratched his initials on it when I gave it to him. Dossie has been telling everyone. She seems to have been under the impression that she was clearing me—I don't quite know why. Anyhow

211

she set the police looking for initials—and there weren't any."

"Is that—bad?"

"It might be. You see, all along I think it stuck in their minds that it isn't so easy to come up beside a man who is seated at his own writing-table, open the drawer in which he keeps his revolver, and shoot him out of hand. I know it stuck in mine. If there was a suspicious bloke on this earth, it was Lewis. It just couldn't have been done."

"Someone brought a revolver in, shot him, and took his away."

"How was it—done?"

"Charles—couldn't it have been suicide?"

"No, my sweet, it couldn't. The fingerprints are all wrong. Besides—"

She pressed closer to him, as if the two of them could be shut in and no one hear what they said to one another. No one really could have heard, she spoke so low.

"Charles—did you know—when you found him?"

"That it wasn't his revolver? Yes."

"Whose was it?"

"Mine."

"What did you do?"

"Nothing I could do. March has gone off to collect Crisp. Then we all go up to Saltings and have a look for the other revolver. I wonder if it will be there."

She said in a most horrified whisper,

"He was shot—with your revolver—the one you kept?"

"He was."

"Do they know it was yours?"

"I think they've a pretty good idea."

"Charles—who did it?"

"Aren't you going to ask me if I did?"

"Charles—"

"Well—ask."

"No—no—no!"

"Not going to?"

"No!"

He said, "Well, well—" His arm dropped from her shoulders. He may have heard a step in the passage, he may have heard the handle turn. She heard nothing herself except the beating of her heart. But as he moved, she moved too, and saw that the door was opening. Lady Minstrell came a step into the room and said,

"Oh, Major Forrest, I'm so sorry, but could you come up to Mama? There's something she wants to see you about."

CHAPTER 27

When Charles Forrest went into her sitting-room Myra Constantine was not in the big padded chair. She was up on her feet and stumping about the room, catching at the furniture as she went, letting it take her weight for a moment, and then rolling on again. There was a horrid resemblance to a bus that had got out of control—one of those brightly coloured buses. She had just turned at the window end when he opened the door. She came charging back to the middle of the room, bumped into the back of a chair, clutched it, and said in a voice like an angry gong,

"What have you been doing? Where have you been? Why didn't you come up when I sent for you?"

Myra's rages were legendary. Charles had seen her in one before. The soft answer, so far from turning away wrath, encouraged it to trample—witness her daughters, Hester stamped completely flat, and Milly reduced to a perpetual "Oh, Mama—"

Charles immediately glared back and said in a loud, rude voice,

"What the devil has that got to do with you? And who do you think you're speaking to anyway?" Then he burst out laughing, flung a careless arm about her, and said, "Come and sit down, old dear! And draw it mild—I'm not Hester."

Just for a moment he wondered if she was going to hit him in the face. Then her glare broke, her eyes crinkled at the corners, the big mouth stretched, and she laughed as heartily as she had stormed. But when he had got her into the chair she fell silent and tragic, her eyes brooding, her whole aspect dark and heavy.

"Hester," she said—"that's what I've got to see you about—Hester. That's a hell of a mess, isn't it?"

He took a moment, and she struck in.

"Look here, Charles—I know, and it's no use pretending *you* don't. It's cards on the table now, and I don't mind putting mine down first. Hester's gone and married James Moberly. And you knew it and you couldn't come and tell me—oh, no! Do you call that being a friend?"

Charles had straddled an upright chair. He sat with his arms folded along the back and looked at her across them.

"Not my business," he said.

The rage had gone out of Myra. Her voice came heavily.

"A bad business—you might have told me—"

"How could I?"

There was a flash from the dark eyes.

"I got it out of her. I'm not a fool—I can see what's under my nose. She's been mooning about like a lovesick rabbit all this month, but to tell you the honest truth I thought it was you."

Charles felt a thrill of horror followed by relief. He was in a mess, but not quite such a mess as that. To have been the object of a fatal passion on the part of Hester Constantine would just about have put the lid on.

Myra's big mouth twisted.

"Go on—say it if you want to! She never did have any sense. If she had she'd have fallen for you. I could have fallen for you myself, as far as that goes, thirty or forty years ago. But Hester, no—she's got to pick on James Moberly, another rabbit that can't stand up and fight for itself any more than what she can. But that doesn't say they won't have anyone to fight for them. I'm no rabbit!"

His quick dark smile flashed out.

"Much more like a charging rhinoceros."

She burst out laughing.

"Oh, yes, I could have fallen for you, Charles."
She dragged out a gaudy handkerchief and wiped
her eyes. "You've not got to make me laugh. It's
all damned serious. You've got to listen to me. I've
got things to tell you—things you won't like, but
they've got to be said, and they've got to be listened
to."

"All right—shoot!"

She looked at him out of her big dark eyes. It
was a dominant look.

"Hester hasn't got any fight in her, and no more
has Moberly. But I have. He's Hester's husband
and my son-in-law, and I'm not having a case
cooked up against him for murdering Lewis, which
he never did and wouldn't have had the guts. Well,
I'm not standing for an innocent man being
hanged, and when the innocent man is my son-in-
law, I'm just about going to raise Cain. Have you
got that?"

"Admirably lucid."

"I mean it."

"I'm sure you do. What are you going to do about
it?"

She sat back in her chair, laid a hand on either
knee, and said,

"I'm going to tell you something."

"Go ahead."

She nodded.

"I'm no fool. Lewis had some hold over Moberly—he used to hint as much. And James wanted
to get away. He wanted to marry Hester—God
knows why, but he did. Lewis was mean, and he
was a bully. He had a bad nature. Everyone will
say James had plenty of motive for killing him. And

he had the opportunity. He had ten minutes after Lilias went and before you arrived, and only Het to say that he was with her all the time and never went out of the study. Mind you, she's speaking the truth. I know Het, and I put her through it. She couldn't stick to a lie with me pressing her like I did. She's telling the truth. She and James were there in the study all that ten minutes, and he hadn't any more to do with Lewis being killed than what I have. But Hester's his wife—who's going to believe her? Any woman 'ud swear her husband never left her if it was to clear him in a murder case. I wasn't born yesterday, and I know how it's going to look."

Charles said,

"That's perfectly true. But if it's any consolation to you, I'm a pretty strong challenger. Lewis was shot with my revolver, I had a better opportunity than anyone, and I'm the only suspect who had any interest in destroying the will which he had made in favour of Maida Robinson."

"And I suppose you think that's going to make me put it on you! Dossie says men are all fools, and there's times when I think she's right. Why, you poor fish, I'd sooner see James hang than you—if it wasn't for Hester. I'm fond of you— didn't that ever get into your head—honest to God fond of you. I don't know what people want having daughters—especially mim-mouthed rabbits. I'd have liked a son, and I'd have liked him to be like you."

Charles looked at her with an odd mixture of feelings. He was touched, moved, but still a little detached—able to survey the scene with the kind of humour which is not so very far from tears. Myra always had been able to move an audience in just that way. He stepped to her side of the footlights to take his part in the show, but he was able to bring genuine feeling to the part as he said,

"Thank you, old dear. You are clever enough to know that I reciprocate."

The big eyes sparkled. She said briskly,

"And now we'll get down to brass tacks. Thursday night, the night before Lewis was shot, he had us all in and showed us that damned Collection. I'd seen it time and again, so I was more interested in watching the people than in looking at his jeweller's window. I watched you for one, and you were so busy looking at that girl Maida you hadn't eyes in your head for anyone else."

Charles laughed.

"She was worth looking at."

Myra tossed her head, very much as she might have tossed it at eighteen.

"Oh, she's got what it takes—I'll grant you that. And a nerve—nerve enough for anything."

"Answer adjudged correct!"

Myra frowned.

"You were looking at her, and everyone else was looking at the jewelry, and I was looking at your Lilias Grey."

His eyes narrowed.

"And what did you see?"

"I saw her looking at you when you were looking at Maida. Hating you quite a piece she was."

"Maida isn't anything to me."

She chuckled.

"You liked looking at her all right."

218

He laughed.

"Who wouldn't!"

"And your Lilias Grey didn't like it a bit. She switched over to the diamonds. Then Maida put on the Forrest necklace and went swanking off to look at herself in the glass, and after a bit when she came back we all got up and moved about. And that's when I saw Lilias pinch the brooch."

Charles stiffened. His arms, lying along the back of the chair, pressed down upon the wood hard—harder. He raised his eyebrows and said,

"Do you mind saying that again?"

Myra flounced in her chair.

"Come off it! You heard me. Your Lilias Grey pinched what Lewis called the Marziali brooch—the one with the five big diamonds that the girl was wearing when her husband stabbed her and the young man she was carrying on with."

"Do you know, I should so very much prefer it if you didn't keep on saying *my* Lilias Grey. She is my adopted sister."

"All right, all right—don't lose your hair! You can call her your grandmother, or your old-maid aunt, or your girl friend, for all I care. I saw her take the Marziali brooch and stuff it into her bag."

Charles was pale. He said in a hard voice,

"And why didn't you say so at the time?"

She gave something between a laugh and a snort.

"You'd have loved me a lot if I had, wouldn't you! The whole cast on the stage, and Miss Lilias Grey unmasked as a thief. Quick curtain!" She laughed again scornfully. "Believe it or not, I can behave like a lady—when I try. I can't always be

219

bothered—I grant you that—but I can do it when I like. So I let everyone get away, and I told Lewis on the quiet."

There was a horrid little silence. What Charles thought didn't bear thinking about, but you can't just shut off your thinking the way you turn off a programme on the wireless. He said quite soon,

"You told Lewis?"

Myra flung out her hands.

"Of course I did. If I hadn't I'd have been a what-you-may-call-it—accessory after the fact, wouldn't I?"

"How did he take it?"

"Oh, quiet—very quiet!" She chuckled. "Said he wasn't surprised, and I needn't say anything, he'd deal with it."

Yes, that sounded like Lewis all right. Charles could hear the way he'd have said it—dry, with the kind of nasty dryness like grit, rubbing the skin, getting into the eyes, catching you on the raw. His chin was down upon those folded arms. Lewis had said he would deal with it. Had he dealt with it, and how? Somebody had dealt with him.

"Give you any idea of what he meant to do?"

"I didn't wait—I'd had enough. I don't mind people when they let off steam and you wonder how much of the furniture they're going to break. It's your quiet ones that get me. I never did like to see a cat go after a bird—soft, you know, and kind of slithery. If I'd got anything handy I'd throw it. Lewis could be like that if he'd got a down on anyone. I tell you what—I never did like Lilias and never shall, but I got pretty near being sorry for her after I'd told Lewis. I mean I'd have given her

220

a good tongue-lashing myself, but Lewis was nasty, if you know what I mean, and I thought I wouldn't care about being in her shoes."

"Did he say what he was going to do?"

"No, he didn't. It's pretty plain what he did do. He rang her up and told her to come and see him three o'clock Friday and bring she knew what with her. And so she did." Myra fixed her eyes on him in their darkest stare. "She came along down at three. I don't know whether she brought the brooch or not. Suppose she brought something else. She says she left him alive. Suppose she didn't."

"I don't think we'll suppose anything of the sort."

"Then the police will. Do you think I'm going to hold my tongue and let them put the murder on James, or on you? I'm not going to, and that's flat! She had a motive, hadn't she? She had taken that brooch, and he was going to be nasty about it. Oh, yes, he was. I know Lewis, and I wouldn't have been in her shoes. Suppose he said he was going to prosecute. I don't say he'd have done it, but she wasn't to know that. Suppose she thought she was for it."

Charles said,

"The will was burned. She hadn't any motive for burning the will."

She shook with laughter.

"She'd have loved that girl Maida to have the money, wouldn't she! It's not Maida's fault if everyone doesn't know Lewis's new will was going to leave her the whole blooming pile. And it was lying there on the table. Wouldn't Lilias have

221

been a chump if she hadn't put a match to it? If the money came to you, she'd get her whack, wouldn't she?"

Charles said,

"Suppositions aren't evidence. I think I've had enough of them." He got up. "March and Crisp are calling for me any minute now."

Her face changed.

"Arresting you?"

"Not yet. Just going along up to Saltings to have a look-see."

She stared.

"What for?"

"The other revolver. I've no idea whether it's there or not. I can't make up my mind what is going to incriminate me most."

"I don't know what you're talking about."

"Oh, it's as simple as mud. I had two revolvers. When I gave one of them to Lewis I scratched his initials on it. Everyone knew he kept it in his drawer. When he was found dead everyone jumped to the conclusion that he'd been shot with that revolver. He hadn't. He was shot with the other one—the one I kept. And, thanks to our admired Dossie, the police have just tumbled to it. So March, and Crisp, and I are going up to Saltings to look for the other one—the one that ought to have been in Lewis's drawer."

Myra took hold of the arms of her chair and heaved herself up. She took a plunging step forward and caught at him.

"Charles—you're not going to let yourself go down the drain for that worthless slut!"

He said, "Hold up, old dear."

"You mean shut up. But I won't! She's not worth it, and you needn't think I'll stand by and see you do it, because I won't! Piling up the evidence against yourself and sticking it under their noses— you damned fool! You needn't tell me—that girl's never been straight. I know a wrong 'un when I see one, and that girl Lilias is a wrong 'un. Broke your marriage up, I shouldn't be surprised—"

He was trying to get her back into her chair.

"Myra, I must go."

She clutched him.

"Now Stacy's a nice girl—nothing low about Stacy. And that's the sort that gets easy taken in by a wrong 'un. Fond of her, aren't you?"

His mouth twisted.

"So so."

She burst out laughing and came down thump into her chair.

"Get along with you for a liar! All right, I mean it—you can go. And remember what I've been saying, because I mean that too."

He was at the door with his hand out to open it, but he turned back.

"Myra, for God's sake hold your tongue!"

She blew him a kiss and said.

"Tooraloo!"

CHAPTER 28

Randal March came back from Ledlington with Inspector Crisp sitting beside him, a small case across his knees. Randal had compared him to a terrier. He does not care about the breed but it has its uses. The resemblance sprang to the eye. There was the wiry hair, the pricked ears, the look of alert efficiency. In one respect the terrier has the advantage. He is not afflicted with class-consciousness, whereas in the Inspector's case it provided him with a conviction that a section of his fellow-citizens were out to down him, and that if he didn't keep a pretty sharp lookout, they might succeed. At the sight of Charles Forrest emerging from Warne House with a certain air of not being in any hurry his hackles rose. He said, "A cool hand," in the voice which always sounded just a little angry, and the Chief Constable nodded and said, "Oh, yes."

Then Charles got into the back of the car and they drove away.

Saltings stood up in the eye of the sun. They left the car and went in, and through to Charles's flat. He might have been the careless host with a couple of friends.

"Bedroom, sitting-room, kitchenette, bathroom. Used to be the billiard-room and things like pantry and offices. Not a bad bit of work for the architect.

Adams is a clever chap. Well, it's all yours—you can do anything you like with it."

March was not feeling particularly happy. There are moments when being a policeman runs counter to one's instincts. He frowned and said,

"Where did you keep that revolver?"

They were in the sitting-room. Charles indicated a bureau of pleasantly mellowed walnut. The flap was down, displaying pigeonholes. Behind the diamond panes above were shelves with painted china birds and figures—a parrot, a canary, green linnets, a charming Industry, and an even more charming Indolence lying asleep in a porcelain chair with ruffled ringlets and one slipper dropping off, whilst a kitten played with the spool which had fallen from her hand. Crisp set them down as gimcracks. He thought the less of Major Forrest for possessing them.

"In one of these drawers?" he said.

There was an elegantly wrought panel on either side of the central pigeonhole. Charles slid a hand into the hole, slipped a catch at the back of it, and brought the panel away, and with it a narrow upright drawer.

"It used to be here," he said.

Crisp made haste to take the drawer from him.

"Nothing there now," he growled.

Charles smiled very pleasantly.

"As you say."

"Does the other side open the same way?"

Charles opened it. There were some papers, a bunch of keys. There was no revolver.

"It's not there."

Charles said, "No. Did you expect it to be?"

"Didn't you?"

"No. I'm quite methodical—I've always kept it on the other side."

"And the ammunition?"

"I hadn't any."

"Why?"

"I hadn't used it since the war."

"Was it loaded?"

There was a pause before the answer came.

"I don't know."

Crisp made an impatient movement, an impatient sound.

"Really, Major Forrest!"

Charles said in a quiet, even tone,

"Well, I don't. It may have been. I came home wounded from France. When I got out of the hospital the war was over. My kit had been sent down here. I shoved that revolver behind the panel with the other one. I didn't look at it again until I had the pair of them out and gave one to Lewis. That's all I can tell you."

"You gave one to Mr. Brading, and you kept the other. Where is the other?"

"I've no more idea than you."

The dark eyes had a faint sparkle. Randal March caught it. He said,

"Just when did you see it last?"

Charles frowned.

"I couldn't say."

Crisp said, "Did you see it when you found Mr. Brading's body?"

"Meaning he was shot with my revolver? What do you expect me to say to that?"

"I'm asking you whether you recognized the

weapon which was lying on the floor by Mr. Brading's body when, according to your statement, you came into the laboratory and found him dead."

Charles gave a short laugh.

"Do you suppose I was fool enough to touch it? What would you have said if I had? I'd something else to do. I suppose, like everyone else, I took for granted that it was his own revolver, and that he had fired it himself."

Crisp came back sharply.

"You say you thought it was suicide?"

"I suppose that was my first impression."

"Do you mean you've changed your mind?"

"I changed my mind when I heard the police evidence about the fingerprints. It agreed with what I knew about my cousin. He was not at all likely to commit suicide."

There were three long drawers in the bureau. Whilst these questions and answers were going on Crisp had the top drawer out and was going through its contents. He worked quickly and neatly. He had everything out, and he put everything back. Then he started on the second drawer. Half way through he said,

"The revolver with which Mr. Brading was shot had no initials on it."

"So I understand."

"But it had a peculiarity—rather a more noticeable one than the initials would have been. Can you tell me whether this missing revolver of yours has any peculiarity?"

"I don't know what you mean by a peculiarity. It has a scrape on the butt."

"How did it get that?"

"German bullet."

"Narrow escape for you?"

"For my father. In the first world war. The revolvers were his."

"Would it surprise you to hear that the revolver found by Mr. Brading's body has a scrape such as you describe?"

"Meaning Lewis was shot with my revolver?"

"Is that really news to you, Major Forrest? If you saw the revolver lying there beside him you'd have noticed that scrape, wouldn't you?"

"I might have done. It would depend which way it was lying."

"It was lying with the scrape uppermost—I saw it at once. But it wasn't until we got the information about Mr. Brading's initials being on his revolver that the scrape became important. You now admit that the initials were on the revolver you gave him, and the scrape on the one you kept for yourself."

"There's no question of admission in either case. Both are facts, and rest on statements which I have made."

Crisp finished with the second drawer and pushed it home. Randal March said,

"Can you make any suggestion as to how your revolver came to be used for this crime?"

"None whatever."

Crisp was at work on the third drawer. March said,

"The bureau is not kept locked?"

"Oh, no."

"And the flat? I noticed that you did not use a key when we came in. Do you usually leave the door unlocked?"

"When I'm in and out—oh, yes. I should lock it if I was going to be out all day or after dark. This week it has been open rather more than usual. I had a friend staying with me, Major Constable. Actually, I put him in an empty flat upstairs—I've only one bedroom here—but he has had the run of this place, and naturally I haven't locked the door."

"I see."

Crisp gave a sharp exclamation. From the corner of the bottom drawer he produced what looked like a mass of crumpled paper. Holding it, he was aware of weight, of a hard core. He pulled at the paper, and a revolver dropped out upon the floor. They all looked at it.

The paper was tissue paper. Crisp used a fold of it to pick the revolver up. He held it delicately by the muzzle and looked at the butt. Then he held it out to the Chief Constable.

"Here we are, sir—L.B. as plain as print. I think Major Forrest has got to explain how this revolver comes to be hidden in his drawer."

March said, "Would you care to make any explanation, Forrest? I must warn you that what you say may be taken down and used in evidence."

Preliminaries to arrest. So it had come. He found it almost a relief. If they arrested him he would at any rate not have to interview Lilias. Quite a large share of the relief came from that. He would have time to think, to see how things shaped. He would see a solicitor. Meanwhile—

He looked at March and said,

"I don't know how it got there. It's the revolver I gave my cousin. I didn't put it there."

Crisp, kneeling on the floor, had opened the case he had brought. He took out an insufflator and blew powder on to the revolver. Charles watched with interest. The powder spread, hung in the air, settled. It lay on the metal surface in an even film. Crisp blew on the film. It scattered. The surface remained unmarked. He turned the revolver over and repeated the process. The same thing happened. He said in a disgusted voice,

"Wiped as clean as a whistle!"

March said, "Is it loaded?"

Crisp broke the breech.

"Every chamber full, sir. Like to make any comment on that, Major Forrest?"

Charles shook his head.

"It's my cousin's revolver. I suppose he would keep it loaded."

The telephone bell rang. Charles turned with a shrug, picked up the receiver, and heard a slight preliminary cough.

"Miss Silver speaking. Is that Major Forrest?"

He said, "Yes."

"Is the Chief Constable there?"

"He is."

"Then may I speak to him?"

He turned to March with the receiver in his hand.

"It is Miss Silver. She would like to speak to you."

CHAPTER 29

Myra Constantine had been adjured to hold her tongue, but she had no intention of doing so. The minute Charles had gone she rang through to the office and demanded that Miss Silver should be found and informed that Mrs. Constantine would like to see her.

Since it transpired that Miss Silver had left the club with the expressed intention of taking a stroll, there was some necessary delay—not unduly prolonged, because the stroll had really taken her no farther than the shady end of a large and well stocked garden, but long enough to exasperate a never very patient person.

On receiving the message Miss Silver replied that she would be delighted, and proceeded, knitting-bag on arm, to the sitting-room, where she was being awaited.

"How kind of you, Mrs. Constantine."

Myra was in her big padded chair. There was the light of battle in her eyes. She said grimly,

"Charles Forrest wouldn't think so. He's just been telling me to hold my tongue, but I'm damned if I will."

Miss Silver coughed. She reprehended the use of strong language. If she had not been so deeply interested she might have made this clearer. As it was, she allowed the interest to appear whilst holding the disapproval in check.

Myra nodded vigorously.

"If you see someone trying to commit suicide, don't you try and stop them? Next door to murder if you don't—that's what I say. And if Charles hasn't any more sense than to go hushing things up and getting himself into Lord knows what sort of a mess, and all for as worthless a girl as you could find—"

Miss Silver coughed again.

"You interest me extremely."

Myra nodded even more vigorously than before.

"I thought I should! And time somebody did get interested in stopping Charles Forrest from making a fool of himself, if you ask me. Who was the fellow who used to ride about on a starved-looking horse trying to push down windmills with a spear?"

With her knitting half in and half out of her bag, Miss Silver submitted the suggestion that Mrs. Constantine might be thinking of Don Quixote, a name which she pronounced in the British manner.

"That's him! Poor Jimmy Downes painted a picture of him spear and all. Used to be a friend of mine donkey's years ago—Jimmy, I mean, not the Quixote man. Nice chap. Drank himself to death. I didn't think much of his pictures, but he liked talking about them, and this Don Quixote, he used to talk about him a lot. Might have been Charles, only a lot older and half starved—this Quixote man, I mean, not Jimmy." She stopped, chuckled, and waved an explanatory hand. "I've got a bit mixed, but the way Jimmy told it, this chap went blundering into one thing after another thinking he was going to help people, and all he did was to do himself in at the end—and I'm not standing by and letting Charles do that. If people do things they've got to stand up to them and take the blame. What's it going to do to them except rot them through and through if they let someone else step in and take what ought to be coming their way? I don't say Lilias Grey shot Lewis Brading, but I do say she pinched a diamond brooch on the Thursday night when he was showing his Collection, for I saw her with my own eyes. She pinched it, and she went off with it in her bag. And when I told Lewis on the quiet, which I did, he said to leave it to him and he'd see to it."

Miss Silver said, "Dear me!"

Myra's conversation had arrested her attention to such a marked extent that she had not even now engaged her knitting-needles, but remained holding them in the correct position with a strand of pink wool suspended upon the raised forefinger of her left hand. After she had said, "Dear me!" she took a fresh breath and remarked,

"A very handsome brooch with five large diamonds set in a row."

Myra goggled.

"Gosh! How did you know?"

Miss Silver inserted the right-hand needle into a pale pink stitch and began to knit.

"A brooch answering to that description was found on Mr. Brading's table—in an open drawer, to be exact. It is, I believe, known as the Marziali brooch."

"Then she brought it back!" Myra struck the arm of her chair with a clenched fist. "He rang her up.

Het says Moberly heard him talking on the telephone."

"When was this?"

"After they'd been talking in the study. It was just before lunch on the Friday—the day Lewis was killed."

Miss Silver inclined her head.

"Yes. Mr. Brading went through into the annexe and put through two calls. In his statement Mr. Moberly says that he followed him in order to compose their dispute. Mr. Brading was telephoning from his bedroom, and Mr. Moberly says he was waiting at the laboratory end of the passage. He heard one call finish and another begin. I have wanted to talk to him about these two telephone calls. It seems to me that they may be of very great importance, and that there may be something which he might care to add to his statement. He speaks of Mr. Brading's tone being an angry one, and admits to having heard the words, 'You'd better.'"

Myra struck the chair again vehemently.

"That's right! He'd be talking to Lilias—telling her to come down after lunch and bring the brooch along. 'You'd better!'" She laughed. "I'd say he was right! He'd got it in for her—I could see that when I told him she'd taken the brooch. He wasn't surprised, you know—that stuck out all over—but he was nasty. I've known Lewis a long time. I was a lot older, but I suppose I could have married him if I'd wanted to a matter of twenty years ago, but I wouldn't have taken it on for all his money twice over. He'd got a nasty cruel streak. I don't know why he and Dossie broke it off, but she was well out of it. You can take it from me anyone would have been well out of Lewis Brading. He was cold and he was cruel, and it's my belief he was going to make things very nasty for Lilias Grey."

Miss Silver was knitting briskly. Her needles clicked. She said,

"Cruelty breeds cruelty."

Myra looked at her. She brought her voice down to something very near a whisper.

"Lewis was shot with Charles's revolver, wasn't he? Not the one Charles gave him, but the one he kept for himself."

"Who told you that, Mrs. Constantine?"

"Charles did, just now. He said the police were taking him off to Saltings to see if the one with Lewis's initials was there."

Miss Silver gave a deprecatory cough.

"It is most inadvisable that that should be repeated."

Myra jerked a massive shoulder.

"Who's repeating it? You know, and I know—I suppose we can talk about it between ourselves. I want to help Charles the same as you do. That's what you're here for, isn't it?"

Miss Silver gazed at her with austerity.

"I do not undertake a case in order to help this person or that. I look for the truth in order that justice may be done. This will help the innocent."

Myra gave an angry laugh.

"And do you think Charles Forrest isn't innocent? You know damned little if you do!"

"Mrs. Constantine!"

"All right, all right! You shouldn't get my donkey up. Anyone who could think Charles would shoot

235

his cousin because he was afraid he was going to be cut out of his will, well, they'd be too much of a fool to be any hand at finding out what was truth and justice."

Miss Silver gave the sudden charming smile which had won her the trust and confidence of innumerable clients.

"You are a very good friend, Mrs. Constantine."

Myra chuckled.

"I'm not so bad. Look here—this thing about Lilias—I told Charles, but you can't trust him to use it. That's why I'm telling you. Lilias Grey pinched that brooch, and Lewis rang her up and told her to bring it back. Suppose that wasn't all he told her—suppose he said he was going to prosecute. He mightn't have meant to do it, but that wouldn't stop his holding it over her—if you knew Lewis you'd understand that. He meant to rattle her. Well, she'd have been rattled all right, wouldn't she? Suppose she took Charles's revolver and came up where Lewis was sitting at his desk. She'd have the brooch in her hand, and she'd put it down and he'd bend forward to pick it up. Easy to shoot him that way. She'd put the pistol in his hand and hope everyone would think it was suicide. And she'd burn the will because it wouldn't suit her to have that girl Maida coming in for the money. And she'd take Lewis's revolver, the one with his initials on it, and be off. And afterwards she'd say she'd left him alive. How's that for a case?"

Miss Silver knitted thoughtfully.

"You have put it in a very lucid manner."

Myra made an impatient movement.

"If it was put to the police, would they arrest Charles Forrest?"

"Not, I think, without further investigation."

She picked up the ball of pale pink wool, ran the needles into it, and put her knitting into the flowered chintz bag, all with a quiet deliberation.

Myra found it exasperating. She said,

"What are you going to do about it?"

Miss Silver coughed.

"If I may use your telephone, I will put through a call to Major Forrest and find out if the Chief Constable is with him at Saltings."

She gave the number, standing primly by a writing-table littered with correspondence, magazines, library books, a geranium which had been moved from the open window to be out of the draught, and two vases exuberantly full of cut flowers. She heard Charles's answer with relief, and was presently addressing Randal March.

"Miss Silver speaking. I am very glad to find that you have not left."

"I was just about to do so."

"Then I am fortunate. I hope that you have not decided upon any definite course of action. Something of importance has emerged. I feel that it should be considered without delay, and before any decision is taken."

There was a pause before he said,

"Very well, I will look in."

Miss Silver coughed.

"You will not, I think, regret it," she said, and rang off.

CHAPTER 30

Randal March gazed in some exasperation at his Miss Silver. Affection for her had survived his schooldays. His respect for her character and his appreciation of the quality of her mind increased steadily with the years which had from time to time brought them to close quarters over some case on which they were both professionally engaged. But there were moments when he found her faculty for suddenly giving a case some completely new turn very exasperating to the natural man. He had no desire, of course, to round off a case by ignoring an inconvenient fact, but Miss Silver's talent for producing inconvenient facts was sometimes felt to be excessive.

He came out of Myra Constantine's sitting-room a good deal disturbed. Now, in what had been Lewis Brading's study, he gazed at Miss Silver and said,

"Look here, is all this on the level?"

Miss Silver was knitting placidly. These little pink vests were for her niece Dorothy's second child—a niece by marriage, and the wife of Ethel Burkett's brother. After ten years of childless marriage—such a terrible disappointment—Dorothy had last year had a little boy, and they were now hoping for a girl. She looked across the pale pink wool and said with mild reproof,

"My dear Randal!"

"Well, you never know with these stage people. They can't help dramatizing themselves and everyone else. If Mrs. Constantine saw Miss Grey take a diamond brooch on Thursday evening, why does she hold her tongue about it for three days and then come out with it pat when one of the chief suspects turns out to be her son-in-law? You don't need me to tell you the whole thing smells uncommonly like a red herring."

Miss Silver found the simile distasteful. She coughed.

"Mrs. Constantine certainly has a vivid and dramatic personality, but I formed the opinion that she was giving an accurate account of what she had observed on Thursday evening. All her mental processes are quick and vigorous. That makes for correct observation, and if an incident is correctly observed it is likely to be correctly described. As to why she did not speak of this incident before, the answer is that she did speak of it, and to the person to whom such a statement was due. She informed Mr. Brading on Thursday evening that Miss Grey had taken the Marziali brooch."

March threw up a hand.

"She says that she informed him!"

"I think there is confirmation of what she says. Why did Miss Grey come and see him on Friday afternoon? I have made enquiries, and I find that she has never visited him in this way before. She is often at the club. She and Mrs. Robinson and Major Forrest have a great many of their meals here. Miss Grey was one of the party who visited the annexe when the Collection was shown on

Thursday evening, but she has never been known to pay Mr. Brading a visit there by herself. Yet she went there on Friday afternoon. Mr. Brading put through two telephone calls just before lunch that day. Mr. Moberly says in his statement that an angry tone was employed, and that he heard the words, 'You'd better!' I think it is no unfair inference that Miss Grey was being told that her theft was known, and that she was expected to return the brooch. There may have been a threat of exposure either then or later. But, to come back from inference to fact—we know that Miss Grey did come down from Saltings to visit Mr. Brading in the middle of that very hot Friday afternoon, that she was alone with him for a little over ten minutes, that we have only her own word for it that he was alive when she left at ten minutes past three, and that the Marziali brooch was subsequently discovered in the open second drawer of his writing-table. Do you not think that Mrs. Constantine's statement receives a good deal of support from these facts?"

"All right—she told Brading that Miss Grey had taken the brooch. Brading rang up and put it across her. She brought it back, and she came away. There's no evidence to show that she shot him. Why should she? It was a family affair. He wouldn't expose her."

Miss Silver coughed.

"I am not so sure. He was a cold and vindictive man. If you think of his conduct with regard to Mr. Moberly you will probably agree with this estimate of his character. Then did you notice that when Mrs. Constantine told him that Miss Grey

240

had taken the brooch she said that she did not think he was surprised? I noticed particularly that she repeated this observation when she told her story to you. It was just one of those little things. I watched for it, and it came out just as it had done when she was talking to me."

He looked faintly startled.

"You think it important?"

"Oh, yes, my dear Randal. If Mr. Brading was not surprised, it was because he knew very well that Miss Grey had this failing. When Mrs. Constantine told Major Forrest of the incident, I do not gather that he showed any surprise either."

"When did she tell him?"

"Just before she told me. He was, I understand, neither angry nor surprised, but merely very much concerned that the story should not be repeated."

"And what do you deduce from that?"

"That it was not the first time that something had had to be hushed up. Perhaps on this occasion Mr. Brading led Miss Grey to suppose that he was not prepared to hush up the theft of the brooch. She might have felt driven to a desperate course. I do not say that she was. I do say that she could have brought Major Forrest's revolver from Saltings and shot Mr. Brading with it."

"You mean it was physically possible."

"She would have known where the weapon was kept. You say Major Forrest's flat was not locked. She could have had access to it. She could have taken Mr. Brading's own revolver away with her and put it where you say it was found, in the bottom drawer of the bureau."

"Yes—she could have done all that."

She coughed.

"There is another point. It is one which engages my attention very strongly. Miss Grey has been accused of theft. She has been summoned to return the stolen property. She is no stranger but a member of Mr. Brading's family circle. The interview which took place was bound to be of an extremely painful nature. Family scenes are apt to be not only painful but prolonged. Do you suppose for a moment that this one would have lasted for only ten minutes? I am perfectly persuaded that Mr. Brading would have no intention of making things easy for her. Remember, he was not surprised at what had happened. He told Mrs. Constantine to leave it to him and he would deal with it. You heard her say that she had never liked Miss Grey, but Mr. Brading's look and manner made her feel sorry for her then. I feel quite sure that Mr. Brading meant to make Miss Grey feel sorry for herself, and I am tolerably certain that he meant to take more than ten minutes over it."

"That's not evidence."

"Of course not, Randal. But I think it should be enough to induce a painstaking search for evidence. A further interrogation of Miss Grey is indicated, and I think Mr. Moberly should be pressed as to those telephone conversations. You have, of course, taken up the matter with the telephone exchange?"

"Yes. It was a busy time—no one remembers." He gave a short laugh. "You know, Crisp isn't going to be a bit pleased. He thought he'd got the case in the bag."

"You have not arrested Major Forrest?"

242

"No. He's over in the writing-room with Crisp. I shall have to detain him unless something comes of this. Now do we go up and call on Miss Grey, or do we have her down here?"

Miss Silver's needles clicked in a very decided manner.

"My dear Randal, you will do just what you think best. But if you ask me—"

"I do. You know how the feminine mind works, and I don't pretend to."

She coughed.

"You cannot divide minds into sexes. Each human being presents an individual problem. But since you ask me, I think it might be as well to send, let us say, Inspector Crisp for Miss Grey, and to interview her in Mr. Brading's laboratory. If she were asked to show you just what she did on Friday afternoon—what her movements were, where she stood or sat—it should, I think, be possible to discover to what extent she is telling the truth. The discovery that the theft of the brooch is known will naturally shake her a good deal."

March got to his feet. He said,

"All right—we'll try it that way."

"You will send Inspector Crisp?"

"Crisp is with Forrest. We were just going to take him to the station and charge him when you rang up. I'm not justified in letting him out of sight unless this turns out to be something."

"You left him here while you went to Ledlington to fetch the Inspector."

"That was before Lewis Brading's revolver turned up at Saltings, and I had Jackson on duty outside. If Forrest had tried to steal a march on us

243

he'd have been stopped. I can send Jackson for Miss Grey."

Miss Silver was putting away her knitting. She coughed.

"I think I have seen him—a pleasant-looking young man. I should prefer that you sent Inspector Crisp."

"Whom nobody could describe as pleasant! Ruthless—aren't you?"

She picked up her pale pink ball.

"I want the truth, Randal."

CHAPTER 31

There are days when time seems to be suspended. Stacy had seen the Chief Constable's car drive away with Charles. She had seen Miss Silver receive Myra Constantine's summons and repair to her sitting-room. After an interminable stretched-out interval she had seen the Chief Constable's car come back. It stopped, and three people got out—March himself, who came upstairs to join Myra and Miss Silver, and, from the back of the car, Charles and Inspector Crisp. Her heart jumped. They had gone away with the Inspector sitting in front beside the Chief Constable, and Charles at the back, but they returned like this. She made herself face what it meant—what it must mean. They wouldn't let Charles sit by himself any more. They had arrested him, or they were going to arrest him. Crisp was there to see that he didn't get away.

She saw them come into the house together, and looking down over the well of the stairs, she watched them pass through the hall in the direction of the writing-room and out of sight.

She had been all this while on the bedroom floor, moving between her own room and the stairs. Immediately opposite the stair head a dressing-room had been done away with to widen the corridor and bring in light and air. A long window looked out over the porch and took the breeze and the distant glitter of the sea. When Stacy stood at this window she could watch who came and went. If she moved to the stair head she had only to lean upon the rail to see what passed below. If she walked to the end of the corridor she could see the glass-roofed passage to the annexe and hear the voices that rose and fell behind Myra's sitting-room door. She could hear the voices, but not what they said. Sound reached her, but no words.

Once, as she walked back along the passage, Hester Constantine stood at her open door. She looked like a dead woman who had dragged herself from her grave to listen, her head bent, one hand on the jamb. She was straining to catch the sound from the room across the way. She and Stacy looked at one another. Then Hester's free hand came up and touched her.

"Who's there?"

"The Chief Constable."

"Why?"

"Charles—"

Hester drew a long breath and stepped back. It

didn't matter to her whether Charles Forrest was hanged or not. She shut her door.

Stacy went back to the window over the porch. It was then that she began to think about going down to the writing-room. If she went down she would see Charles again. She didn't see how they could stop her. Even if he was under arrest, she might be able to speak to him, and she would at least see him again. It began to matter more than anything else in the world.

When the door of Myra's sitting-room opened and Miss Silver came out with the Chief Constable she felt an agonizing pang, because she thought that she had lost her chance. She stood rigid in the recess and heard Miss Silver say,

"If you can spare me a little time—no one will disturb us in the study."

She let them go down, leaned over the balustrade to watch them out of sight, and then ran down herself. Where time had lagged endlessly, it was now slipping away—the last remaining time in which she could see Charles, touch him, hear him speak. She ran, and came into the writing-room with quickened breath and colour in her cheeks.

Charles stood on the hearth with his back to her, apparently engaged in the contemplation of the gloomy battle picture which lowered from the chimney-breast. He had a turn for quotation, and was thinking that it would be aptly described by that passage in the Bible which speaks of a confused noise and garments rolled in blood—"Every battle of the warrior—" he thought that was how it began—"is with a confused noise and garments rolled in blood."... . No, he wasn't sure if he'd got it right now. These things came floating up out of your mind like jetsam.

He was thinking quite dispassionately that it was odd to be worrying about a quotation while you were waiting to know whether you were going to be arrested for murder, when he heard the door fly open and turned to see Stacy come running in. She pushed the door to behind her and came to him, breathing quickly, her colour wavering, her eyes wide and startled.

"Charles!"

Inspector Crisp came forward from the strategic position which he had been occupying midway between the door and the window with an eye to each. Stacy hadn't even noticed him. She didn't notice him now. She held on to Charles with both hands and looked at him with all her heart in her eyes.

Crisp forced himself upon the attention with a brisk, "I beg your pardon, Miss Mainwaring—"

Stacy did not look at him or speak to him. She said under her breath,

"Send him away."

If Charles's voice was not quite steady when he answered her, it was due to the fact that the emotions have a way of being interchangeable in moments of stress. The interval between laughter and tears can be traversed without intention. He said,

"I'm afraid he wouldn't go."

"Miss Mainwaring—"

Stacy went on taking no notice. She held on to Charles with desperation.

"They haven't—arrested you?"

247

He looked over her head at Crisp, the angry terrier to the life, with a rat just out of reach.

"I believe not—technically. But we are on debatable ground. What would you call it, Crisp? Detained for further questioning is an expression I seem to have read in the papers. Or am I on the way to the station to be charged? That also has a familiar ring."

The tone did nothing to sweeten Crisp. He said in his stiffest and most official manner,

"I must ask Miss Mainwaring to leave."

Charles said, "All in good time. If I'm not actually arrested, you know, I have an idea that I still have a few rights." He dropped his voice for Stacy's ear. "You'd better go, you know."

Her hands clung.

"Are they going to arrest you?"

"We're on the way. I gather that a red herring has crossed the path. It may, or may not, divert us."

"Miss Mainwaring—"

Stacy continued to take no notice.

"If they—if they do it—will—will they let me come and see you?"

"Do you want to?"

"Charles!"

"Nasty sordid business, you know. I sit at one end of a table, and you sit at the other, and a warder listens in."

"Major Forrest, will you kindly ask Miss Mainwaring to go. I've my duty to do."

"I don't think it extends to putting her out by force, does it? And so far moral suasion doesn't seem to be getting us anywhere." He dropped his voice again. "You'd really better go, Stacy. This is trying us a bit high, don't you think?"

"You?"

"Me."

She said, "I'll go," and took her hands away so suddenly that he thought she had lost her balance and would fall, but before he could touch her she had steadied herself. Her colour was all gone. She said, "Goodbye—" in an exhausted voice which hardly reached him. Then she turned round and went out of the room.

Crisp held the door and shut it after her rather forcefully. No one could say that he had banged it, but it had that effect. Stacy had not looked at him when she came. She did not look at him as she went. He might not have been there.

When he turned round from not banging the door Charles Forrest was once more standing with his back to him looking in the direction of the battle picture on the chimney-breast, but this time it is to be doubted whether he really saw it.

CHAPTER 32

Lilias Grey pulled back the curtains from her sitting-room windows. The sun was off them now, and there was the beginning of a breeze from the sea. The day really had been stiflingly hot, but in the next hour or two the air would freshen. She went over to the door and opened it to make a draught in the room. It was a grievance that her flat opened directly from the sitting-room upon the corridor. In his downstairs flat Charles had a nice little lobby entrance. She had not seen, and never would see, why she could not have one too. Facts adduced by Mr. Adams, the architect, made no difference to this point of view. It was, and remained, a grievance. On a hot day like this, of course, there was a certain advantage in being able to achieve a through draught.

She came back from the door to stand by the window again. It had been such a very long day. Charles had not been to see her. She felt angry and resentful because he had not been. She had seen him for a moment in the hall on his way out to lunch with Major Constable, and that was all. She wouldn't have seen him then if she hadn't heard Major Constable go down and followed him, because of course she guessed at once that Charles would be taking him out to lunch. She felt a grievance about that. Charles hadn't asked her to come too. She would have said no of course. If anyone saw her, they might think it strange so soon after Lewis's death. Oh, no, she wouldn't have gone, but she would like to have been asked. No one would think anything of Charles and Jack Constable having lunch together in Ledbury—even nowadays men were much freer than women— but it would not be prudent for her to be seen at an hotel or a restaurant until the funeral was over. She would have to go to the funeral of course. However hot it was, she would have to wear her black coat and skirt, because she had nothing else that would be suitable. Fortunately, it wasn't very thick, but it was wool—and in this weather! But she would have to wear it—and at the inquest too.

All the time these thoughts were going through her mind they were getting nearer to the inquest. She would have to go to it, and be sworn, and give her evidence. When she got to this point everything in her shook and was confused. That was what frightened her about the inquest. She would have to stand up in that sort of box with a ledge in front of it and read the oath from the printed card they gave you and give her evidence. The room would be crowded, and everyone would be looking at her. The black coat and skirt was becoming. It threw up her fair hair. She could wear the little black hat which hardly hid it at all—just that flattering tilt over the eyes, and the scrap of veil to soften the brim. She had a comforting picture of herself standing there, rather pathetically slim and fair, doing her best to be brave. Then the shaking and the fear came back. Suppose this horrid frightened feeling came over her when she was giving her evidence and she got confused and didn't know what to say. It had all been such a horrid shock. And no one came near her. Charles didn't come near her.

She stared out of the window. There wasn't a cloud in the sky, or a shadow on the sea.

Someone was coming up the stairs—a man. Charles? Major Constable? The sound came in through the open door. She turned round and went to it, and saw Inspector Crisp step up on to the landing.

In the annexe the stage was set when Crisp brought her in. The glass passage was like a furnace, just as it had been on that dreadful Friday afternoon. To step from all that heat and glare into the room which Lewis Brading had designed for his Collection was to lose a good ten degrees of heat and to drop into what seemed for the moment to be darkness. Only one light burned high up, and the black-hung walls muffled it. Lilias Grey caught her breath, checked, felt Crisp's touch on her arm, and went on again. He said, "This way, Miss Grey," and they came into the lighted passage beyond.

The door of the laboratory was ajar. Crisp opened it and stood aside for her to enter. All the laboratory lights were on. The room seemed dazzlingly bright, like a room in a hospital—white walls and ceiling, and a chill upon the air.

She turned to the right as she came in, and saw the Chief Constable facing her across Lewis's table a dozen feet away. He was sitting where Lewis had sat. Away on his left there was a little dowdy woman with some pale pink knitting in her lap. That would be Charles's private detective. Somehow the sight of her, sitting there looking so exactly like somebody's governess, was a relief. The cold, fluttering sensation which had been making her feel quite sick began to subside. It was tiresome to be dragged down here on a hot evening, and with no reason given except that the police wished to check up on some of the statements which had been made. But there was nothing to be frightened about. Her nerves were just playing her tricks, and no wonder after the shock she had had. It was all just a routine matter, as commonplace and ordinary as the dowdy little governess person sitting there knitting up pale pink wool.

March said, "Come in, Miss Grey. There are just a few questions I must ask you. Crisp, will you be ready to take notes?"

The fluttered feeling returned. Very foolish of course—just her nerves. Randal March was a good-looking man. He had been Superintendent at Ledlington before he became Chief Constable. He looked like a country gentleman—big, fair, becomingly bronzed.

The Inspector had settled himself and taken out a notebook. It was these formalities which made you feel nervous. And no need for them that she could see. Why couldn't Mr. March just call on her in her own drawing-room? So much more suitable. He said quite politely, but in what she could only call an official voice,

"Now, Miss Grey, I have your statement here. I am sorry to trouble you, but it will help us if you will just run through the whole thing again. By the way, I don't know if you have met Miss Silver. She is a private enquiry agent. Mr. Brading approached her in the first instance, and she is now representing Major Forrest. If you have no objection, I should like her to be present."

"No—no—of course—I mean, I don't mind at all. Charles told me."

"Then if you don't mind, Miss Grey, I should like you to go back to the door and come in again. I want you to imagine that I am Mr. Brading sitting here. And then I want you to do and say what you did and said on Friday afternoon."

Miss Silver had thought Miss Grey very pale

when she came in. She became perceptibly paler now.

"Oh, I couldn't—I don't really think—"

"I would like you to try, Miss Grey. If what you say in your statement is correct, I do not quite see why you should make any objection."

She put her handkerchief to her lips. Behind the linen screen she moistened them.

"I'll do what I can—"

She went to the door, still holding the handkerchief. As she turned to repeat her entry, March stopped her.

"Had you a handkerchief in your hand?"

"No—no—oh, no."

"We will try to be as exact as possible, so will you put it away. You had that bag?"

"Oh, yes."

"In your left hand?"

"Under my arm."

"Well then, you came in. What did you do?"

She tried to remember what she had said in the statement. The words were there, written down, but between those words and her recollection of them there rose the picture that was never far from her mind. Her lips were so dry that she had to moisten them again. She didn't know what to say—but she must say something, or they would think—they would think—

She came half way to the table and stammered,

"I don't know—you're making me nervous. I suppose I said, 'How do you do?'"

"And Brading?"

"I suppose he did too."

"And then? What did you do?"

"I can't remember every single thing."

"Just do your best. Show me what you did next."

She came the rest of the way, nervous, hesitating, her eyes on March. When she reached the table she stood there. Her hand came out and closed on the table edge.

Crisp looked at her sharply. He had been thinking all this a piece of tomfoolery, but now he wasn't so sure. He had an accurate mind, and he remembered her statement. It said that she came in and sat down to the table and talked to Mr. Brading about a bit of business, which is what she would have done if she had had a bit of business to talk about. Well, now she had been asked to show just what she did, and she hadn't so much as looked round to see if there was a chair, she just came up to the table and held on to it.

The Chief Constable said,

"You were touching the table like that?"

She let go of it in a hurry.

"No—no—I don't think so."

"Well, try and stick to just what you did on Friday. Did you stand like you're doing now?"

A feeling of panic came to her. She tried to remember just what she had said.....Something about talking to Lewis—sitting down and talking to him. She said as quickly as she could get it out,

"No, no, I sat down."

"Where?"

There had been a chair. Every time she shut her eyes she could see the table, and Lewis. There had been a chair—a little to the right of where she was standing now. She moved a hand and said,

"There."

At a look from the Chief Constable Crisp got up and set a chair where she was pointing. She was very glad to sit down.

March said,

"And then?"

"We began to talk about business. I had come to ask him about investing some money."

That was what she had said in her statement. She was doing all right now. If she stuck to that, they couldn't trap her. She had only got to say that bit about a mortgage falling in, and wanting Lewis to advise her about investing the money. She began to say it.

When she was about half way through she saw that Miss Silver was looking her. Such an odd look. Not unkind, not exactly stern. More as if she was sorry about something. Her voice began to falter.

"He said—to put it—into government—securities—"

"And then?"

"That was—all. I mean—of course—we talked about it a little—"

"What did you say?"

"Oh, just—what did he think would be best—that sort of thing."

"And what did he say?"

"To put it—into—government securities—"

"That was all he said?"

She felt relief. They were coming to the end. She had got through. She said,

"Oh, yes."

"Nothing about the Marziali brooch?"

She gazed at him with dilated eyes. Her tongue

crept out and touched her lips.

"I don't know—what you mean—"

"Don't you, Miss Grey?"

She shook her head.

Miss Silver put down her knitting and came over to her. She had a glass of water in her hand.

"I think you had better drink this, Miss Grey."

The water was held to her lips. She drank. Some of it spilled. She drank again. Miss Silver set the glass down on the table and said in a kind, firm voice,

"Now you must listen to the Chief Constable."

March said,

"On Thursday evening you were present with a number of other people in the outer room of the annexe when Brading showed his Collection. The Marziali brooch is listed as part of it. It has five large brilliants, and it is of considerable value. Mrs. Constantine deposes that she saw you take it and put it away in your bag. What have you to say to that?"

"Oh—it isn't true—" She reached for the water, gulped a mouthful, and almost dropped the glass upon the table.

March continued in an even voice,

"Mrs. Constantine says she waited till everyone was gone and informed Brading of what she had seen. She says, Miss Grey, that he did not appear to be surprised, but stated that he would deal with the matter. He telephoned to you, did he not, just before lunch on Friday?"

She said in a choking voice,

"It was about the investments—about my coming down to see him—"

257

"Now, Miss Grey—you need not answer unless you wish to. I have to tell you that anything you say may be taken down and used in evidence. And I must tell you that this statement of Mrs. Constantine's and your own attitude bring you under very strong suspicion in regard to Mr. Brading's murder. He had reason to believe that you had stolen a valuable brooch. He had sent for you in order to deal with the matter. You came, and you saw him. You brought back the brooch, because it was found in this drawer, which was standing open. If he threatened you with exposure, you had a strong motive. The weapon with which he was shot was brought from Saltings. The weapon which was in his drawer was taken back to Saltings—"

She cried out, "Stop—stop! I didn't!" She clutched Miss Silver's arm in a bruising grip. "Don't let him! Make him stop! I didn't!"

Miss Silver detached the clinging hands in a perfectly kind but firm manner. For his part, Randal March, who had sometimes wished her away, was at this moment quite unfeignedly glad of her presence. Hysterical women were the devil.

Miss Silver said in her voice of authority,

"Pray calm yourself, Miss Grey."

"But I didn't—I didn't touch him—or the revolver! I couldn't! Things like that frighten me to death! Oh, you don't think I shot him! Mr. March, you can't—you can't think I shot him!"

He made no reply. Miss Silver said,

"Miss Grey, you must please control yourself. If you are innocent you have nothing to fear. If you wish to make any explanation—"

"He won't listen to me! No one will listen! You

won't believe me! Oh, can't you make him listen!" She was sobbing in a helpless, terrified manner.

Miss Silver put a hand on her shoulder.

"Anything you have to say will be listened to. You will not be compelled to speak, or pressed to do so, but you are perfectly at liberty to make a statement. Inspector Crisp will write down what you say. Afterwards it will be read over to you, and you may sign it if you are willing to do so. No pressure of any kind will be put upon you. Now just take another drink of water, and make up your mind if there is anything you wish to say."

Lilias put out a shaking hand for the glass, drank between sobbing breaths, and set the glass down again. Some of the water had spilled and was running down her chin. She dabbed at it with her handkerchief and said,

"Oh, Mr. March, I didn't shoot him. He was dead when I came."

There was a definite feeling of shock in the room. Miss Silver said, "Dear me!" Standing beside Miss Grey, she observed her with the closest attention. She was no longer collapsed and unstrung. It was as though the shock produced by her words had had the effect of steadying her. She was trembling a little, but she no longer sagged in her chair. She had ceased to sob.

Randal March said,

"Do you wish to make a statement to that effect?"

"Yes—yes—of course I do. I must. I can't let anyone think—oh, it's horrible!"

"Brading was dead when you came into this room on Friday afternoon?"

259

Her words came with feverish energy.

"Yes, yes, of course! Don't you see, that's why I couldn't tell you what he said, or what I said. He was dead. It was the most horrible shock I've ever had. I just came into the room, and he was dead."

Miss Silver came quietly back to her seat and took up her knitting. Miss Grey was quite steady now. She would not become hysterical again. This one most startling admission made, the rest would be easy. She quoted a French proverb to herself—"*Ce n'est que le premier pas qui coûte.*"

Randal March was going over the arrival at the annexe.

"Who let you in, Miss Grey?"

"The door was ajar," she said.

"Did that surprise you?"

"Yes—no—I thought Lewis had left it like that for me."

"Was there a light inside?"

"Yes—like it was today."

"Only one light burning?"

A shiver went over her.

"Yes—it was dark coming in—"

"Was the passage beyond lighted?"

"Yes—just like today."

"And the laboratory?"

The shiver again.

"Oh, yes—dreadfully bright."

"Tell me exactly what you saw when you came in."

Inspector Crisp was writing it all down, but she didn't mind. She couldn't get it out fast enough now that she had begun.

"I came round the door, and just for a minute I

thought he was asleep. His head was down on the table. I came a little nearer, and I saw that he had been shot."

"Why didn't you give the alarm?"

She said in a queer slow voice,

"I—don't—know. It was—a shock. I just stood there—I didn't seem to be able to move."

"But that passed—you did move?"

She said, "Yes. I went to see if he was—dead."

"Will you show me just how he was lying."

"His head—was just on the edge—of the blotting-pad."

March pushed back his chair and got up.

"I should like you to come round and show me just how the body was lying."

She came round the table and showed him, taking up very exactly the position in which Lewis Brading had been found.

"Thank you, Miss Grey."

She went back to her seat, and he to his.

"The right arm was hanging down?"

"Oh, yes."

"Did you see the weapon?"

"It was lying there on the floor—as if he had just dropped it. I thought he had shot himself."

"Did you know of any reason why he should shoot himself?"

"Oh, no."

"But you thought it was suicide?"

"Yes, I did."

"Then why didn't you give the alarm?"

"I—I—"

"Miss Grey, the first shock had passed. You had begun to reason. Your mind was sufficiently active to formulate the theory that Brading had committed suicide. Your natural course would be to run over to the house and give the alarm. Why didn't you do so?"

Her hands were picking at her wet handkerchief.

"I was afraid."

"Why?"

"I was afraid they'd think—" She stuck there.

"You were afraid they would think you had shot him?"

She caught her breath.

"Well, you did think so, didn't you?"

"Because a very strong motive had emerged."

Miss Silver coughed. She addressed the Chief Constable with polite formality.

"Pray forgive me—may I ask Miss Grey a question?"

"Oh, certainly."

She looked across the pink wool and said,

"Had you any reason to suppose that this motive would appear? When Mr. Brading talked to you on the telephone, did he tell you that Mrs. Constantine had seen you take the Marziali brooch?"

There was a moment when March feared a recurrence of the hysterical sobbing. But it passed. Lilias Grey said, "Oh!" on a note of outrage. Then she drew herself up and had recourse to words instead of tears.

"Myra Constantine is a vulgar, interfering old woman. She thinks everyone has the same low motives as herself. And Lewis has always listened to her. He was *most* unkind, *most* unfair." She tried for, and actually achieved, an air of dignity. "I *borrowed* the brooch because it interested me very much and I wanted to make a sketch of it. I was thinking of writing some articles on jewelry. I didn't ask Lewis, because he was sure to make difficulties. I meant just to make a joke of it and return the brooch next day. And then he rang up and was *most* disagreeable. And of course I knew Myra would make mischief about it if she could. So when I found Lewis dead like that I thought it would be much simpler if I just slipped away and didn't say anything."

It was at this moment that March really began to believe that she was speaking the truth. Only the natural processes of a completely inconsequent mind could have produced so perfect an example of unreason. He could not bring himself to believe that it could be simulated. He had to make an effort in order to focus his own thought again.

"You made up your mind that you would just go away and say nothing?"

She said in quite a pleased voice,

"I thought it was the best thing to do."

What a woman! Well, he must get what he could out of her.

"Now, Miss Grey, you were here for about ten minutes. What did you do after you had made up your mind to say nothing?"

"I put the brooch into that second drawer. It was open."

"Was there a revolver in the drawer?"

"No—it was on the floor."

"Did you see a second revolver anywhere?"

She looked surprised.

"Oh, no. I'm sure he only had the one."

"Well, you put the brooch in the drawer. What else did you do?"

A startled expression came and went. It was so slight, so fleeting, that only Miss Silver noticed it.

"I don't know what you mean."

"You have ten minutes to account for. I don't think you have accounted for them yet. What did you do after you put the brooch in the drawer?"

This time he was aware that she was rattled. She said,

"I came away."

March shook his head.

"Oh, no, not immediately. You have that ten minutes to account for. Perhaps I can help you. Did you see a metal tray on the table?"

"I—I don't know—I may have done."

"Come, Miss Grey, I think you must have seen it. Where was it?"

"Over—over there." She pointed to an empty space on his left hand.

"Was it empty?"

"I—I think so."

March said, "You see it's all coming back. Just go on trying. Did you see Brading's will?"

She said, "Oh!" like someone who has missed his footing.

"Did you see it, Miss Grey?"

She stared at him helplessly and burst into tears.

Miss Silver laid down her knitting and said very firmly indeed,

"Miss Grey, if you do not tell the truth you will, I believe, bring very serious trouble on yourself. I think you did see Mr. Brading's will. I believe that it was lying there on the table. You saw

264

it, and you read it. It made you very angry to think that Mrs. Robinson would come in for all that money. I do not suppose that you reasoned any farther than that. If that will were destroyed, the money would come to Major Forrest, and if the money came to Major Forrest, you would certainly get a share of it. Shall I tell you what you did? The will-form was not very large. You took out your handkerchief and you lifted the metal tray across to the far right-hand corner of the table. You were collected enough to remember that you must avoid leaving fingerprints. You laid the will-form on the metal tray, and you struck a match—since you smoke you would probably have matches in your bag."

"How do you know that I smoke?"

Miss Silver coughed.

"I asked Mrs. Constantine. You struck a match, set light to the will-form, and watched it burn. That is what you did, did you not?"

Lilias threw out her hands. The shredded handkerchief dropped to the floor.

"Oh—oh—oh!" she cried. "How did you know?"

CHAPTER 33

"Well, what do you make of that?"

March was alone with Miss Silver. They were in the laboratory. Lilias Grey, at Miss Silver's suggestion, had been invited to retire to Lewis Brading's room, where there was a very comfortable couch. An elderly chambermaid had been placed in charge of her. Miss Grey made no objection. She had cried a good deal, but dried her eyes when it was suggested, also by Miss Silver, that she might care to have a cup of tea. Crisp went away when she did, leaving March alone with Miss Silver. She was considering how difficult it was to disentangle the lie that was half a truth from the truth that was half a lie. She recalled with admiration the lines in which Lord Tennyson had dealt with this fact. Leaning back in one of those low armless chairs which she preferred, she continued to knit. She answered March's question with another.

"What do you make of it yourself?"

He lifted a hand and let it fall again.

"It all depends on whether she is telling the truth. Is she?"

"I think so, Randal."

His voice took a cynical tone.

"All that rubbish about the brooch being borrowed, and wanting to make a sketch of it?"

Her needles clicked.

"Oh, no, of course not. That was just a smoke-screen. She is the type who will never look a fault in the face and admit to it. It is the common shop-lifting type. They must excuse what they do, put a good face on it, and keep their self-respect. It is a kind of muddled thinking which corrodes the whole character. Miss Grey exemplifies it at every turn. She stole Mr. Brading's brooch, but I am quite sure that she did not shoot him."

He was inclined to agree. He said,

"Your reasons?"

She was knitting with a certain brisk cheerfulness.

"My dear Randal, this crime was very carefully premeditated, very cleverly plotted. It bears the marks of a clever mind working swiftly and ruthlessly—quick to turn circumstances to account. Can you see Miss Grey's mind operating in any such manner? Pray consider the situation in which she found herself. She had robbed Mr. Brading. He had found her out. She knew that Mrs. Constantine was aware of her theft. Mr. Brading had rung up to tell her she must bring the brooch back. She did so. Do you suppose for a moment that she had provided herself with a weapon and had come down here with the intention of shooting him? I do not suppose that she had ever handled a firearm in her life. With her capacity for self-deception it would be impossible for her to believe that Mr. Brading really meant to expose her. She expected an unpleasant scene, but not that he would proceed to extremities. Had he convinced her that she was in real danger, she would have had recourse, not to Major Forrest's revolver, but to Major Forrest himself. She would have informed him in a deluge of tears of the cruel and unsympathetic attitude which Mr. Brading was taking up. I can assure you, Randal, that she is—though for different reasons—quite as incapable of shooting anyone as I am myself. The sight of Mr. Brading's dead body terrified her, and, true to her type, her sole idea was to pretend that nothing had happened. She does not think clearly or intelligently at any time. Under the influence of shock she does not really think at all. She acts from instinct and habit. I am sure it did not occur to her that by stating Mr. Brading was alive when she left him she would be throwing suspicion on Major Forrest."

March said drily,

"She was capable of sufficient thought to destroy the will."

Miss Silver shook her head in a very decided manner.

"Not thought, Randal—instinct. Her whole course of conduct shows her to have been strongly acquisitive. She read the will, and saw that Mr. Brading had left everything to Mrs. Robinson. She had only to strike a match in order to counteract what must have appeared to her to be a monstrous injustice. You have seen her and heard her. Is it not perfectly clear that she would consider such a course to be quite justifiable?"

"Oh, she would justify anything."

"Exactly."

After a moment he said,

"If you're going to take her evidence, it clears Charles Forrest. That's what you came down here to do, isn't it?"

Miss Silver did not rise. She said sedately,

"I came down here to serve the ends of justice and to discover the truth. You know me too well to believe that I could have any other motive."

He smiled.

"You have just produced an extremely able piece of special pleading."

She coughed.

"You asked for my opinion. I have given it."

He sat for a moment, chin in hand, studying her.

"It has not occurred to you that there might be quite another explanation for, shall we say, this variation from Miss Grey's original statement?"

She returned his look with bright intelligence.

"What explanation do you suggest?"

"She is Forrest's adopted sister. She is supposed to be devoted to him. As you have said, she is not a very clear thinker. At the time that she made her statement it would not occur to her that to say she left Brading alive at ten past three would be liable to throw suspicion upon Forrest, who says he found him dead at twenty past. When she does begin to realize it she is frightened, and when she finds that Forrest is on the brink of arrest she comes out with this story of Brading having been dead when she got here just before three."

Miss Silver smiled in a perfectly amiable manner.

"That is quite ingenious, Randal, but it will not do. In the first place, I do not suppose for a moment she knew that Major Forrest was in danger of being arrested. In the second, she did not come out with the statement about finding him dead. She was surprised and startled into admitting it. And in the third, I really do not see Miss Grey thinking of anyone's interests in an emergency except her own."

"You think she was surprised into making that admission?"

"Certainly. I was watching her very closely when she came in. Did you not see how she checked involuntarily as she came in sight of the writing-table? She checked. Her eyes dilated. She stared at you in a horrified manner. She found it difficult to advance. I was quite sure then that she had seen Mr. Brading lying there shot. You asked me whether I thought she was telling the truth when she admitted this was the case. I think the fact that she was doing so is corroborated by her description of the position of the body. It was correct in every detail, was it not?"

He nodded.

"Forrest might have told her that."

"It is not very likely. He would not describe such a distressing scene to a person of so hysterical a temperament."

"Well, I agree with you there. I am not sure that I do not agree with you all along the line, in which case Forrest is in the clear." He smiled. "You are a very efficient advocate."

The pale pink vest revolved. She coughed reprovingly.

"Major Forrest does not need an advocate. The facts speak for themselves. Have you considered, Randal, that the changing of the revolvers is an actual proof of his innocence?"

"My dear Miss Silver!"

She coughed again.

"If you have not considered it, pray do so. Mr.

Brading's visitors on Friday afternoon all came from Saltings. Any one of them might have obtained possession of Major Forrest's revolver, the one with the scrape on it, and have exchanged it for the one which had been given to Mr. Brading and which bore his initials. Since Mr. Brading's revolver was on the spot—and it is agreed that this fact was generally known—why was it not used for the murder? As an attempt was made to pass the death off as suicide, we must agree that Mr. Brading's own revolver was not used because it could not be used. The murderer would have been unable to take it out of the drawer and fire it at the very close quarters necessary to support the idea of suicide. He, or she, had therefore to provide another weapon, and, in the event, to use it. But, alone amongst those four visitors, Major Forrest had no need to provide himself with another weapon. He could have stood by his cousin's side, turned the conversation to the revolver he had given him, and found some pretext to open the drawer and take it out. It would all have been perfectly natural and easy. Major Forrest could have shot his cousin without arousing the slightest suspicion. He did not need his own revolver, and he is a good deal too intelligent to have employed it."

March was looking at her very intently.

"Someone employed it. Who are you suggesting?"

"Someone who could not count on getting hold of Mr. Brading's own revolver. Someone who planned the whole thing very carefully, but was so hurried in the performance that the fingerprints which were to convince the police that Mr. Brading had committed suicide slipped and were smudged. Someone who was obliged to remove Mr. Brading's revolver and leave the other because Mr. Brading's revolver was fully loaded and there is simply no place in this room where he could have got rid of a shot."

March put up a hand.

"My dear Miss Silver!"

She smiled at him, kindly but with gravity.

"It is all true, is it not? Whilst you are thinking it over I would suggest that you send for Mr. Moberly."

His brows drew together.

"Moberly?"

She coughed.

"There are one or two questions I should like to ask him. I have abstained from putting them until I could do so in your presence."

He said, "Moberly—" again in a meditative voice. And then, "Oh, well, I don't mind seeing Moberly myself. He's got the wind up, and we may get something out of him. I've an idea there's something to get."

He picked up the house-telephone and spoke into it.

After he had laid it down again he turned round smiling a little and said,

"Observe—I send for him first and ask questions afterwards. What do you want to ask him about?"

She coughed.

"The letters which came by the second post on Friday."

"What letters?"

"You will remember the waiter's excuse for having overheard part of a conversation between Mr. Brading and Mr. Moberly. He said he was bringing in Mr. Brading's letters."

He looked at her with a faint shade of surprise.

"Is there any reason to suppose—"

"I think so." She was knitting steadily and briskly, her small neat features composed, her aspect purposeful. "You see, one of those letters was from Mrs. Robinson."

"How do you know?"

"I asked the waiter."

March was frowning.

"Would he know her writing?"

"Oh, yes—he seemed to be quite familiar with it. She has been here a great deal. She has written letters and given them to him to put in the postbox. It is down by the gate."

"But—"

She inclined her head.

"I know, Randal. Mrs. Robinson was here until fairly late on Thursday evening. She was one of the party to whom Mr. Brading showed his Collection. She walked home along the cliffs with Major Forrest. This letter must have been written after she reached Saltings. That is why it interests me. I find that there is a pillar-box about a quarter of a mile from Saltings where a lane comes out upon the main road. Anything posted there after five in the afternoon would be collected early next day and delivered locally by the second post. This would count as a local delivery. I am indebted to Miss Snagge for these particulars. She sorted the letters when they came in on Friday, and she corroborates Owen in saying that one of Mr. Brading's letters was from Mrs. Robinson. I think we are entitled to conclude that it was written after she got back to Saltings."

He said, "Oh, well, they were engaged. People do that sort of thing."

She coughed rather sharply.

"I think there is more in it than that. Mrs. Robinson walked home with Major Forrest. He has said that she told him Mr. Brading had asked her to marry him and had executed a will in her favour. You will observe the form of her communication— he had asked her to marry him. I think it is possible that she had not up to that time given him a definite answer."

"He wouldn't have signed a will in her favour if she hadn't."

"Then perhaps it was merely that she herself was still hesitating. I must tell you that Mrs. Constantine, who is very acute, and Miss Dale, who is an indefatigable gossip, have both been at some pains to inform me that Mrs. Robinson is very much attracted by Major Forrest."

March laughed.

"And you believe everything you hear?"

She said primly, "I do not find that at all difficult to believe. Major Forrest is an extremely attractive man."

"And what conclusion do you draw from that?"

"None at present. But that is where I hope Mr. Moberly may help us. She had that walk with Major Forrest, and then she wrote and posted a letter to Mr. Brading. After he had received it he put through two angry telephone calls. We know that one was to Miss Grey. We do not know whether the other was to Mrs. Robinson. I suspect that her letter was either a refusal or a definite acceptance. In neither of these cases does it account for what followed."

March nodded.

"Look here, I think we'll have Forrest in before we see Moberly."

He spoke into the house-telephone again.

"Just keep Mr. Moberly back till I ring. And ask Major Forrest to come over."

Charles Forrest came into the room rather wondering what he was going to find there. Crisp had left him some time before, but he had been asked to remain in the writing-room, and he had done so. There seemed to be some constabulary activity. From the window sounds reached him of comings and goings. Opening the door, he could observe a policeman in charge of the house-telephone. Stacy was not in sight. He shut the door again and remained alone with his own thoughts until summoned to the laboratory, where he was received by Miss Silver with a smile, and by the Chief Constable with a pleasant "Come and sit down, Forrest."

The last thing he had expected was to be taken through that embarrassing walk with Maida, but he came out of it without going beyond what he had said in his statement. She had told him that Lewis Brading had asked her to marry him, and that he had made a will in her favour. The will was to be signed next day. They had discussed the whole thing. He had remarked that she would not find his cousin very easy to live with, but he had been very definitely under the impression that she

275

intended to accept him. When March said, "You didn't think she had already done so?" he replied, "Well, as near as makes no difference."

It was at this point that Miss Silver put her first question.

"Did you know that she intended writing to him that evening?"

He didn't know where all this was getting them. He said,

"She did write to him."

March exclaimed, "You know that?"

"I posted the letter."

"Do you mind telling us just what happened?"

Charles looked the surprise he felt.

"Nothing happened. After we got in I wrote a letter myself and was going out to post it. Maida was on the stairs with a couple of letters in her hand. I offered to post them for her, and she gave them to me. That was all."

"Any conversation?"

He was frowning. No harm that he could see in repeating what she had said. He let them have it.

"She just gave me the letters and said, 'Well, you're going to have me for a cousin,' and I said, 'And very nice too.'"

"You're sure she said that?"

"Oh, yes."

"Then you took it that the letter she gave you to post was her acceptance of Brading's offer?"

"Of course."

March thought, "Well, that's that. So it wasn't her letter that made Brading angry, and we're barking up the wrong tree."

Miss Silver gave a gently interrogative cough.

"There were two letters, Major Forrest?"

"Yes, two."

"Did you notice to whom the second letter was addressed?"

"Oh, yes. It happened to be uppermost—I couldn't help seeing it."

"And to whom was it addressed?"

For the life of him March couldn't see what she was getting at. He heard Charles say,

"To a friend of hers, a Mrs. Hunt."

"Did you notice the address?"

"Oh, she's a Londoner. She's been down once or twice. I couldn't tell you the exact address. If you want it you can get it from Maida."

Miss Silver coughed again, this time in a deprecating manner. She pursued her questions.

"Is Mrs. Hunt an intimate friend?"

Charles laughed.

"Oh, I should think so. The kind you'd be bosom friends with after a bus ride—hearty, genial—more or less all over everybody."

March let it go at that.

"Well, I think that's all we wanted to know. I had better tell you that there have been—developments. I must ask you just to stay in the club for the moment, but apart from that there is no reason why you should not behave as usual."

Charles took this with rather a straight look.

"Meaning that I'm not under detention any longer?"

"Meaning just what I said."

"Do you know, I should rather like an explanation."

March frowned.

"Miss Grey has made a statement."

He saw the dark face harden.

"What has she said?"

"That Brading was dead when she got here."

That Charles was completely taken by surprise was beyond doubt. He said,

"*What!*"

March nodded.

"That is what she says. If she is to be believed, it would of course exonerate you."

"Lewis was dead when she got here—"

March said, "Go away and think it out."

Charles got up.

"Where is she?"

It was Miss Silver who answered him.

"She is lying down. One of the chambermaids is looking after her. She was a good deal upset."

He took himself out of the room in frowning silence.

CHAPTER 34

James Moberly came into the laboratory with the air of a man who has braced himself to meet disaster. Whereas in the ordinary way he stooped a little, he now held himself stiffly upright. Miss Silver smiled at him as he came in. The tone in which she invited him to be seated recalled her schoolroom days. March, glancing from her to Moberly, wondered just what she took him to be—the tongue-tied boy paralysed with shyness—the ingenious one ready for emergency with a lie—the dunce who does not know his lessons—the idler who has scamped his work—or the mutineer who defies authority? Next moment he was recalling Moberly's story and setting him down as the boy who has blotted his copybook.

Miss Silver said,

"Pray sit down, Mr. Moberly. You must, I am sure, be even more anxious than we are to have this distressing affair cleared up. I believe that you may be able to help us, and the Chief Constable is very kindly allowing me to put some questions to you in his presence."

James Moberly said nothing. There was a chair on the far side of the table. He sat down upon it without relaxing those taut muscles or appearing to afford himself any ease. With a slight preliminary cough Miss Silver addressed him.

"Will you take your mind back to Friday morning, Mr. Moberly. Mr. Brading had been out, and he had returned. Just before twelve you were having an interview with him in the study."

He said in a dry, stiff voice,

"I have made a statement about that interview. I haven't got anything to add to it."

She continued to smile in an encouraging manner.

"I shall not ask you to do so. Your conversation with Mr. Brading was interrupted by a knock on the door. A waiter of the name of Owen came in, bringing some letters which had arrived by the second post. Mr. Brading took the letters, and the

279

waiter retired. Did you happen to notice what letters there were?"

"Not at the time. I had my back to the room."

"But you did notice them afterwards?"

"Yes. Mr. Brading was at his table. I turned round and came back. The letters were lying there. There were two of them. One looked like a local bill, and the other was from Mrs. Robinson." He spoke in short jerky sentences, his voice under constraint.

March said, "Sure about that? You knew her writing?"

"Yes—it is very distinctive."

"Did you see Mr. Brading open the letters?"

"No. He referred to the conversation we had been having about my wanting to leave. He said, 'I don't want to hear any more about it. The matter is closed.' Then he picked up Mrs. Robinson's letter and went over to the annexe."

Miss Silver coughed.

"You followed him, did you not? How much time had elapsed before you did so?"

"Between five and ten minutes. I could not accept what he said. I could not accept that the matter was closed. I went after him to tell him so, but that of course I would remain for a reasonable time until he was suited."

"Did you in fact tell him these things?"

He hesitated. The nervous strain under which he was labouring became more apparent. He said at last,

"I had no opportunity."

"You say in your statement that he was telephoning when you came into the annexe—he was using the instrument in his bedroom and the door was open. You say that you retired to the end of the passage beyond the laboratory door in order to avoid overhearing his conversation. Why did you not simply enter the laboratory?"

Moberly's eyes went past her. He said,

"I don't know."

She laid down her knitting for a moment and leaned towards him, her hands on the pale pink wool.

"Mr. Moberly, I am going to beg you to be frank. In your statement you say that Mr. Brading made two calls, that the tone of his voice was angry, and that only two words reached you. They were, 'You'd better!' Pray consider whether the time has not come when you should tell us what you really heard."

"Miss Silver—" His voice broke off on something like a groan.

She gave him another of those encouraging smiles.

"The truth is always best, Mr. Moberly. I know that you heard more than you have admitted."

He said, "Yes," still in that groaning voice. And then, "What was I to do? I knew that I was suspected—he had taken care of that. He used to tell me to pray for his long life, because his death would ruin me whatever way it came. I thought, 'The less I say, the better for me. It will only look as if I was trying to put the blame on someone else.' And I did not like her very much. Everyone knew that."

March said, "Miss Grey?"

James Moberly shook his head.

"Oh, no. That was later. When I first went in he was talking to Mrs. Robinson."

"How do you know?"

"He used her name." The strain had gone out of his voice. It was just tired and toneless.

"Go on."

"It was the first thing I heard—'My dear Maida!' I went away down the passage. I didn't wish to overhear. But then I stopped. It was his voice that stopped me, because he was speaking to Mrs. Robinson, but his voice—"

He had been sitting forward, shoulders hunched, hands between his knees. Now he straightened a little and looked at them. It was a look full of remembered pain. He repeated the last two words.

"His voice—that's what stopped me. He was speaking to her the way he used to speak to me when he wanted to—remind me—to hurt. It was the way he had been speaking to me in the study when I told him that I wanted to leave." A kind of shudder ran over him, his eyes went blank. He said half under his breath, "He knew how to hurt."

Miss Silver said,

"Yes, there was a love of cruelty."

He turned to her with a startled expression.

"He liked hurting people—he liked hurting me. It made him feel what a lot of power he had. He liked that. But he was in love with Mrs. Robinson. When I heard him speak to her like that I was afraid. I wondered what had happened. I listened—it doesn't sound nice, but that's what I did—I stood there and I listened."

March said, "What did you hear?"

282

"I told you. He said, 'My dear Maida!' in that voice. Then there was a break—she was saying something. And he said, 'That is most interesting. Do you expect me to believe it? You can come down here this afternoon and say it all over again. Then you can judge for yourself just how much ice it cuts.' Then he laughed and said, 'My dear Maida!' again, the same as before—'My dear Maida! You put those two letters in the wrong envelopes, and there's an end of it! Your "Dear Poppy" may be interested in what you wrote to me, but I assure you it's nothing to the interest I feel in what you said to her. Perhaps you have forgotten the terms in which you were pleased to describe me. You can revive your memory when I return you the letter this afternoon. I should also like to show you the will I signed this morning. I should like you to watch its obsequies. There's many a slip 'twixt the cup and the lip, isn't there?' Then he rang off and gave Miss Grey's number. I went farther off down the passage. I didn't want to hear what he said to her—I'm not an eavesdropper. All I did hear was that his voice went on being angry, and once he said, 'You'd better!' That's all I heard."

March said, "Are you prepared to write all that down and sign it?"

He nodded.

"I have done so. I wrote it down on Friday night whilst it was all fresh in my mind. My wife has the paper. I gave it to her to keep in case—"

"Then it did occur to you that this was evidence of the first importance?"

He shook his head.

"I don't know. I wanted to safeguard myself. I

283

didn't want to accuse anyone else. I was afraid of what might have happened when Mr. Brading and Mrs. Robinson met. But then Miss Grey said that he was alive when she left him at ten minutes past three."

March looked at him hard.

"She doesn't say that now. She says she found him dead."

James Moberly stared back at him for a moment. Then he gave a groan and put his head in his hands.

March said, "I'd like to have that statement, Moberly."

When he had gone out March turned to Miss Silver. She sat there knitting, the second pink vest almost finished. She might have had no more on her mind than the impending baby and its outfit. He contemplated the clicking needles, the small busy hands, the unruffled demeanour. He may have been recalling how she knitted her way through the case of the Poisoned Caterpillars in which she had saved his life, or that much more recent case in which his own deepest feelings had been involved, and from which he had emerged with a wife.* He may have been thinking merely of the case in hand. He said,

"Well, it looks as if that ace of yours had taken the trick. We'll have to have Constable and Mrs. Robinson here and put them through it. If she did it, he must have been in it up to the neck."

"Oh, yes, Randal. It must have been very carefully planned."

*Miss Silver Comes to Stay

"Do you think Maida Robinson did the shooting?"

"I fear so. I fear that she came here meaning to do it. Mr. Brading intended to show her the will he had made in her favour and to destroy it in front of her eyes. She came here determined to prevent his doing so. She had Major Forrest's revolver in that large white bag under her bathing-dress. Mr. Brading meant to punish her. He meant her to read the will before he destroyed it. It would be quite easy for her to come up beside him and lean forward to look at it. He would suspect nothing. His mind was full of the desire to punish and humiliate her. She shot him like that, dropped the revolver on the floor, took his own revolver out of the drawer, put it in her bag, and came away, leaving the bag behind her. Her part is done as far as the annexe is concerned. She comes through the glass passage into the hall, exclaims that she has left her bag, and sends Major Constable back for it. Now observe, Randal. I told you that the murderer had been hurried. Major Constable has to be very quick indeed. You must remember his training in the Commandos. He has it all planned, all timed, but all must be done at lightning speed. I feel sure that he would not trust Mrs. Robinson to remove her own fingerprints, or to place Mr. Brading's upon the revolver. It is there that hurry betrays him—those fingerprints are not quite right. He has to be absolutely certain that Mrs. Robinson has left nothing that will compromise her. He would have to wipe her fingerprints from the drawer as well as from the revolver and substitute Mr. Brading's. And in the middle of all that Mrs. Robinson rings through from the office, and he has to answer her and provide a man's voice which will pass with Miss Snagge for Mr. Brading's. You will remember that she heard no words, only a man's voice answering Mrs. Robinson. I feel sure that that scene must have been very carefully timed and rehearsed. The telephone receiver here was probably protected by a handkerchief—it must bear Mr. Brading's fingerprints and no others. And with all this, Major Constable must be absent for no longer than was necessary to fetch Mrs. Robinson's bag and perhaps say a few polite words. The margin of safety was an extremely narrow one, and every second's delay would cut it down. A very bold and carefully premeditated crime."

March said, "An extraordinarily cold-blooded one."

She said, "Yes. Crimes perpetrated for money are usually cold-blooded. There is an element of deliberate choice which is absent from the crime of passion."

He said, "But Constable—what brings him into it? They were the barest acquaintances."

Miss Silver coughed.

"Do you believe that? I find myself unable to do so. You will remember that I have not seen either of them, but from what I have been able to gather, there was—I hardly know how to put it—an effect of intimacy. Perhaps suggestions would be a better word—Major Forrest's remark to me that his friend had 'fallen hard' for Mrs. Robinson. Stacy Mainwaring said they seemed like old friends. Mrs. Constantine concluded quite bluntly that they were having an affair. I think you will find that there is some link, some previous contact. That sort of thing is very hard to disguise, and it must be remembered that the absolute necessity for disguising it arose quite unexpectedly and with great suddenness. They have not appeared together anywhere since Mr. Brading's death."

March said, "I'd forgotten you hadn't seen them. She is—rather beautiful. It's hard to believe—"

She looked at him with a faint pitying smile and coughed.

"Oh, my dear Randal!" she said.

CHAPTER 35

Stacy had been sitting in the farthest corner of the hall when Charles went by to the annexe. She could not bear to be upstairs or in any of the rooms in case—Thought stopped there, because what lay beyond was too frightening. She couldn't give it words.

She held up a paper, and hoped that the people who came and went would think that she was looking at it. She saw Charles go by without looking to left or right. He was alone, and she took what comfort she could from that.

After a moment she got up with the paper in her hand and came to where she could see the short length of passage between the billiard-room and the study, and the door leading to the glass passage beyond. At the far end she could see Charles just going into the annexe. That meant that they had sent for him again. If there was no one in the study, she could wait there until he came back and find out what was happening. You could see the whole of the glass passage from the study window, so she would know when he was coming back, and if he was alone, she could find out what was happening.

She went quickly to the study door and opened it upon an empty room, the writing-table stripped and tidy, the chairs in order, the window wide to the summer evening air. She stood there, looking out, waiting for Charles to come back. The time dragged. There seemed to be no end to its slow passage.

When he came at last he was, as he had gone, alone, his face frowning and intent. She ran to the door and opened it. And then he was coming through out of the glass passage, and she couldn't get her voice above a whisper to call to him.

"Charles—"

The sound seemed to fail. She couldn't think that it had reached him, but he saw her, leaning against the jamb in her white dress. He said her name, took her back into the study, and shut the door.

She found a small choked voice.

"What's happening?"

His arm was round her shoulders.

"No gyves on the wrists for the moment. No one quite so hot on arresting me as they were an hour ago. Even Crisp appears to have other interests. But it mayn't last. Let's make the most of it and go and have some food. It must be after seven."

Stacy took no notice. She had turned to face him. She pulled at his coat.

"What's happening? You're not telling me. I must know."

He stood frowning down, a hand on her shoulder.

"Lilias has made a statement. She says he was dead when she got there at three o'clock."

The colour rushed into Stacy's face.

"That lets you out!"

"If they believe her."

"Don't they?"

"I wouldn't like to bank on it. I don't know whether I believe her myself. That's the trouble—she's such a damned liar."

"Is she?"

He could only just hear the words.

"Oh, from the nursery. Didn't you know?"

All her bright colour ebbed. Her hand fell from his coat. She said,

"No—you never told me."

He was watching her closely.

"Why should I tell you?"

There was no answer. Her eyes were dark and startled.

He said again, "Why should I tell you? Would it have made a difference if I had?"

"Charles—"

"All right—I'm going to tell you now. It wasn't the sort of thing one wanted to talk about. I don't know how many people have guessed, or known. We've always put our heads in the sand and hoped for the best. And everyone loved my mother—her

289

friends stood by her. Some people do stand by their—friends."

It was like a knife going through her when he said that. And that was just what he meant it to be, because she hadn't stood by him, she had panicked and run away. Whatever she said or did, that was something he couldn't forget. She didn't say anything.

He went on.

"You know Lilias was adopted. My mother wanted a child—they'd been married some time. She saw Lilias and fell in love with her—she was a very pretty child. Then three years later I came along. I expect that's what started the rot. You see, she had been the centre of attention, and then all at once she wasn't. She was the adopted child, and I was the real one. It wasn't that my mother changed towards her—she didn't. At least, not any more than any mother changes when she has two children instead of one. But the situation changes. The first child isn't the only one any more—it has to share. Well, that's always been the bother with Lilias—she wants the centre of the stage, she wants the limelight, she doesn't know how to share. When she couldn't have what she wanted she tried to grab it. She started showing off to get noticed—it's a thing lots of children do. My mother tried to check it, but it got worse. There were one or two very bad patches. She told lies, and she took things. She was going through a plain stage and she wasn't getting much notice. Then in her teens she got very pretty again and it stopped. We thought it was going to be all right. Then she had an engagement that went wrong, and another—

rather stupid affairs—and it all started again. I think it helped to kill my mother. Then there was the war. Lilias went into the hospital at Ledlington, and then to a convalescent home for officers. She dramatized it all a lot and got no end of a kick out of it. Then the war came to an end and everything was deadly flat again. And that's where we were three years ago. I hoped when I married—but it didn't turn out that way."

All this time his hand was on her shoulder. Now it became a grip under which she couldn't move. Holding her like that, he said harshly,

"Just what lies did she tell you about me?"

"Lilias?"

"Yes, Lilias. You were very quick to believe her, weren't you? Well, now we're going to have a show-down. What did she say to make you go off as if I'd got the plague?"

Stacy had never been able to imagine herself telling Charles what Lilias had said. It had always seemed to her that the shame of it would be dreadful enough to kill them both—not physically, perhaps, but to kill all that mattered in them and between them. But now all the barriers were down. It was just as if her tongue didn't belong to her—as if it didn't matter what it said. Mattering, and caring, and being ashamed were gone by. She spoke in a low, quiet voice,

"Lilias said you took things—money, or anything that would bring money. She said you had always done it, and she and your mother had to put the things back and hush it up."

"And you believed her—just like that?"

"I don't know. She had been hinting ever since

we came—a little bit here, and a little bit there. We hadn't been married a month. I didn't know much about people, and I didn't know much about you. I don't know whether I would have believed her or not. I was frightened—angry—jealous. Oh, I don't know what I would have believed. You had gone up to town to see solicitors and people about Saltings—I knew you wanted to keep it and didn't see how you could. Lilias wanted me to promise that I wouldn't tell you what she said. I wouldn't. I said I had a headache and went to bed. It was true, you know—it ached dreadfully. I meant to stay awake and tell you when you came in, but I went to sleep. I had a dream, and I woke up. There was a light in your dressing-room and your door ajar. I got up to go to you—"

"Yes? What stopped you?"

She said, "Nothing—." It was more an exhausted sigh than a word. The picture rose so plain—the lighted room, and Charles at the bureau with the necklace in his hand.

His bruising grip was on her shoulder. He said, "What happened?"

She took a long shuddering breath.

"I looked in. You were standing by the bureau. You had Damaris Forrest's necklace in your hand. Lewis showed it to us in his Collection. I saw it in your hand."

He laughed without mirth.

"And instead of coming in and saying what about it you went back to bed and pretended to be asleep, and cleared out at cockcrow next morning! It never occurred to you that you might give me a chance to explain?"

She looked at him then, her eyes wide and dark with pain.

"I don't think you know—what a shock—it was. I couldn't think at all. I wanted to get away—and hide." She looked aside. A burning blush came up to the roots of her hair. "I—I was so—ashamed."

He said, "I see. You didn't think much about me—did you?"

"No. Charles, let me go!"

"In a minute. We've got to have this out."

He had both hands on her now, hard and heavy.

"Charles—"

"We've got to have it out. Look at me!"

She raised her eyes.

"No—don't look away! Just keep on looking at me and tell me the truth! You left me because you thought I was a thief, and you believed that I had stolen the Queen Anne necklace. Do you still think so?"

She did look at him. She said,

"No."

"Why?"

"I'm not so young or so stupid as I was—three years ago."

"You don't think Lilias was telling the truth?"

"Oh, no!"

"And the necklace?"

"I don't know. You didn't steal it."

"Quite sure about that?"

Her voice was steady and composed now.

"Quite sure."

He took his hands off her shoulders and stepped back.

"All right, then I'll tell you. The necklace is a

Forrest heirloom. Lewis never had it. His mother was a Forrest, so I let him have a copy made for the Collection. It was the copy you saw when he showed us his stuff. The necklace was at the Goldsmiths and Silversmiths being cleaned—for you. I brought it down with me, and I got it out to have a look at it. I thought if you woke up, I'd give it you then. My mistake! When you cleared out I let Lewis have it for eight thousand. He'd always wanted it, and I used the money to reorganize Saltings—I didn't want to sell if I could help it. There you have it. Rather a stupid business, don't you think? Well, come along and have some food."

She stood where she was, very pale again.

"Charles—"

"What is it?"

"You couldn't—forgive me?"

He gave her the most charming of his smiles, just tinged with malice.

"But, my sweet, of course. All valuable experience, and no harm done."

She knew then that it wasn't any good. You can't have a thing, and throw it away, and just whistle it back again. And she had done it herself—she couldn't blame anyone else. She turned to the door, and felt Charles's light touch on her arm.

"Food," he said. "Let's pray they haven't run out of ice."

CHAPTER 36

It was about half an hour later that Inspector Crisp arrived back at the club with Mrs. Robinson and Major Constable. A police sergeant drove with Major Constable beside him, while Crisp sat behind with Mrs. Robinson and kept his eyes open. Nothing had been said, except that the Chief Constable would be glad to see them at Warne House. So far from evincing any reluctance, both had appeared to welcome the suggestion. Mrs. Robinson in particular had quite brightened up. "I don't suppose he'll keep us long, will he, and then we can get a decent meal. And no one can say anything if we've been sent for, can they?" A rhetorical question to which Crisp had not felt obliged to reply. Cool hands, the both of them, was what he thought, and he'd best keep his eye lifting.

He took them through to the study by instructions. The Chief Constable had been having something on a tray with that Miss Silver. They had finished, and the waiter was just coming away as Crisp turned into the passage. He opened the door, stood aside for Mrs. Robinson and Major Constable to go in, and on a look from the Chief Constable came in himself and shut the door.

March was at the writing-table. He asked them to sit down, speaking gravely and pleasantly. The room felt cool with its north window wide and a breeze coming in. Maida was in black—something thin with open sleeves which showed how white her arms were. She wore very little make-up, and needed none. As she sat down she opened a lizard-skin bag, fished for a cigarette-case, and flicked it open. She chose a cigarette and turned to ask Jack Constable for a light, all very deliberately, as if she were going through a scene in a play. March, watching her, wondered if that was how it seemed to her. She tilted her chin, drew at her cigarette, and let out a little cloud of smoke to spread and hang in the air.

"Well, Mr. March," she said, "what is it? I hope you're not going to keep us too long, because I'm starving. I haven't had a decent meal for days. I've no cook, and I didn't like to shock people by coming out—though what good you do anyone by sticking indoors and moping, I can't see."

The deep, full voice took some of the edge off the words. She sat easily in the chair which had been set for her, pulling it out of the straight and leaning an arm upon the back. Her bright hair shone in the room.

Miss Silver was looking at Jack Constable. He too sat easily, but he was not smoking. He looked the plain, blunt soldier, florid and sunburned in his open-necked shirt and flannel slacks. There was nothing to show that he differed from thousands of other young men who had been through the war. Broad-shouldered and well set-up, with rather more than the usual allowance of good looks, and perhaps rather less than the usual allowance of brains.

And then, as if he felt that direct enquiring gaze

of hers, he turned and gave her a long, cold look. Just for a moment her busy needles checked. She revised her first estimate of Major Constable. That look had betrayed him. The bright blue eyes had a steely tinge. There was a brain behind them, keen, capable, ruthless. The impression was instantaneous and indelible. If there had been a shadow of doubt in her mind, it was removed. She pulled on her pale pink ball and continued to knit.

March said,

"I have asked you to come here because two statements have been made which throw rather a different light upon Mr. Brading's death."

Maida's shoulder lifted.

"Well, I suppose you have to keep going on about it. But what's the use—he's dead. After all, I'm the person most concerned. I've lost a husband—and a fortune. Look here, perhaps you can tell me. He made that will in my favour, and he signed it. Won't I have a chance of getting what he meant me to have, if I bring a case? Jack says not, but I don't know—I should think—"

Jack Constable said,

"I didn't say you hadn't got a chance. You'll have to consult a solicitor—that's what I said. She will, won't she?" He addressed March, who said,

"We'll keep to the point if you don't mind. Miss Grey has made a statement to the effect that Brading was dead when she went over to the annexe at a few minutes to three. Since you were both with him just over ten minutes before that time, you can see that your position is very materially affected."

Maida drew at her cigarette and blew out the smoke.

"Lilias would say anything," she said in a drawling voice. "The world's champion liar. Haven't you found that out? You will, you know. A nice spot of limelight—that's all she wants."

March went on as if she had not spoken.

"Your position is affected. I have to tell you that anything you say may be taken down and used in evidence."

Crisp sat down near the door and took out notebook and pencil. Jack Constable stared.

"But it's all too ridiculous. You don't mean to say you think Maida—why, I saw him after she did!"

"What I said was addressed to you as well as to Mrs. Robinson."

Jack Constable continued to stare.

"But, my dear man, it's crazy! I went back to get Maida's bag, and everything was absolutely O.K. Why, he spoke to her on the telephone while I was there."

"Somebody spoke. It is you and Mrs. Robinson who say that it was Mr. Brading. Miss Snagge only heard a man's voice. The police case will be that it was yours."

Constable said slowly,

"The police case—you've got as far as that, have you?" He threw back his head and laughed. "I say, you must be pretty hard up for evidence! Perhaps you wouldn't mind telling us what motive we're supposed to have had. Maida had just got engaged to him, and he'd made a will in her favour. I didn't know that, mind you, I only heard about it afterwards. And then she's supposed, not only to have bumped the poor chap off, but to have destroyed the will. A damned good case, I must say! Makes a lot of sense, doesn't it?''

March looked at him steadily.

''It makes quite good sense, Constable. It was Miss Grey who destroyed the will.''

Maida withdrew her cigarette to say,

''Lilias is crazy. I've thought so for a long time. I expect she shot him.''

''Why would she shoot him?''

''I don't know. Why should I? I'd every reason not to.''

''Had you, Mrs. Robinson? We can go into that if you like. I think you wrote two letters on Thursday evening—''

The hand with the cigarette moved towards her lips again.

''What if I did?''

''One of them was to Brading.''

She drew in a mouthful of smoke and let it out again slowly.

''I was engaged to him, you know. One does write to one's fiancé.''

''You wrote a letter to Brading, and Forrest posted it.''

''Certainly.''

''There was another letter—to a Mrs. Hunt.''

''How very incriminating!''

March said, ''I'm afraid so. You see, you put them into the wrong envelopes.''

She just stared at him.

''I *what*?''

He said in a measured voice,

"You put the letter which you had written to Mrs. Hunt in the envelope addressed to Brading. He got it by the second post on Friday, and he went into the annexe and rang you up. Moberly overheard his side of the conversation. You know best what was in the letter you wrote to your friend Mrs. Hunt. Moberly heard Brading say, 'You put those two letters in the wrong envelopes, and there's an end of it. Perhaps you have forgotten the terms in which you were pleased to describe me. You can revive your memory when I return you the letter this afternoon.' And then something about wanting you to watch the obsequies of the will he had signed that morning, and a bit about there being many a slip between the cup and the lip."

Jack Constable was watching her. She said scornfully,

"Moberly! He'd say anything! He's in a jam himself. Naturally, all he wants is to put it on someone else." The cigarette went to her lips again.

It was at this moment that the telephone bell rang. March picked up the receiver and listened. To the rest of the room the voice of Sergeant James speaking from the office was a baritone murmur. To March it conveyed the intelligence that there was a lady in the hall asking very urgently for Mrs. Robinson.

"Name of Hunt, sir—Mrs. Hunt."

March said in a non-committal voice,

"Say what she wants?"

Sergeant James cleared his throat. What he considered the lady wanted was to go home and sleep it off, but he didn't like to say so to the Chief Constable. He compromised on,

"Well, she's calling for drinks, and she says she wants Mrs. Robinson—something about a letter, sir. There are two men with her."

March said, "All right," and hung up. He scribbled on a bit of paper and handed it to Miss Silver.

"Perhaps you wouldn't mind taking this on."

She read it with grave attention, put it into her knitting-bag with her needles and the pale pink wool, and left the room. The whole thing had taken very little time.

Crisp finished writing and glanced up. Jack Constable looked as if he was going to say something, but it did not get said. Maida went on smoking. As March addressed himself to her again, Miss Silver emerged upon the hall, and was aware of commotion. The Chief Constable's note had informed her that Mrs. Hunt would be there. She had no difficulty in identifying her. She was, in fact, making her presence felt in an extremely vivid and spectacular manner. There was a good deal of her, encased in cherry-coloured chiffon, with several rows of artificial pearls reposing upon an enormous bosom. She had masses of black hair, and eyes that had to be seen to be believed—so big, so dark, so rolling. She carried a white diamanté bag, and she was decidedly more than half-seas over. It was a pity that March was not there to watch the meeting between her and Miss Silver, but it had an appreciative audience in Charles and Stacy, who were coming out of the dining-room.

With an introductory cough Miss Silver addressed the ebullient lady, who had just remarked in a singularly carrying voice that if everyone *was* dead and buried in this forsaken dump, she meant to have a drink "if I have to raid the bar to get it."

Miss Silver said, "Mrs. Hunt, I believe."

She received an expansive smile.

"That's me—Poppy Hunt. Call me Poppy— everyone does. Are you the manageress? Because if you are, I tell you what—the service is damned bad. Five solid minutes I've been here and can't get a drink. Three of us, and all our tongues hanging out! Meet the boy friend—meet my husband. And we all want drinks."

The boy friend was a thin, haggard man with a gloomy eye. He had reached the melancholy stage and was propping himself against the office counter with the air of one who would welcome almost any kind of death.

In contrast, Mr. Hunt was not drunk at all. He had a worried, inefficient look, like an ant that has strayed from the nest. He gazed through crooked pince-nez at his wife and murmured, "Perhaps a little soda-water, my dear—"

Miss Silver coughed with great firmness.

"Come and sit down at this table, Mrs. Hunt. I believe you were enquiring for Mrs. Robinson."

Poppy let herself down with a run which shook the proffered chair.

"That's right," she said. "I want a drink, and I want Maida, and I can't get either. What sort of a dump do you call this anyhow?" It was said quite without rancour. Drunk or sober, there was no ill will in Poppy Hunt.

Miss Silver coughed.

"Your order will be attended to. Is Mrs. Robinson expecting you?"

Poppy laughed.

"Not a bit of it! Surprise for her—joke, if you know what I mean—best joke you ever heard. Here—she writes to me, and I'm away. Letter goes home, but I'm not there, so my hubby brings it along with him when he comes to pick me up this morning. Me and the boy friend, we were off at my sister's. Ledbury—that's where she lives. Nice little place. All friends together—usual crowd—plenty to drink. Well, Al brings my letters along, and when I open Maida's, what d'you think?" She had her elbows on the orange table. A chin or two were propped on stubby hands glittering with rings. "Best joke ever! What d'you think she'd done? Put the wrong letter inside! There it was on the envelope, 'Mrs. Al Hunt.' And inside it was, 'My *dear* Lewis,' and saying she'd have him! I don't know when I laughed so much!"

She was laughing now, swaying backwards and forwards, and the chair creaking with her weight.

"Bit of a mix-up, I don't think! Me getting 'My *dear* Lewis,' and him getting 'Dear Poppy,' and Lord knows what about his being a dry old stick but the best she could do! So I said to my hubby, 'What's the odds? No distance to Saltings. We'll take her on the way back—chip her head off—all have drinks together.' And then she wasn't there. 'Well,' I said, 'never say die. She'll be at that club she's so fond of. We'll get her there, and we'll get the drinks too.' And here we are!"

She repeated the last phrase slowly. There was the effect of something running down. And then with a hiccuping laugh she was off again.

"Funny, isn't it? I'll say it is! Because if she put

in *his* letter to me, well, what's the odds she put in *my* letter to him? And Lord only knows what she said in it!'' She pulled herself up with a jerk, staring at Miss Silver. ''I'm not saying what she said, mind you, because I don't know, but if it's anything like what she's said before, it's going to take a bit of explaining. All out to get him, of course, and I don't blame her. Money's money, and a girl's got to look out for herself. So let's hope she didn't say the half of what she's said before.'' She paused, stared owlishly, and shot a final dart. ''And I tell you what—half 'ud be a hell of a lot too much.''

Miss Silver said, ''Have you seen a paper today?''

She got another stare.

''Don't read the papers. We'd a thick night. Here—isn't that drink coming?''

Miss Silver coughed in a very delicate manner.

''You did not see a paper today. Did you see one yesterday?''

Poppy Hunt sat up straight with a hand on either arm of her chair. Everything rocked a little—and they wouldn't bring her a drink. She said more in sorrow than in anger,

''Never—read—papers. Lot of—tommyrot. Where's Maida?''

Miss Silver rose to her feet.

''I will take you to her. Where is the letter you spoke of?''

There was a rummage in the diamanté bag. The contents spilled. A lipstick rolled one way, a compact the other. Mr. Hunt, who had been hovering, went down on his hands and knees to pick them up. The boy friend continued to prop the office counter, his melancholy still farther advanced along the road to coma.

Miss Silver stooped, secured a rather bright blue envelope, and said briskly,

"Come, Mrs. Hunt, I will take you to Mrs. Robinson."

CHAPTER 37

In the study the Chief Constable was engaged in marking time. He had left a particularly delicate and difficult hand to Miss Silver to play. He did not doubt her ability to get as many tricks out of it as was humanly possible, but he found it difficult to keep his mind from straying. He had just finished a series of questions to Major Constable, designed to elicit previous knowledge of Charles Forrest's revolver and of the place where it was kept. They were answered with a frank nonchalance which appeared to rob them of their importance.

"But of course I knew he had a revolver. He used to yarn about it—belonged to his father—saved the old man's life—all that sort of thing. Did I know where he kept it? Well, there you have me. Drawer in the bureau, I think, but I wouldn't like to swear to it. Just one of those things you take for granted, and, if anyone asks you all the whys and wherefors you're stumped."

Nothing could have been more open and ingenuous.

Maida Robinson tossed the stub of her cigarette in the direction of the waste-paper basket. It struck the edge and fell back upon the carpet. Without giving it a glance she lit another.

March addressed Jack Constable.

"How long have you known Mrs. Robinson?"

He laughed.

"How long is it, Maida?"

The tip of the cigarette glowed. She held it away.

"Oh, back, in the war sometime—a few dances, a few drinks—"

"And how well did you know each other?"

"Like I said."

"Nothing more?"

Jack Constable's blue eyes stared.

"Is that meant to be offensive?"

"Not unless you take it that way."

Maida waved a hand to clear the smoke between them.

"What are you getting at anyway? Because Jack and I run into each other now and again, we are in some ridiculous plot to kill Lewis? Use your head, Mr. March! I've danced with quite a lot of men in my time, and had drinks with them too. I married one of them, and I was sorry enough for that. Well, I got my divorce, and I was going to marry Lewis. I'm not going to pretend I was in love with him, and it wouldn't cut any ice with you if I did. I liked him all right—he wasn't such a bad old stick. And he was in off the deep end about me. Look at the way he rushed and made that will. Now is it likely I was going to throw all that away?"

306

She laughed and drew on her cigarette. "It's all nonsense about those letters. Moberly made it up to save his skin. Everyone knows how Lewis bullied him, poor wretch. I always told him he'd push him too far some day. But suppose it was all true, and Lewis was in a rage with me—he wasn't, you know, but just suppose for a moment that he was." She gave that low laugh again. "Why, I could have talked him round in five minutes. I didn't need to shoot him—he'd have eaten out of my hand. You're just being silly."

March said,

"That would depend on what you said in your letter to Mrs. Hunt—the one Brading got by mistake."

She said, "There wasn't any letter," and the door was flung back to reveal Poppy Hunt.

It was Poppy herself who had flung it. The smell of alcohol and scent enveloped her. She stood swaying on the threshold in her red dress. The room with its north window darkened by the hill looked shadowy to her. The smoke of Maida's cigarette hung in the air. Her mind was hazy with drink. Everything was blurred at the edges and a little out of the straight. There were people there— a man at a desk—another man—a policeman—but still no drinks—

Miss Silver came past her and put the blue envelope into Randal March's hand. It was addressed to Mrs. Hunt, and it had been opened.

He had just slipped out enough of the sheet which it contained to read the words, "My *dear* Lewis," when Poppy saw Maida—the bright hair first, and then the hand with the cigarette, the thin black dress, the eyes.

The eyes stared at her. Horrid and pale the girl was. Come to think of it, she'd never seen Maida pale before—always a lot of colour and no need to put it on.

It was all gone as Randal March leaned forward with a sheet of rather bright blue paper in his hand.

"Mrs. Hunt has brought you the letter which you put into her envelope by mistake."

The words touched everything off. Poppy Hunt held on to the jamb of the door and saw things happen. Somebody called out, "The window!" Somebody threw a chair. A regular rough house, that was what it was, and Maida jumping out of the window and legging it, and a man going after her. She began to let out a succession of piercing screams.

It was Jack Constable who had shouted and thrown the chair. He had thrown it in Crisp's face, caught him half way to his feet, and knocked him sprawling. March saw a second chair coming and dodged, but it got his shoulder, spun him about, and checked him. When he reached the window Maida was out of sight and Jack Constable rounding the corner of the house.

March went out over the sill and after them, whilst Crisp was getting to his feet with the blood running down his face and taking the other way out along the passage and through the hall.

They came to the porch more or less at the same time. Crisp saw his own police car go sliding down the drive. The blood dripped into his eyes, but it didn't need that to make him see red. Take the police car, would they, that he'd left all turned and ready to go! And nothing to go after them in but the Chief Constable's Vauxhall, which was facing the wrong way. They wouldn't get away of course, but they'd give them a run. And the out and out nerve of it, that's what got him!

He threw himself into the car, and whilst the Chief Constable turned it he cleared the blood from his eyes with an angry hand and shouted instructions to Constable Jackson.

"Tell James to ring all stations! Give the number of the car! It's to be stopped and the occupants detained! You, Hewett, jump in behind!"

And then the bonnet of the car swung round and they were off down the drive. As they cleared it and ran down into Warne, the police car was just in sight on the long, slow hill climbing up on the other side. Bound to take that way, and bound to run through Ledstow. It was after that it would be tricky.

March looked sideways and said, "All right, Crisp?"

"Yes, sir—only a cut."

"You look like another murder. Here, Hewett, get a handkerchief round his head and keep the blood out of his eyes. You can do it from behind there."

The police car was out of sight, gone over the brow of the hill and running for Ledstow. March said,

"They won't stop them there, and they've got a fair start. What will they do next? They won't risk Ledlington—all those narrow streets, and the alarm out. I'd say they'd turn inland out of Ledstow

309

and take the old smugglers' road that runs through Cliff past the Catherine-Wheel—a good straight run with nothing you can call a turning till you get away from the cliffs and go inland again, a good four miles. They'll reckon to gain on us there and get rid of the car when they are in amongst the lanes. At least that's what I should do in their place."

"They won't get away," said Crisp in a dogged voice. His head was being tied up, and Constable Hewett was being extraordinarily clumsy over it. All the first-aid classes in the world couldn't produce fingers when what a chap has got by nature was a couple of bunches of awkward thumbs. He said, "That'll do!" in an infuriated voice and shook his head exactly like a terrier coming up out of the ditch where he had failed to catch a rat.

They came through Ledstow at a speed that brought heads round to look at them. As they shot by the police station, a constable waved them to the Ledlington road, which is just beyond. The smugglers' road takes off in a couple of miles, running between hedges until it comes back to the sea at the village of Cliff, and from there runs bare and exposed on the mounting line of the coast.

On the rise past the Catherine-Wheel of smuggling reputation they saw the car again. March said,

"We've pulled up on them," and Crisp said, "Not enough."

After that neither of them spoke. The needle of March's speedometer ran up to sixty-five, trembled there, and climbed point by point to seventy. The black car in front of them went down over the brow of the hill and out of sight. At sea level there would be a choice of three diverging lanes—a two to one chance of missing and being missed.

They came to the top of the road themselves, and saw the long incline run down on the edge of the cliffs, falling with them to soft, broken country with trees and hedgerows. They had caught up on the stolen car, but as Crisp said, not enough. It was a third of the way down, and might be out of sight for long enough to slip into one of the three lanes beyond the bend at the foot if they could make the turn in time. With a clear road they could.

But the road wasn't clear. A lorry came grinding up on the crown of the road. In a flash Crisp was leaning well out on his side, showing his uniform, pushing up his hand like the arm of a semaphore. March began to brake. The lorry driver hesitated, looked at the two cars rushing down towards him, thought of getting off to the side of the road, saw Crisp's frantic signals, the police uniform, and checked. With Jack Constable roaring at him like a bull, he stopped there in the middle of the road. He didn't like being roared at. He stopped and got ready to jump.

But there wasn't any need. Jack Constable measured the gap on either side with his eye. He would have taken any chance, but there wasn't one. He laughed, and Maida screamed. Then he put the car at the cliff. She screamed again as they went over.

CHAPTER 38

It was going on for nine when Charles Forrest was called to the telephone. Rumours had been drifting back to Warne House. The police had left in a hurry. Major Constable and Mrs. Robinson were said to be dead. Their car had gone over the cliff and smashed on the rocks below. It was a collision with a lorry. It was a collision with the Chief Constable's car. It was suicide.

In the middle of all this Charles had to go and listen to Lilias, who needed someone to whom she could explain how pure all her motives had been, and how little one could expect to be understood or appreciated in a world peopled by unsympathetic characters like the Chief Constable. He heard with relief that he was wanted on the telephone, and proceeded to the study, where he took the call.

"March here. I'm speaking from Ledlington hospital. Can you come out at once? I expect you know who shot Brading. They made a dash for it in a police car and got blocked on the cliff road. Constable put the car over. He's dead. She isn't—yet. We want a statement, and she won't make one unless you're there. Be as quick as you can—there mayn't be much time."

March was waiting for him at the hospital.

"She's broken her back. Perfectly clear in the head, and no pain. They say she can't last the night, and it may be sooner. We're bound to have that statement, and she wouldn't say a word until you came."

Up a stair, along a cool antiseptic corridor, and round a screen. Maida's bright hair on the pillow. Not a mark on her face. Her eyes looking a long way off. They came back to see him.

There was a chair by the bed. He sat down.

She said, "Charles—"

Her hand moved a little. He took it. It was cold. She said,

"They want me to make a statement."

"Yes. Will you?"

"I wouldn't till you came. I don't trust them. You'll tell me—is Jack dead?"

"Yes—he was killed at once."

"I'm—dying?"

"Yes."

"Sure—it's not a trap?"

"That's what they say."

She shut her eyes for a moment.

"All right—"

A police stenographer slipped in round the screen, sat down on the other side of the bed, took out his notebook. Maida opened her eyes and said,

"I shot Lewis—you know that. I wouldn't have done it if he hadn't said what he did. We planned it—after we knew about the letters—but I don't know that I'd have done it—really—not when it came to the point—I don't know. He said—oh, well, I've got a temper—I had the revolver in my bag—I came up close and shot him. He thought I was going to look at the will—it was there on the table—but I shot him."

313

Her voice was low and steady, but there wasn't enough breath to carry it for more than a few words at a time. She held his hand. After a moment she said,

"Are they writing it down?"

"Yes."

"I don't care—it doesn't matter now. It was Jack's plan—from the beginning. We'd been in jobs before. I came down—to get in with Lewis—because of the Collection. That was the first idea—to get away with the stuff. Then Lewis—fell for me—in a big way. I told Jack I could—marry him—it would be better that way. He didn't like it—at first—but he agreed. He liked me—a bit—himself." She shut her eyes again. The cold fingers moved in the warmth of his hand. Then her lashes lifted. "Liking people is—the devil. That's what—queered the show. Not Jack, but me. You came along—and—I liked you. If you had liked me—we could have—made a go of it. I'd have sent Jack—away—and let Lewis and his Collection go—down the drain. I as good as told you so—when we walked back together—on Thursday night. But you weren't—having any. It's that girl, I suppose—the one you were—married to—"

Charles said, "Yes."

She gave a faint ghost of a laugh.

"That's—the way—it goes. It doesn't matter—now—but I was mad—at the time. I went in and—blew off steam—writing those two letters—one to Lewis saying—I'd have him—and the other to Poppy Hunt saying—just what I—felt about it. And I put them in the—wrong envelopes. I'd had a drink or two—and I was mad—with you."

314

She moved her head a little on the pillow and said, "Oh, well—"

A nurse came round the screen and felt her pulse. When she had gone away again Maida said,

"Lewis got my letter—by the second post—on Friday. He—rang me up. He was mad. He said he'd—signed his will, and I'd better come down and—'assist at its obsequies.' I thought that meant he wouldn't—destroy it—till I came. I thought—perhaps—I could talk him round—but Jack said no. He—made the plan. It—all—went—quite—smoothly—"

There was a long pause. She lay with her eyes open, looking past Charles as if he wasn't there. The nurse came again and stood there. The statement was read over to Maida. She made a mark. Charles and the nurse witnessed it. The nurse slipped away. The stenographer went too, trying not to make a noise. Time went by. Only her eyes moved. They turned on Charles, and seemed to see him. She said slowly,

"Do you think we—just—go out?"

"No."

After some time she spoke again.

"Then—what?"

"I don't know—pick up the bits and go on."

Her lip twitched. It was something like a smile. She said,

"Some bits—Lewis—Jack—" And then, "I'd like you to—see me out. Your hand is—warm—"

It was three in the morning when he came out of the hospital and drove back to Saltings alone.

315

CHAPTER 39

The inquest was over. Wilful murder and suicide in the case of Jack Constable. Wilful murder and accidental death in the case of Maida Robinson. Charles gave his evidence, interviewed lawyers, interviewed James Moberly, interviewed Miss Silver.

"I don't know what to do about Lilias, and that's a fact."

Miss Silver coughed. They were in the study. She was well away with a third vest and knitting briskly.

"She has had a severe shock. She will, I think, be a good deal more careful for some time to come. I have seen her and talked to her. I hope that I may have made an impression. Not only has she herself formed the habit of covering up her faults, but those around her have done so too. She has desired to attract attention to herself, to transfer her faults to others, and she has sought to be loved and esteemed for qualities which she does not possess."

It was sententious, it was almost pre-Victorian, it was a survival of the great Moral Age. Even in the middle of one of the stickiest days of his life Charles was able to admire where he could not emulate. He could only say,

"That's about the size of it. But where do we go from there?"

Miss Silver coughed in a gently encouraging manner.

"She requires more interests, occupations—something which would give her the satisfaction of feeling that she can win approbation in a legitimate manner. If she has any talents, any capability, let her develop it and use it for others."

The only thing that Charles could think of appeared painfully inadequate.

"She worked with the Red Cross during the war, but that has rather faded out. And before that she used to play for a dancing-class—something to do with the village institute—I don't know—"

Miss Silver beamed upon him.

"That would be admirable for a start. Give her all the encouragement you can. And now, if you will forgive me, I am going over to see Mrs. March. Such a charming person."

"Yes, I've met her—Pallas Athene."

She was putting away her knitting.

"A most appropriate nickname. 'A daughter of the Gods, divinely tall—' as Lord Tennyson puts it." She rose to her feet and extended her hand. "I shall be leaving tomorrow. I do not know if this is goodbye or not."

Charles didn't know either. He hadn't seen Stacy yet. He had wanted to see all these other people first and get clear of them before he saw her again, and then—well, that was just where he couldn't look ahead.

Miss Silver was referring in a grateful and dignified manner to "your very generous cheque." It was necessary to respond. He did so in all sincerity.

"I owe you more than I can possibly repay.

March has made no secret of it."

She smiled.

"He is always more than kind. May I say, Major Forrest, that I wish you every happiness?"

He let her get away, rang the bell. The waiter who came was Owen. The man who had brought those letters in on Friday—talk of haunted houses! He said,

"Could you find Miss Mainwaring and ask her if she can spare me a few minutes?"

The door shut him in again with his thoughts. Every house where things have happened is a haunted house. But in all old houses everything that can happen has happened already—and again—and again. Birth and marriage and death, good and evil, and the drifting thoughts of men— an old house sees them all. Lewis and Maida and Jack Constable, James Moberly and Hester Constantine, Myra, Lilias, Miss Silver, Stacy and himself—they were part of the pattern of this generation. There had been other generations, there would be more to come—"All the rivers run into the sea, yet the sea is not full." If you make too much of your own bit of the pattern—

From where he stood he could see the annexe, blind in the shadow of the hill. He thought about getting windows knocked in those blank walls— good big ones. The club could do with the extra rooms. Get light and air into the place—they'd let you have permits for that all right. Disperse that horrible Collection—some of the things to museums, the better stones sold separately. Get rid of the associations and they'd be like any other bits of stone. What a damnable thing for a man to have made the centre of his thoughts—grubbing in old crimes, raking up their follies, their passions, their agonies. Get rid of it all—let in the light— He began to plan where the windows would go.

Stacy came in. She had shadows in her eyes and under them. The white dress made her look pale—but perhaps it wasn't the dress—

He was over by the window. She came close and stood there, waiting for him to speak. All the feeling between them was sad and quiet. At last he said,

"Well, it's all over."

"Yes—Miss Silver told me."

He went on in an abstracted voice.

"I gather the police won't do anything about the will. Even if Maida had lived and not been suspected of having anything to do with Lewis's death, there was really no one except herself who had actually read it. I think she would have found it very difficult to establish any claim on the estate. As it is, there is no one to make one—and of course nobody is allowed to benefit by a crime. Lilias practically admitted that she had destroyed the will, but she didn't sign anything, and if there were any question of taking proceedings, she would simply deny the whole thing. Everyone knows she burned the will, but if she were to say the police bullied her into hysterics and she didn't know what she was saying—well, there would be plenty of evidence about the hysterics, and a nasty double-edged sort of case for the police to handle. Counsel could make out at least as strong a probability that the will had been destroyed by Lewis, or by me. They won't touch it. Nobody's been done out of

319

anything, and they'll just let it go."

There was a long silence. Then Stacy said,

"Charles, you look so tired."

"I was up most of the night."

"With her?"

"Yes. How did you know?"

"Edna Snagge's sister is a nurse at the hospital."

"I see."

Then she would know that he had sat there hour after hour holding Maida's hand until she slipped away. It came to him that this was where he would know whether they could take up their life together again or not. There was no emotion between them—just tiredness, and sadness, and a kind of groping in the dark. If she understood, the groping hands would meet, they would find each other. If she didn't understand, there were no ways so wide as those in which they must walk apart.

She said, "Were you—fond of her?"

"Not like that."

She took that simply. She said,

"She was—fond of you. I'm glad you were there."

The groping between them had stopped. Everything cleared. He said,

"She didn't feel anything. I held her hand—"

Stacy said, "I'm glad."

He put his arm round her, and they stood like that for a long time. Life began to come back—life and feeling. It was like the blood running back into a numbed limb. There was a tingling and a pain, a pressure of feeling and emotion, a sense of something flowing in. At last he said,

"Why would you never see me?"

"I was ashamed."

"Of what?"

"I cared—so much—"

"Rather an—odd reason, don't you think?"

His arm dropped from her shoulders. His hand moved to touch hers. He could feel that she was trembling. She did not look at him, nor he at her. They looked at the blank walls of the annexe and at the shadowed hill. They did not see these things. They saw three wasted years which need never have been, three years when they might have been together. Stacy said in a voice which shook as her hand was shaking,

"If I'd seen you—if you touched me—I shouldn't have cared if you'd stolen a million necklaces. That's what made me—so ashamed."

The hand that was touching hers turned and caught it in a grip so hard that it hurt.

"Well, what about it now? Have we wasted enough time, or haven't we? And what happens next time Lilias lets her imagination loose on me— do you swallow everything whole and let us in for another divorce?" He let go of the hand and put his arms round her. "Well?"

"Charles—"

"Yes, I'm Charles, and you're Stacy. But the question is, are you Stacy Mainwaring, or Stacy Forrest? Every time I've heard someone call you Miss Mainwaring I've wanted to hit them over the head."

Stacy stopped trembling. It was extraordinarily heartening to hear Charles say things like that. And then she had a picture of Charles hitting a waiter over the head with a dinner plate, and she began

321

to laugh. She said, "Oh, Charles!" and she laughed, and the tears ran down her cheeks. And they kissed and held one another tight. The empty years were gone.

The End